Sign up for our newsletter to hear about
new releases, read interviews with
authors, enter giveaways, and more.

www.ylva-publishing.com

THE
RETURN

ANA MATICS

For all those who find their way to Heron Island

HAWKE LEADS SMALL-TOWN TEAM TO SHOWDOWN WITH PHS

Portland Press Herald

March 7th, 2002

AUGUSTA – With the host school's team eliminated in a double-overtime frenzy yesterday evening to the upset-minded Near Haven Lady Knights, all that stands between them and the state title are defending state title holders, the Portland High School Lady Bulldogs. The game is scheduled to be played at a neutral location, as the schools are on opposite ends of the state and the state athletics board has made an exception to keep the teams on more equal footing.

Near Haven, coached by long-time veteran Charlie White, starts four seniors and holds a 30-4 overall record (26-4 regular season). Led by starting point guard, Elizabeth Hawke (averaging 17 points, 5.2 assists, 2 steals), Near Haven has come out of nowhere to blaze their way through the Northeast Division playoffs and to find themselves on the brink of history. It has been over ten years since a team outside of Portland, Bangor, or Augusta won a basketball state title.

Hawke, a 5'9" senior, leads the team in scoring and assists, and holds the all-time points record at Near Haven High School with over 2,000 points. She is averaging just over seventeen points a game and has received a good deal of out-of-state attention for her backcourt leadership. She currently has offers from Fresno State and Portland State (Oregon) to play at the collegiate level, as well as from the University of Maine.

HAWKE PICKS PORTLAND

Near Haven Mirror
May 2002

NEAR HAVEN – With the deadline to determine her destination nearly up, Near Haven's star point guard has selected to play her collegiate ball at Portland State University. Hawke spoke to a small gathering of reporters and well-wishers with her coach, Charlie White, yesterday.

When asked why she chose to go to college so far away, Elizabeth Hawke explained, "Some people live and die in Near Haven, you know? I want to get out, to make a name for myself, to put this place on the map. The first step was winning state; the next step is to take my game as far as it can go."

Hawke, an orphan and ward of the state, has spent the better part of her high school career living with her coach, Mr. White, and his daughter. She attributes her success in basketball to the constant immersion of strategy that she receives from being around her coach every day. Mr. White is a twenty-five-year coaching veteran who also serves on the school board since retiring from teaching civics at Near Haven High School.

Hawke will join a veteran club that plays in the Big Sky Conference and says that she hopes to make an immediate impact on the team.

PORTLAND 60, MONTANA 45

From Basketball Roundups
USA Today, January 2003

Freshman Elizabeth Hawke (5'9" Near Haven, ME) scored 17 in just twenty-five minutes of play in her Big Sky debut against rival Montana. Portland State is currently 5-9 after a grueling preseason that included trips to Georgia, Tennessee, and Notre Dame; they are currently the favorite to win the Big Sky.

BASKETBALL STAR DISMISSED ON ROBBERY CHARGES, HEARING PENDING

Kennebec Journal
September 2003

PORTLAND, OR – Police filed charges Saturday against local basketball talent Elizabeth Hawke, nineteen, following her arrest Friday evening. Hawke, according to police reports, is charged with possession of stolen goods and evading arrest. Portland State has officially dismissed Hawke, a rising sophomore, from their basketball team following notification of her arrest.

"We regret that we can no longer welcome Ms. Hawke to represent our community and school," the school's official statement read. Further comment was declined.

Hawke averaged 10 points and 2.3 assists with twenty-four minutes of playing time per game her freshman year.

HAWKE SONG – NEAR HAVEN'S HAWKE GUILTY

Near Haven Mirror
January 2004

PORTLAND, OR – Former Near Haven High basketball star, Elizabeth Hawke, was convicted in a public hearing yesterday of possession of stolen property. She is facing up to five years in prison and will be sentenced sometime next week, according to court papers.

Hawke, twenty, was arrested in September of last year after police found her loitering in a restricted area. Upon a search of her person, an undisclosed number of watches with an estimated value of close to $100,000.00 were found on her person. Hawke testified in court that she had simply collected them for a friend and had no idea that they were stolen, but upon cross-examination it came to light that many of Hawke's associates in Portland possessed police records and long rap sheets. As this is Ms. Hawke's first conviction, there is some expectation of leniency from presiding judge Martha Rogers.

HAWKE RELEASED ON GOOD BEHAVIOR

National Briefs

Near Haven Mirror

August 2006

OREGON – Local basketball hero Elizabeth Hawke (twenty-two) was released from prison in Oregon yesterday based on good behavior and new developments in the case. Hawke was sentenced in 2004 to serve five years for possession of stolen property and served one and a half years of her sentence before being released. Police suspect that Hawke was telling the truth during her trial when she said that she had no idea that the property she was holding had been stolen, as several similar cases have occurred around the Portland area since her conviction in 2004. Ms. Hawke declined to comment to the press upon her release.

CHAPTER ONE

HOMECOMING (25 MAY, 2012)

CHARLIE DIDN'T ANSWER WHEN LIZA called him collect from a pay phone in Boston and the operator wouldn't let her leave him a message. She slammed the receiver down in disgust and stared at it for a long time before turning away and scowling at the rain-slicked bus station parking lot that she had sprinted across in order to chance this call.

It wasn't like she had much else to do. The bus to Bangor didn't leave for another hour and she figured that it was a common courtesy to call before showing up in the town whose name you've disgraced. Maybe she was just hoping for too much, going back there, but she was out of options now. It was home or nothing, with the last of her money gone, funneled into this bus ticket to Bangor.

Liza ran a tired hand through her two-day-dirty blonde hair and scowled up at the sky. The rain pelted down hard; cold droplets of water fell around her and she was growing more and more desperate by the second. She had half a mind to try calling Charlie again, to tell him that it was

Maine or nothing, and no matter what she had done to them, it couldn't be worse than what she was coming from.

Ten years later and she was still running. Liza chewed on her lip and contemplated the payphone. She had burned all of her bridges at home; she'd done that a long time ago. Now she was just trying to remember if there was anyone in that godforsaken village that would care if she lived or died. Names of former friends, teammates, and the few people she'd stayed with who weren't god-awful swam through her mind and she struggled to remember if any of them even cared the last time she was fucked six ways to Sunday and desperately needed help.

There was one name, but it was far too early in the day for him to be back at port. Liza sighed again, staring up at the rain once more. *Stupid lobstermen and their stupidly rigid schedules.*

It always rained in May, but at least in Boston there was some semblance of a spring. Liza hitched her bag further up her shoulder and scowled at the rain. The jacket she was wearing wasn't that great at keeping the wet out, but it was better than nothing. It was made of cheap, fake leather in the most obnoxious shade of blue imaginable. She had found it in Vegas, after they'd let her out on good behavior—when they'd finally figured out that Liza was just a patsy. There had been some restitution money from the state after that, and the chance to look across a courtroom and tell twelve of her peers that her asshole ex-boyfriend, Jared Dickens, was a manipulative douche who'd let her fall on the sword for him.

The judge hadn't expunged the records though, and her restitution money soon ran out when it became obvious that no one was going to offer Liza a job with that criminal history. She had been stuck with the idea of lying about it, which she couldn't stomach, or simply fumbling her way through life, hoping there'd be someone like Charlie, her former coach, who she'd chance upon again.

Kicking a rock and sending it skittering across the bus depot's parking lot, Liza shivered. It was fifty-five and rainy, and she had spent the better part of a year in Raleigh couch-surfing with friends and working basketball concessions, as no one ever asked twice in a place like that. It'd had been eighty when she'd left North Carolina and now she was stuck in a New England not-quite-spring. She was gonna get sick.

Over the loudspeaker, there was an announcement that they were boarding the bus and Liza hurried out into the rain once more, her boots splashing water up her pants legs. She sighed when she looked down at the rainwater slicked with motor oil that now dotted her nice boots and the one pair of jeans she owned that she actually liked. Just another fuck-up, she supposed.

Maybe in Portland, Charlie would answer his phone. Or it would be late enough that she could try the second option, the one that she still wasn't entirely sure she wanted to try.

It seemed like no matter where she ended up on I-95, it would always be clogged with traffic. Central Boston was no exception to that rule. Liza shifted back in her uncomfortable bus seat and stared out over Boston Harbor listlessly, her chin resting on her palm. It had been *forever* since she'd seen this place, and it felt as though nothing had changed at all. She fiddled with a fraying thread from the seam of her jeans and sighed.

As the bus merged at a snail's pace over to I-93 and pointed north towards Concord, she was once again lost in thought. Liza had avoided New England for so long, and hated the idea of coming back to a place where people might know her. Now though, she stared at the clouds of fog rolling in off the water and realized that she'd missed the sight and smell of the ocean.

And the bus ride dragged on.

In Manchester, Liza debated getting off the bus and trying to call Charlie again. But the layover was only twenty minutes and she knew that she would go and waste what precious little cash she had left at the McDonald's that was nestled inside the bus station and end up hungry again in twenty minutes. She kicked off her boots and curled her legs underneath her, trying to force herself to concentrate on the novel in her lap. It had been free in a bin outside the library in Raleigh and she took it knowing that it was good and long and would probably take her the entirety of the bus ride to read it.

"Whatcha reading?" asked the kid who'd been kicking her seat incessantly since they left Boston. He was half-hanging over the seat, a Nintendo DS in his hands and Mario half-heartedly paused in mid-jump away from Bowser's flames. It looked like Mario was about to die.

Liza felt for the kid, because towards the end of those games, Bowser could be a real bitch to beat. She didn't have the heart to glare at him, and just shrugged and flipped the cover for him to see.

"Mu-tin-a-y on the Bounty." The kid sounded the words out slowly.

Liza thought that he was a little old to still need to sound out words, especially now that she was back in New England where there were actually decent public schools. Her eyes narrowed. Video games were ruining children to this day, it seemed. "Mutiny," she corrected.

"What's it about?" The kid was absorbed in his game again, but he was obviously expecting Liza to entertain him as the bus rolled forward and on towards Concord once more.

"Sailors who didn't like their captain," Liza explained. Guilt flooded over her as she struggled to force down the memories of her teammates' adoration when she'd been captain. Once, she'd been a leader on a state championship-winning basketball team and people had looked up to her. Now she was just fallen from the town's grace, and as the Milton of Manchester sped by out the window, Liza worried her lip and wondered if going back there was even the right thing to do.

She was returning home, defeated.

And Charlie still wouldn't answer his phone.

The bus stopped at a Mobil station in Bow, New Hampshire, to get gas before going up the road to Concord to pick up even more passengers. Liza didn't really understand why there were two stops so close together. She stared out the window as the Mobil station and hotels that dotted the juncture of I-89 and I-95 gave way to residential homes. This was the sort of look that she had always taken for granted in New England.

New Hampshire had always been something of a mystery to her. It bordered all of Maine and yet the people here, she reasoned, would be more at home in Alabama than in Maine or Vermont, or even Massachusetts. It was a place to start for her. As the bus wound its way up Route 13 towards Concord, the view was startling. She didn't understand why this place was so different from the rest of New England.

In Concord, Liza watched with raised eyebrows as a beat-up Chevy with a stars and bars sticker on its back dash drove down the street across from the bus station; she said nothing as the bus started to slowly empty. There was a long way to go until Portland, and then it was on to Bangor for this bus. More people would probably get on in Portland, she figured, and the bus route ended in Canada.

She sat back and continued to read about breadfruit and the increasingly harsh conditions on the ship, her mind drifting as the rain continued to fall outside. She fell asleep with her finger tucked into the book to mark her place, her hair falling into her eyes and her breathing finally even for what was probably the first time the entire trip.

Liza dreamt vividly. She always had.

She was standing in the house where she lived when she was three, just barely old enough to remember the feelings of betrayal as the man she'd thought to be her father and his tired wife drove her up to the social services office in Bangor. They had a child of their own now—a newborn, Liza's file read, and they could no longer take care of two children. Liza would be better off with a different family, and they urged the social worker to place her quickly so that there would be no bad memories. That had not happened. Even as a child, she had been so angry at the family that had loved her so strongly until she no longer served their purposes. Now that they had a child that was their flesh and blood, Liza no longer had any value in their lives.

They'd thrown her away like trash, and the emergency placement at ten o'clock on a Friday night, just before Memorial Day, had been every bit as bad.

The place that they'd sent her to haunted her to this day. She could not escape the stale smell of that house and the oppressive weight of the air around her as she moved from room to room. She was careless, a child, and her little body tripped on a rug and knocked a vase loose from its shelf. It crashed down around Liza, so like and yet unlike the rest of her life.

And Liza ran, skittering to a halt at the stairway, debating whether to go up or down. Fear was everywhere in this memory—in this dream—and she was afraid to move.

At the base of the stairs was an older girl with dark hair in a braid that ran down her back. She smiled and her warm brown eyes crinkled at the corners when she looked at Liza. Liza reached out, desperate to get away. The girl looked away when the hand on the small of Liza's back struck hard enough to bruise.

She had broken a vase, running indoors, and her foster sister would do nothing to stop her mother's wrath.

"-land," a voice crackled through the haze of dream and memory and Liza jerked awake. She blinked, surprised to see that they'd pulled into Portland just as the growing, rainy dusk had settled more firmly into night. "Portland, everyone out. Those traveling on to Bangor or Eastport can get back on in twenty minutes."

There was a line of pay phones across the street and Liza heaved her bag over her shoulder once more. It cut into the skin through her jacket and the sweater beneath it, and she winced. She hadn't had a dream about that place in months now, and as she inched ever closer to where it all began, she was not sure she wanted to keep going. Portland was as good a place as any to start over.

Liza could stay here. She'd be able to find a job and could perpetuate the lie of normalcy for a little while longer. Her money was completely gone—she'd spent it on her bus ticket and she wasn't particularly keen on repeating the same process that had plagued her since she'd been released from jail. She *had* to go back home to try and sort herself out in the one place she could think of where doors probably wouldn't be slammed in her face as soon as people figured out who she really was. She needed to go back there, even though she didn't want to; it was the only place where she might have the chance to become whole again.

Charlie didn't pick up when she called, but this time the operator allowed her to leave a message, free of charge. Liza didn't really know what to say, and swallowed desperately against her dry mouth, praying for the words to tumble forth and out into the world. "Coach..." Her tongue felt thick and heavy as she spoke. "It's Liza Hawke. Look, I... I don't really know where else to go anymore. I'm on a bus headed home. I'm going to need a place to stay." The words stretched out into silence and the answering machine clicked off into an empty, almost ringing sound. Charlie wasn't going to do her any favors, Liza knew this now.

"Can I try one more number?" she asked. She'd hung up the phone and dialed zero one more time, and the operator had politely informed her that she could not redial the same number collect if there was no one on the other end who would accept the charges.

"No messages this time," the operator replied. Liza gave her the name of the only other person in all of her godforsaken hometown that might still give a damn about her.

She stood in the rain in Portland, squinting across the street at the bus station, making sure that the bus wouldn't leave before she was on it, as she listened to the phone ring. After the tone pulsed twice, she found herself smiling as a harassed-sounding Kevin Jaspen told the operator that yes, he would accept the charges to speak to Elizabeth Hawke in Portland.

"Hey Kevin," Liza said. She didn't really know how to ask him what she wanted to ask.

"Hawke." His tone was curt, but not without warmth.

Even over the phone, Liza could tell he was smiling, just a little bit.

"What has got you calling me from Portland of all far-too-close-for-comfort places?"

Sighing, Liza wrapped a strand of hair around her finger and watched as it curled, straw-yellow against her skin, and then fell flat and limp once more. She needed a shower and a decent night's rest. "I'm coming there." She glanced at the bus station once more. They were starting to line up, but she was pretty sure that it was just the bus for Boston. "I want to try and start over."

"Then why the hell are you coming *here?*" Kevin wanted to know.

Liza didn't think there was an answer for that. It was seven-thirty on a Thursday—right before a holiday weekend. The roads were clogged with early vacationers headed to and from their homes and destinations. She just wanted to stop, to rest. She wanted, and the thought terrified her beyond all measure, to go home.

"Dunno if you've been keeping up, but this place is dead nine months out of the year, love."

"I know." She cradled the phone between her hands. "I'm getting in at nine; can I crash at yours for the night?"

"Is one night going to turn into many?" he asked. His tone was mild and not accusatory, which Liza was thankful for. She didn't really want to have to explain to him that she had nowhere else to go. Not just yet at any rate.

Liza rolled her eyes. "I'm calling you because you were a friend, Kevin. A really good friend, once upon a time. I've already tried Charlie…but he won't pick up, and I don't dare call Nancy, not after what happened." Liza wasn't above asking for help, but she *was* above begging. She would find a place to stay even if it wasn't with Kevin, and they both knew that.

He chuckled. "Nice to know I'm still playing second best to Charlie White."

Liza could feel the sarcasm dripping through the phone and rolled her eyes once more, even though he couldn't see her.

"I'll be there. You can still mend traps right?"

"And man the boat if you need me to," Liza replied. She hung up, listening to the sounds of the city streets. Portland was a nice city, and Liza had lived in enough of them to tell the good ones form the bad. When she'd been seventeen, Portland had seemed like the greatest city in the world, but then she traveled across the country to the other Portland and had found everything that she'd never wanted in a city that was supposed to represent her freedom—her escape.

Boarding the bus once more, she tried not to think about what might be waiting for her when she returned to Near Haven. She went back to reading about breadfruit and Tahiti and shit getting real on the Bounty and tried not to think about anything at all.

She had left Maine on a day like this in May, ten years ago. It was raining when Charlie and his daughter had driven her to Portland with only one suitcase and a new pair of Jordans in Near Haven High's colors. Back then, Liza had stared down at their black, white, and deep purple the whole drive, a swell of gratitude welling up within her.

Charlie had smiled at her and had hugged her at the airport. Having never had a father, she figured Charlie was the closest she'd ever had. All she could think about today, despite the book and the same beat-up pair of Jordans jammed into the top of her bag, was how she'd let him down. He'd done so much to get her out—and she'd thrown it all away for the first guy who told her she was beautiful.

Liza pushed all thoughts of *that* from her mind and watched out the window, as the rainy city gave way to the thick pine forests of northern coastal Maine.

Kevin's beat-up old Isuzu pickup was still running, apparently. It was the same car he'd had in high school, bought off of his father before he'd left the town to go further south and attempt to start a carpentry business. Liza remembered driving out of town to go camping in New Hampshire with Kevin and how it rained so hard they'd set up a tarp over the truck bed and slept there, drinking stolen Bud Light and singing along to Green Day on the radio.

Liza was the only one to get off the bus in Near Haven and she didn't thank the driver when she departed. Her heart thudded in her chest and she was suddenly very grateful that Near Haven was such a small town. No one, save Kevin, who was leaning against the hood of his truck, was there to see her arrive. No one had to know just yet. Liza liked that. She liked the feeling of anonymity. Maybe this way it would be easier for her to lie to herself and pretend that this was just another place that she'd come to, like any of the places before that. This wasn't a place where she'd had endings or beginnings. If she lied to herself hard enough, she could almost believe that she was starting over here with a blank slate.

The bus roared off down Main Street, pausing at the single stoplight before disappearing into the inky night.

Liza inhaled the smell of the salt air and stepped towards Kevin, hand raised in greeting.

He raised one in return, but it was the sudden sight of the other that had Liza hissing, "*Jesus*, what the fuck happened to your hand?"

"Stuck in a pot that Billy was throwing overboard," Kevin said. He glanced down at the prosthetic that formed his left hand. Liza's eyes widened as he shrugged nonchalantly and pulled her into a tight hug. "I nearly drowned."

"Shit, man." Liza said. She let out a breath of air at the tightness of his embrace and kissed him on the cheek. Once she'd thought that they'd be lovers, but that had been a long time ago. Kevin had been an odd kid when they were in school, and Liza always figured that he'd be an odd adult too. Now he was just a face from her past, and Liza was not entirely sure she knew what to say to him. It had been a very long time since she'd felt this awkward. She shifted from foot to foot, looking at Kevin's black leather jacket and ratty Sox T-shirt beneath it. He had on black jeans that had seen better days, and he looked a lot more like the bad boy from a boy band than a lobsterman with only one hand.

"I renamed the boat." He stepped back, grinning at her.

"Did you now?" She raised an eyebrow. When they were kids, the boat had been named for Kevin's mother. "To what? The *Black Pearl*?"

"Well, given that Billy's last name is Schmee, I went with the *Jolly Roger*." He nearly pouted as Liza threw back her head and laughed and laughed. Of course he had.

Billy and Kevin had been inseparable since childhood. Their fathers had both had lobster boats, as well as a tidy side business renting skiffs to tourists during the summer and doing island-hopping day trips on the weekends. Billy was a few years older than Kevin; she couldn't remember exactly how many years off the top of her head. She thought it might have been three, since they'd been in high school together, but Billy had always had trouble in school. There was no telling if he'd been held back due to academics. He was a good friend to Kevin, better than Liza had ever been, at any rate.

"You got a sick sense of humor, Jaspen." She clapped him on the shoulder and grinned at him. Raising an eyebrow, a smirk playing on her lips, she added, "Or should I say, Captain Hook?"

His eyes glittered dangerously in the light of the streetlamp above them. "Speaking of *children's* films," he said glaring at Liza, "get in. I have to drop something off for a friend."

Still chuckling, Liza threw her bag into the back of Kevin's truck. It smelled like fish and the ocean and she wrinkled her nose and adjusted the bag so that it wouldn't touch the collection of rain- and seawater-wet leaves that had piled up in the bed of Kevin's truck. She hopped into the cab where Kevin was already fiddling with the radio. He produced a cassette from above his sun visor and popped it into the tape player. When the opening chords of *Blue Highway* filled the cab, Liza couldn't help but smile. Ten years later and Kevin's taste in music was pretty much the same. Somehow, she was not really all that surprised.

Kevin drove up Main and turned left on Park.

Liza peered around at the brightly-lit windows of the town as Kevin drove slowly through the streets. There was a brown paper bag on the seat beside him that moved occasionally and Liza knew that there was at least one lobster in it. She was tempted to open it up and have a look, curious if the sea crustaceans had changed at all.

The town was pretty much the same. Liza still held her breath as they drove by the church graveyard; she very pointedly didn't look at Charlie's house as they passed it heading up the hill that overlooked the town. They moved on to High Pine Street. She still remembered this street and the time she'd spent briefly living on it when she was barely old enough to count her fingers and toes. It wasn't really all that different, and Liza was about to disregard the street when Kevin pulled up to the one house that Liza had no interest in ever entering again. Staring up at the house, Liza could feel her heart hammering in her chest as though she'd just played a full forty minutes of basketball with no break. It dwarfed all of the other structures on the street in size and prominence and belonged to the senator's wife, who'd taken over his job after he had a heart attack some five years before.

Sitting in St. Paul, Liza had been surprised to open the newspaper and read about the sudden and rather traumatic death of a Maine senator who'd had a massive coronary on his way back to his home state. She shook her head, for her involvement with that family had been a lifetime ago. Another family *had* to be living there now. Leaning forward, Liza reached for the crank handle to lower the truck's window, desperate to get rid of the smell of fish and sweaty man that seemed to cling to the truck's interior.

"Be just a sec," Kevin said. He took the brown paper bag and stepped out of the cab, then slammed the door shut and let himself into the gated yard.

From the doorway, a small figure shot across the lawn. The little boy was wearing his pajamas and was barefoot as Kevin scooped him up with his good hand.

"I have a present for you." Kevin spun the kid around for a second.

Liza was pretty sure that this was the strangest thing she'd witnessed yet. Kevin wasn't supposed to be good with kids. He was *supposed* to be her weird friend from high school who used to wear eyeliner and listen to Insane Clown Posse and Slipknot to the point people started to worry about him. They'd been kids in the Nineties; everyone was on the lookout for teenagers who wore all black and listened to the wrong sort of music in those days.

Regardless, being an adult wasn't a good look on him... on either of them really.

"This little guy wasn't going to make it if we put 'im back," Kevin said. He deftly opened the bag with his prosthetic and reached in to pull out a small white bundle. "So I thought that you could look after him in your tank?"

The little boy nodded solemnly and took the bundle from Kevin—it was not a lobster—Liza leaned forward and caught sight of the stark white of a shell. It was a hermit crab...had to be.

"Did you ask my mom?" the kid asked. Kevin grinned in response.

"I'm sure that your mother will understand doing a good deed." Kevin winked and pushed himself back to his feet.

The little boy turned with carefully cupped hands and made his way back to the door.

That was when Liza first caught a glimpse of the boy's mother standing in the doorway and dressed to the nines. She didn't look particularly familiar and a wave of relief floated easily over Liza. If she didn't have to deal with *that* family while she was sorting her shit out, it would be a blessing.

Liza glanced up through her curtain of hair and caught the woman's face as she stepped under the porch light. She was *gorgeous*. She was Sofia Milton and she had aged fucking beautifully.

Liza slumped down in the seat as Kevin climbed back into the cab.

"Not hiding, are you?" he asked, with a raised eyebrow. He moved the gear shift and pulled the truck back onto the road proper. He peered over his shoulder at the house that they had just left and shrugged. "Pretty sure that she doesn't bite."

Groaning, Liza shook her head and forced her attention back out the window again. She watched the familiar houses as they passed them, running through the multitude of names of their residents that she had never been that good at recalling to begin with, trying to remember who lived where. People never left Near Haven.

Liza had been desperate to leave, and now she was sitting in Kevin's truck like she was still a junior in high school. This place had a terrible pull. "I take it she married Dave then?"

Kevin nodded and turned down Harbor Way, heading towards the house his father had built before either of them were born. It was Kevin's now, like the boat and the fishing business. His father had never made it in the carpentry business and ate his gun not long after Liza left for Oregon. She still hated to think about that phone call, Nancy begging her to come back, to console Kevin. Liza had started against Montana that night and Nancy hadn't called again.

"Lost him too," Kevin said, as he turned into his driveway.

Lobster pots and buoys littered his front porch and Liza collected her things from the back of the truck without a word. She brushed off the wet leaves and slung the bag over her shoulder.

"Dave drowned; they were out on a sailboat—the whole family was there, even the senator—and got caught in a squall. It took the coast guard three hours to find him." Kevin shook his head and kicked a damaged pot out of the way as he crossed to his front door. It skittered to a halt against a four-high stack of them, wobbling precariously against the railing that wrapped around the porch. He turned to Liza after he'd unlocked the door, hand still resting on the handle. "There's a lot of talk in town—that it wasn't really an accident, and you know better than most how Sofia's mother is."

And Liza did know. She'd felt that wrath and knew Sofia had felt it too. It was a secret that Liza intended to take to her grave, and she made sure that her CPS records had been sealed once she aged out of the system. No one had to know the secrets of the Milton family, even if Liza was far too young at the time to know many of them at all. Still, she'd felt the sting and had endured the bruises until a more permanent solution was found. She'd done it because it meant that Sofia, all of seven years old at the time, would smile at her. She'd smile and just for that instant, the pain would leave her eyes.

"What do you think?" Liza asked. She followed Kevin inside. The house was largely unchanged. The wide stone fireplace still dominated the living room, but Liza could see that Kevin had decorated the mantle with various things he'd found over the years. The antique glass Asian buoys—that Liza remembered helping him untangle from a truly frightening-looking piece of seaweed when they were six—were still there, but now there were a few old-looking bottles and some interesting driftwood as well.

"I haven't really ever thought about it." Kevin shrugged. "But you'd best get to bed if you're going to be helping out on the boat in the morning." He gestured vaguely towards the couch and yawned. "We can fix the pots tomorrow night."

He disappeared into his bedroom and came out a minute later with a pillow and a blanket that Liza gratefully took. She was okay with the couch; it was better than sitting on an uncomfortable bus seat for damn near two full days. She was exhausted and world weary on top of it.

It hadn't really sunk in that she was back yet, and Liza wondered if she would dare stay long enough for it to.do just that.

CHAPTER TWO

Summer (17 June, 2012)

LIZA FELL INTO ROUTINES EASILY. She supposed that her childhood had created her need for things to stay regimented. Her life had been in flux so often that the simple act of Kevin dumping rain gear on her at four thirty in the morning was the routine that she latched onto.

She stumbled into the kitchen and made coffee as Kevin, out on the porch in nothing but his boxers, scowled up at the pre-dawn sky. He was trying to determine if they should wear their raingear out to the car or simply bring it with them and put it on when they got down to the boat. The last thing any of them wanted was to spend the day cold, damp, and miserable because the freezing Maine rain had gotten into their hoodies and socks. This was a morning ritual, and after he'd made his determination, he would come in and down two cups of the coffee Liza had made, black and strong.

Mornings were usually a mixture of Kevin opening the fridge and staring blearily at its contents before slamming it shut and announcing, as he did most mornings, that they would be getting take-out sandwiches for lunch. They never lingered after Kevin's announcement of their lunch plans and Liza's subsequent eye roll. They hurriedly got dressed and then drove down to the docks to meet Billy.

Billy usually had more coffee, and the sandwiches that Kevin decided they would have for lunch, when he met them at the docks. Liza always liked Billy because he never judged. He had a nervous personality that sometimes made her wary, but he never once commented on her being back in the one place that no one ever thought she'd return to.

When she was seven, Liza had lived with Kevin and his father for a spell while Child Protective Services attempted to work out a placement for her. The Milton family obviously hadn't been an option anymore, and there didn't seem to be many other places for her to go. Kevin's father, despite his flaws, was a good man. He had done all the paperwork before Liza had even screwed up the courage to ask if she could stay with him and Kevin while CPS sorted it out.

He taught her how to fish and how to fix lobster traps. She could sew canvas and weave a net by hand if she had to. It came in handy, as Kevin had never learned and had no money to repair the holes in his traps with anything but the least expensive materials he could buy at the Home Depot up in Bangor.

Liza told herself that she was just earning her keep, but she liked it. There was no one to judge when she was hanging off the side of a boat, trying to hook a buoy with one hand, while desperately flinging the other hand out to keep her balance. She was always good at balance drills, and she had excelled at off-balance shots when she'd played ball. Now she was just hauling in traps and throwing the small lobsters back, keeping half an eye out for more hermit crabs for Kevin's little friend. It all seemed so simple.

It was late in the evening when they returned to shore, hungry, exhausted, and desperate for a shower. Liza usually let Kevin go first, and puttered around the kitchen figuring out what to cook for dinner while she waited for him to finish.

Cooking came naturally to her. She'd worked a good bit in kitchens as she'd traveled across the country. It had always seemed to her that most back-of-the-house employees had records of one sort or another. Liza hated that the record stuck with her, following her around, even though the circumstances of her initial arrest were so convoluted and stupid. She had always been too proud to lie about it on her application, and while some states had specific timeframes for reporting criminal records, there wasn't any sort of consistency state to state. She figured that when she was ten years removed from the incident, she could potentially pass it off like a foolish collegiate mistake—like a DUI with more jail time or something. Maybe by then she would have her shit together enough to know what she wanted out of life.

That morning, when she'd eaten breakfast, she had used the last of the milk. They needed to get more. Liza stood in front of the refrigerator in an old T-shirt that she thought might have belonged to her freshman roommate at Portland State and gym shorts, contemplating the dismal lack of food contained within the battered, old relic from the seventies. Scowling, she pushed the door closed and crossed to stand in front of the half-closed bathroom door. She knocked and called, "I'm going to get some groceries."

The sounds of water splashing inside stopped and Kevin shouted over the still-running showerhead, "What?"

Puffing out her cheeks in exasperation, Liza reached for the door handle, thought better of it, and raised the volume of her voice instead of opening the door further. She didn't need to see any of that, *again*. "We have nothing to eat. I'm taking the truck and going to the store."

The splashing started up again, and Kevin's reply was nearly lost as the sound echoed off the thin bathroom walls. "Go ahead. Get me some apples."

Rolling her eyes, Liza retreated into Kevin's room and fished his truck keys out of his work pants that he had left in a heap in the middle of the floor. She found them after trying two pockets and hesitated for a minute before turning away from the wallet jammed into the back pocket where she'd found the keys. She had earned enough cash during the three weeks she'd worked with him to afford to buy groceries if she wanted to.

The truck, p.o.s. that it was, started on the first try and Liza couldn't help but think that this was the first time she had driven anything with more horses than a golf cart in nearly a year. The last time, if she recalled correctly, had been in Knoxville, when she helped drive some drunken college students home after a football game for ten bucks and a couch to crash on for the night. At the time, Liza had been very caught up in the injustice of it all. It had been strange to be back on Tennessee's campus, given that the last time she'd been there, she'd gotten her ass handed to her on the court by a gargantuan guard who must've had at least six inches and thirty pounds on her, and was playing shooting guard.

Now though, she was plagued with a different sort of injustice. She didn't know what she was doing, walking into a grocery store that was sure to be full of people who hated and resented what she'd done to the town's good name. No amount of pointing out that she was released, that it was part of a bigger conspiracy, and that she had just taken the fall for a guy she was stupidly in love with seemed to work. The judgmental gazes had gotten better in recent days, but Liza could still feel the sting of their anger even now, as she walked through a mostly empty parking lot.

Even Kevin and Billy, though they avoided the topic like the plague, both mentioned that her name was no better than Sam Mud's these days in Near Haven. Despite this, Liza reasoned that she had money and it was legal tender. They were not going to turn her away from buying groceries.

Memories in a small town were stupidly long-lasting.

Though there was a chain store just up the road, maybe ten miles away, that probably boasted better prices, Liza pulled into the small lot in front of Sprat and Co. instead. For as long as anyone could remember, Sprat and Co. had been the grocer of choice for all of Near Haven. They were a local company, owned by a man named Jack and his wife. Liza remembered saving up the dimes and nickels she found on her runs as a teenager for the dollar soft-serve they had in the back corner of the store. It would sometimes take a week or more to save up enough, but she always took her time and savored the treat like the rarity that it was.

She swung the truck into a parking spot next to a very nice older Mercedes, taking care to leave enough room so that no one's door got dinged and headed inside.

She knew the store well; nothing had changed in the years of Liza's absence, and it was easy to move through her list without feeling overwhelmed the way that she sometimes did when she went grocery shopping. They had not moved anything around since Liza was just a kid when that nor'easter and the not-hurricane had collided into the perfect storm. Back then, the store got flooded when the tide washed right over the bulkheads and into town proper. She remembered how outraged everyone in town had been when that storm wasn't named as the final hurricane of the season. It had been too late, the meteorologists said, but the people here knew better. It took the better part of two years for the town to completely return to normal.

Still trapped in her thoughts, Liza bent down to contemplate the choices of pasta on the bottom shelf. She was debating angel hair pasta over regular spaghetti when she caught sight of the small boy with brown hair from her first night in town, standing at the end of the aisle. He was wearing a bright red T-shirt, pushing a cart as his mother walked beside it. Liza swallowed, reaching out with a shaking hand to pick up the box of pasta and put it into her basket.

They were walking right behind her now and she felt woefully underdressed and smelly, given how she'd been out on the water all day. She likely had lobster gunk in her hair, or maybe seaweed. Probably both.

She was trying to look wholly interested in the pasta sauce selection, but curiosity was getting the better of her. She kept sneaking glances over her shoulder, watching the slow progression of mother and son as they made their way down the aisle. The little boy was walking on his tip toes as he pushed the cart, and now that he was closer, Liza saw the all-too-familiar emblem of her former coach's summer basketball camp printed in white across the front of his shirt. The red, if Liza remembered correctly, meant that he was still in elementary school.

Sofia Milton paused, staring at something on the shelf to Liza's left.

Liza shuffled out of the way, trying not to draw attention to herself.

Sofia was dressed to the nines and her heels looked like they were designer made.

Liza squatted down to select a jar of cheap, off-brand pasta sauce. She had nearly gotten it into her basket and was moving to stand once more when the kid, half-hanging off the back of the cart, wrinkled his nose and stared in obvious disgust at her beat-up old Jordans.

"Your kicks are old." He was half-swinging off the cart handles with his own pair of LeBrons, looking like he had just walked out of the store with them on.

Liza picked up her basket and stood, grinning at him despite her fear of what his mother would no doubt say to her. "They do their job," she said. She forced herself to smile as pleasantly as she could with her stomach all twisted up in knots as she turned to his mother. "Charlie doesn't like it when kids wear their shoes outside. He says that the dirt and stuff from outside messes up the gym floor."

"I'm sure that you, of all people, are not in a position to comment on what that old man says or does not say."

There was such utter dismissal in Sofia's tone that Liza didn't even bother to fight it. She simply shrugged and turned away, taking her basket and heading towards the front of the store without looking back. She grabbed a bag of apples from an end-cap display and moved through the motions of the checkout, paying for the food out of her own pocket. It was strange, handing over her hard-earned money and knowing that she wasn't just barely subsisting for herself. Liza felt really good about it for the first time in a long time.

She was out in the parking lot and loading her bags onto the passenger's seat when someone tapped her on the shoulder. Liza slammed the door shut and turned, fully ready to give that woman a piece of her mind for being so exceptionally bitchy. The words died in her throat when she saw who it was, and her stomach dropped to somewhere around her knees. "Hey," she said quietly, almost shyly.

Nancy White stared back at her for a long moment with disbelief evident in her green eyes before she launched herself at Liza. She didn't seem to care that Liza probably still had seaweed or maybe even lobster goop in her hair. She just hugged Liza as close as she could, face buried in the sandy-blonde hair that was frizzing out of the plait that ran down her back.

Liza didn't make friends easily. She had never been able to. Friendship didn't come naturally to kids who had never had a permanent fixture in their lives. The only two pieces of her life that had remained the same, no matter where she went, were her baby blanket and a stuffed bear.

Despite this, friendship had always come so easily with Nancy. She was younger than Liza by about four years, and by the looks of it, just out of college and back in this godforsaken place. Liza had tossed away that friendship, like so many others, on her way to the airport that had taken her from one Portland to another and far away from Near Haven.

And yet Nancy was hugging her as though Liza was the only thing keeping her grounded.

"You came back," Nancy said almost breathlessly. She had cut her hair stylishly short, and still dressed like she'd fallen out of some hipster store catalogue. She was dressed all in white and lace, and looked like a fairy-tale princess and not the little fourteen-year-old that had seen Liza off at the airport in Portland some ten years before. "Oh Liza."

This time the reunion hug came easier to Liza. With Kevin, it was easy to avoid. She could scowl and point out that he had a weapon of maiming for a hand and he could wink lewdly at her and ask if she wanted to know what else it could do, which was *horrible* to think too much about. Liza thought that she was pretty good on that front, never thinking about *that* again, but she would still roll her eyes and act horrified. It was almost like it was before.

The "almost" was what had kept her from venturing into town until now. It had kept her down Harbor Way and out on the boat with the lobsters and the seals that popped their little whiskered faces up out of the bay and watched with doleful, curious eyes as Liza and the others moved from pot to pot, checking the day's catch. It was easier out there on the water; there were no expectations except to not fall overboard.

"Nancy." Liza hugged her back just as tightly. Liza was gross and she didn't care. This girl, who was now a woman, was the closest thing she'd ever had to a sister. She'd grown up and Liza had missed it all; she almost hated herself for staying away as long as she had.

No one ever left Near Haven, and if they did leave, they came back. It was like every other fishing town, or every other mill town that Liza had ever been to: a vicious circle of hell that no one could escape. The pull of the small town was just too great.

"As tender as I'm sure this reunion is, you are blocking access to my car."

It was the cool, clipped tone that made Liza back away slowly from Nancy, guilt flooding her face as she complied without question. She was not sure if it was the tone or the delivery or both, but Liza couldn't help but think that Sofia sounded so much like her mother—who was (thankfully) far away from here, pretending to be an upstanding citizen.

"Miss White." Sofia had an armful of groceries and a child in tow, but she looked every bit the woman her mother had raised her to be.

Liza really wasn't sure what to make of her and stared openly. She was struck by how sad Sofia Milton seemed, and by how hauntingly beautiful she was.

Liza was about to open her mouth to reply, when Sofia's nose wrinkled and she added with a note of distaste clearly evident in her voice, "Miss *Hawke*."

"Sorry, Madam Mayor," Nancy said and shuffled out of the space between the two cars.

Liza followed her, scowling and not quite able to shake the gut-punched feeling that came with the title that Nancy had used to address Sofia. She would never, not in a million years, have thought that Sofia would follow her parents into politics. Sure, it had been the assumption that the daughter of a senator and an absolute witch of a debutante would do something *meaningful* with her life, but from what Liza recalled of Sofia—from the summers she'd returned to town from whichever Seven Sisters school she'd gone to (Holyoke? Or maybe Vassar? Liza couldn't remember, it somehow had never seemed important for her to know.)—she had been more interested in Dave and their future life together.

The little boy in his too-expensive shoes was clutching a gallon of milk to his chest and Liza was about to smile at him, but Nancy spoke first.

"You're Nathan, right?" She gave the kid that same kind smile that Liza had seen in her throughout their many years of knowing each other.

Nancy had grown up, and somehow Liza had missed it.

He nodded. Looking up at Nancy with solemn eyes.

Liza's eyebrows shot up. She wasn't sure why, but she thought Sofia would have named her child after her late father, or maybe her husband. Liza stood awkwardly off to one side, leaning on the back of the truck as the little boy—*Nathan*—scrutinized Nancy.

"You're Ms. White. I'm in your class next year."

Nancy flashed him a smile that painfully reminded Liza of Nancy's father and nodded decisively. "Yup, I got the class lists yesterday in the mail."

Nathan hiked up the milk jug, holding it more comfortably in one hand so that he was able to hold out the other for a proper handshake. The condensation from the milk stained his red shirt maroon. "It's nice to meet you," he said. He was the picture of politeness.

Nancy shook his hand with a small and private smile on her face.

Liza jammed her hands into her shorts pockets and stared off into the distance. She felt like she was intruding, and from here she could almost see the ocean if she looked just right. She didn't know why she felt so awkward now. This was normal. Meetings like this were a normal part of life here. Everyone was connected; everyone was caught up in everyone else's business. There could be no expectation of privacy in a place like this.

"Nathan." Sofia had rolled down the Mercedes's window. "We have to go home now."

He smiled brightly at both of them and then scampered off to the passenger side's back seat, calling good-bye over his shoulder.

Liza almost smiled as she watched him strap himself into a booster seat under his mother's watchful gaze. He must be just at the end of having to need one of those, judging by his height and weight. Liza wondered if it was some sort of a paranoia on his mother's part that kept him in it.

Sofia shifted the car into reverse and pulled out of the space expertly, not even bothering to spare either of them a glance as she drove off.

"*Bitch*," Nancy muttered under her breath.

Liza turned to her, her mouth half open in shock. Her friend *had* grown up, it seemed, even if she still dressed like she'd fallen out of some college hipster's sixties wet dream. Liza remembered joking once, when Liza was sixteen and wearing belly shirts and baggy pants and Nancy was just entering adolescence and embracing the flowing look of the hippy movement, that Nancy had been born into the wrong decade. Liza shrugged, the soft cotton of her T-shirt scratching at her ears and a slow smile growing across her face. She didn't know why the easy feeling of friendship was coming back so effortlessly. She had been out of the loop of Nancy's life for so long now that it almost felt like she was intruding. An awkward silence fell around them, and Liza tried to figure out what to say next.

"What are you doing for dinner?" Liza asked after a long pause of awkward silence.

Nancy spent the time chewing on her lip and staring at the ground. She was being very careful not to meet Liza's gaze.

"I'm staying at Kevin's."

"I had gathered." Nancy looked up then, a wry smile playing on her lips. She jerked her head to the truck. "You were always going off with him in this thing back then too." She sucked in a deep breath of salty-smelling air, hesitation clearly evident on her face, and then asked, "You aren't sleeping with him, are you?"

Shaking her head violently, Liza let out a bark of laughter that felt stupidly good after being glared at by Miss High-and-Mighty (who was apparently the mayor of this shithole town—when the fuck did that happen?).

"Nah, just the couch. Which is lumpy and smells like beer and piss."

"Well you smell like lobster boat, so there is that," Nancy pointed out. "And I don't have any plans for dinner."

"Did you drive?" Liza asked. She moved towards the cab once more, pulled the door open, and shoved all the groceries towards the middle of the bench seat.

"Walked." Nancy returned her earlier shrug with one of her own.

"Get in then," Liza replied. "I'll cook."

"This I gotta see." There was a wicked glint in Nancy's eyes as she scrambled into the passenger side of the truck and poked through the grocery bags with curious eyes.

Liza wanted to point out that ten years was plenty long enough to acquire a hobby, thank you very much, but the retort died on her lips when Nancy smiled at her, warm and true.

Maybe this was the feeling that she had been missing.

Kevin was (thankfully) dressed when they got back and seemed genuinely happy to see Nancy. Liza left them to their strange local beer that he had produced from the refrigerator and took a quick shower. Dinner came easily after that, conversation and food prep seguing beautifully into Kevin doing the dishes and Liza and Nancy sitting out on the porch, watching the fireflies dance over the harbor.

Liza pulled one of the busted-up traps that Kevin had clearly avoided fixing towards her, and inspected the damage. It looked like something had chewed its way through the netting, which was a little bizarre, since there wasn't much in the water here capable of doing that. She turned the trap this way and that, not really sure what she was supposed to say to Nancy now.

"My dad wanted to go to your parole hearing," Nancy offered after a few moments of drawn-out listening to the crickets chirp. She sipped her beer and stared out over the harbor.

She was not looking at Liza, and Liza was grateful for it. She couldn't imagine what her face looked like right now—a grimace of pain and anguish, probably. "I talked him out of it."

Liza's hand faltered and stilled on the top of the trap. "Why?" She was not sure that she wanted to know the reason, but the curiosity burned within her all the same. With slightly shaking hands she reached for the scissors that were set on the window next to her beer. She was sitting on an overturned fruit crate as if it were some high society throne, while Nancy leaned against the porch's support pillar, still not looking at her.

Liza measured out two arm lengths of wax-coated nylon cording and waited, fingers twisting the frayed edge of the twine and slowly unraveling it.

"When the news broke here that you were going to be released due to new evidence in your case, no one knew what to make of it. My dad especially." Nancy shrugged. "I know you though, and we looked up the details of what's-his-face…"

"Jared," Liza growled with more malice than she thought herself capable of.

Nancy started, as if surprised, and stared at Liza across the porch.

Liza's knuckles were white as she gripped the twine, halfway into making an accidental knot. "Jared fucking Dickens, may he rot in jail for the rest of his unfortunate life." She didn't say that she wished she could kill him twice over, just for what he had taken from her. Her future was gone, snuffed out in an instant. She had been unwitting, but an accomplice nonetheless. Liza hated that she could not escape the conviction, no matter how innocent her intentions had been. The watches that had been found in her possession were still stolen, and she was not the first girl Jared had duped into taking the fall for him.

Liza tied the knot off and looked up at Nancy. "You should have let him come. It..." She looked away, frizzing bangs falling into her eyes. "It would have been nice to see someone I knew there."

No one had been there for her at the hearing. It had been two women and a grizzled old man asking her if she'd learned her lesson and if she was ready to be a useful member of society even though it was blatantly obvious to everyone involved that she'd been framed by her horrible boyfriend. She'd answered as truthfully as she could, and the state had cut her a check for her trouble and the loss of her career, but would not strike the conviction from her record. It was—still was really—a fucked-up situation.

Nancy turned her attention back to the harbor and the dancing fireflies. She didn't speak for a long time, sipping on her beer as Liza reweaved the busted net on the lobster pot. There wasn't anything to say. Liza had said her piece, and Nancy had explained her view.

Liza used to think that Sundays were the easy days. Nothing ever happened on Sundays. Well, now she knew better, and was grateful when Kevin came out, towel still slung over his shoulder. He stood with his hands on his hips and announced to the pair that he was going to attempt to make cookies, if they would like to supervise. It broke the ice, and soon Liza and Nancy were laughing together again, maybe not able to forget, but starting to forgive.

It was much later when Liza drove Nancy back to her dad's place when the conversation turned back to what it had at dinner. Nancy was telling Liza about how she had a lease starting in August, but she was apparently staying with her dad until the apartment was ready. "Actually," Nancy said, pasta expertly twirled around her fork, "I'm probably going to need a roommate."

Liza told her that she'd think about it. Now though, as she dropped Nancy off outside her father's house, she couldn't help the little urge in her stomach that was desperately wanting to tell Nancy no. She didn't want to be here that long, no matter how easy it would be to fall back into the pattern of this place.

The people here understood, and yet didn't understand. Liza didn't think that she would ever truly understand or fully comprehend how utterly her involvement with Jared Dickens had destroyed her life.

Liza looked up from where she was studying the nicks in the leather of the steering wheel cover that Kevin had had since forever.

Charlie White was standing on the porch, staring at her with a sad-looking smile on his face.

Liza reached forward and slowly cranked down the window in time to hear him call her name.

"Hawke!" he shouted, his voice sounding far older than she ever remembered it sounding. "Can you still play?"

The question wasn't one that had ever been an issue. Liza had always been able to play ball. Maybe she was a little rusty, but it was like riding a bicycle. She'd never forget sitting around as a kid watching Jordan do layup after layup until she fully understood the mechanics of it. "Yeah, coach," she called back.

"Camp starts after the fourth. I expect you there to assist." He scratched at his grey beard and she could tell he was smiling beneath it. Charlie had always been a good guy, and she was eternally grateful for all he had done for her during her childhood. "One-fifty a week, you can still gallivant with your lobster boy in the mornings."

Liza reached forward and started the truck's engine. "I'll be there, coach."

CHAPTER THREE

Camp (4-11 July, 2012)

THEY SPENT THE FOURTH ON the boat, drinking
Miller High Life and shooting off illegal fireworks that
Billy produced from the trunk of his car. Liza brought
Nancy along, and with her came her friends—friends that
Liza scarcely remembered from the last time she'd lived
in Near Haven. They were all grown up, and it was very
jarring for Liza. Rachel, who had always been quiet and
reserved as a kid, had grown into a woman who obviously
was far more comfortable with her sexuality than Liza was
herself. Ashleigh had a child and was married at twenty-
four, which was fucking bizarre. Liza thought of Ashleigh
as a round-cheeked kid who'd played dress up with Nancy
in the seventh grade when Liza had snuck them into the
high school's theatre costume room after school.

With all the unseen underwater obstacles that dotted
the water outside of Near Haven's tiny cove and harbor,
Kevin probably was too drunk to be driving a boat around.
Liza didn't stop him though, because, if she was honest,
she had no clue where any of the rocks were anymore.
They talked and laughed and Liza dove into the water on

a somewhat drunken dare. The water was freezing and she came up for air shivering and covered in goosebumps, but in the heat of the mid-afternoon sun, it felt good.

She dove down once more, pushing herself into the deep water and the gently swaying seaweed. Her eyes stung as she moved around the brown and yellowish, slimy feeling leaves. She was looking for something in particular, among the seaweed, something that she was not sure she would find without a mask and snorkel. Still, there it was, swimming in her murky vision, clinging to a rock. The salt water stung her eyes. Liza reached forward and pulled the tiny starfish from its spot on the rock and clutched it close to her chest as she kicked her way back to the surface.

"Thought you'd gotten stuck under the boat," Kevin said. Liza hauled herself up and out of the water and padded, dripping wet, over to Nancy.

"Do you remember these?" Liza asked. She pressed the starfish into Nancy's hand and wrung the water from her hair and onto the Roger's deck, shivering in the bright July sunlight as Nancy cradled the tiny creature cupped between her hands.

"You used to fish them out for everyone." Nancy laughed, prodding at the creature with one finger. "And named them," she added with a raised, skeptical black eyebrow.

"That one's Claude," Liza answered smoothly, and everyone laughed.

Nancy, after a moment's pondering, delegated an empty bait bucket to play house to Claude the starfish. She leaned over the side and filled it with water for their temporary friend. Claude slowly righted himself and attached himself to the side of the bucket as the night progressed.

The salt water dried in Liza's hair and she tilted her head back, staring up into the night sky thoughtfully. It was an odd feeling, tinged with the flavors of happiness. Maybe she just didn't know who she was anymore, and this was as good an identity as any.

She was more than a little drunk when she told Nancy that she'd be willing to room with her once her apartment was ready. They were walking back—she, Ashleigh, and Rachel, with Nancy trailing half a step behind them—heading to town to see the real fireworks display, when it just sort of slipped out. The words were leaden, uncomfortable on Liza's tongue, as she stared at Nancy.

"I'd wondered what was holding you back." Nancy confessed with a small, closed-off smile.

They were leaning back against the trees atop the hill; Ashleigh and Rachel were talking a little ways down the hill from them, in a second outcropping of broad, hundred-year-old maples.

As the fireworks erupted above them, Liza realized that she didn't really have an answer for Nancy's non-question. Or at least, not one that she felt as though she could share with Nancy. She had hoped that returning to Near Haven would simply be a stopping point on the way to somewhere else—somewhere better—but with the money from helping Kevin out and the promise of a place of her (almost) own come late summer, Liza was finding that she almost didn't want to leave. Memories and her own curiosity gripped her, and she desperately wanted to stay long enough to find out more about this town and all that had happened since she had left.

"I don't know." Liza shrugged. Her shoulder was tight against Nancy's shoulder. She ran a tired hand through salt-dry hair. She leaned in close when Nancy raised her arm and pressed a kiss to her friend's cheek. This transgression, at least, was easy to forgive. Not having an answer was, by far, the least complicated part of Liza's plans. The others would be harder.

After the holiday vacationers cleared out of town on Monday, Liza wandered towards the high school at Charlie's appointed time. Her shoes were tied at the laces and slung over her shoulder; she had spent the better part of an hour scrubbing the bottoms of them clean of dirt and rocks that could scratch the gym's floor. Socks and a water bottle she had liberated from the *Roger* were tucked inside of them.

Near Haven's high school was an old brick building that Liza thought was built in the forties, back when Near Haven was a prosperous fishing village that doubled as an idyllic vacation destination for all the big city folks from Boston and New York. The building was full of asbestos and the auditorium probably should have been condemned, but she found that it still held that pull for her.

Once, she used to run this school. She hadn't been the best student, and needed tutoring during the summer to ensure that her grades stayed good enough to get her a decent SAT score and a no-worries transcript to send out to potential college coaches. Liza bit her lip, fingers looping through the twisted shoelaces that were cutting into her shoulder. She knew that it was stupid to even entertain the idea, but maybe *that* was why Sofia Milton was so snippy with her now. Liza *had* spent two summers under her tutelage, being brought up to speed in chemistry and then physics—her two worst subjects—by Sofia, who was then a college student.

It didn't seem like it could possibly be the entire reason, though. But Liza had other things to worry about. Charlie's old Crown Vic was parked by the gym entrance. He was unloading supplies from it as she approached, passing them into the waiting arms of a lanky-looking guy in mesh shorts and a beat-up Patriots T-shirt. Liza's brow furrowed and she stared hard at the guy, trying to place his face as she approached. She was still struggling to recall where she'd see him before when Charlie righted himself, slammed his trunk closed, and slung a second equipment bag over his shoulder.

"Ah, Hawke."

Charlie's face hadn't aged as well as she would have expected. As a kid, she had always thought he was immune to aging, all black hair and beard. Now though, his hair was more salt and pepper and his beard was more unkempt. His hair had grown out of the Marines-style buzz that he'd rocked all throughout Liza's childhood and now curled up and over his ears. His hair and the deep lines at the corners of his eyes and mouth made him look old—far too old to line up with the mental image that she always had of him.

"Grab the ball rack, will you? You remember Ted, right?"

The guy with the sandy-blonde hair and the charming smile flashed a little half wave; most of his fingers were still wrapped around the bag he had slung over his shoulder.

It took a moment, but then Liza remembered. Ted Frederick was the former quarterback of the football team (back when the school had enough kids to have a football team) and—if Liza's memory from Nancy's drunken ramblings the other day served her well—he was the current gym teacher at the elementary school.

"Hey Liza," he said. There was a kind tone in his voice that went a long way to make her feel better about agreeing to Charlie's request. "How've you been?"

Liza reached for the ball rack and adjusted her shoes so that they hung around her neck and dangled into her armpits. She knew she looked ridiculous, but she'd done it so that she could steer the rack better. "All right," she answered. She started to push the rack towards the gym entrance. "Back home for a change."

Ted's head tilted back and he laughed lightly, a smile blossoming across his face. "And here I thought you were one of the lucky ones who got out."

Rolling her eyes, Liza held the door open for him. "Yeah, out. Only then I got my ass landed in jail." She snorted derisively. There'd been a bit of a snafu with that when Charlie was setting up her employment paperwork. It was all under the table, but the school board of old men and women who were institutions in the town wanted all their ducks in a row. A felon should not be working around children, but it seemed as though Charlie had called in every political favor he had to get them to look the other way. Liza was grateful for it, more than she could ever say.

Ted just laughed at Liza's derisive comment. He used free hand to maneuver the front end of the ball rack over the slight lip on the gym floor meant to stop the cold and wet from getting into the gym.

Liza smiled at Ted, despite the memory, happy that he was still every bit the good guy that she remembered him being in school. He had been a year behind her, and friends with pretty much everyone.

Charlie disappeared off into the locker room and Liza lingered at the door until he came out.

Ted wandered off to the equipment room and soon returned with a hand drill and the crank that Liza knew from experience would help them to lower the rest of the baskets.

She watched him with her arms folded across her chest for a few minutes, before she sighed and pushed the door to the locker rooms open. Near Haven High only had one locker room, and the rules were that the girls changed first, the boys second, and if it took more than five minutes for either gender group, there would be laps around the gym for everyone. Mrs. Harden, the high school gym teacher when Liza was at school, was an old battle-axe of a woman who took no crap from anyone and made due with what she had available to teach the best class she could.

Charlie was sitting on one of the long locker room benches, lacing up his sneakers. He looked up when Liza opened the door and then went back to lacing his shoes.

Liza crossed the room in three easy strides to sit next to him and tried to ignore the incredible feeling of awkwardness that rolled over her as she settled down to change out of her flip-flops and into her shoes. It was only when she got her socks on and was moving to untie the shoelaces holding her shoes together that she realized

Charlie was watching her. His eyes were sad as he regarded her, weather-worn old lips pursed into a thin line.

She raised an eyebrow and met his gaze head-on. "What?" She figured that it was way too early in this rekindling of their relationship for there to be awkward silences like this. Charlie was one of the few people Liza thought might actually miss her if she were to die tomorrow.

"You still have the shoes we got you..."

There was something in Charlie's tone, and the way his eyes crinkled—it wasn't happiness per se—but the kind of contentment that came right before it. He had never been happy for as long as he'd known her, always wanting more and more, his expectations growing ever higher. She didn't like how he seemed to have slowed down, or how he was able to sit and smile at her as though nothing had ever gone wrong between them. It felt alien to Liza, uncomfortable in how it didn't fit neatly into her carefully constructed worldview.

Liza nodded and pulled her laces tight. "I don't have much," she confessed. She didn't want to elaborate on the fact that all she owned in the world fit into a single bag. Liza couldn't have had more, and she didn't want to linger on the subject. Even still, while she'd been back in Near Haven, she had acquired the next in the series of *Bounty* books and was working her way through it in her spare time. She liked it: the story of a man who had done all that he could to keep his men alive and still fell short. She liked to think that Kevin might be like William Bligh, but she knew that he was not *nearly* that much of an asshole.

Still, Kevin was the closest thing she'd ever had to a brother, let alone a person who cared enough about her to drop everything and come out into the dark to pick her up when she had needed a ride. Liza didn't make friends well. Trust issues, said the therapists when she was a child, and then again in prison. She was still smarting, twenty-eight years after the fact, from the parents who abandoned her at the fire station, and she didn't think that she would ever understand why they had done what they did to her that fateful day.

Finishing the knot, Liza glanced back up, her gaze once again meeting Charlie's. He had that unnerving, almost *touched* look in his eyes, and the look made her uncomfortable. She knew that she didn't deserve that sort of affection from anyone, let alone a man as great as Charlie White. "And these have lasted a long time," she finished quickly. Her cheeks burned and she felt stupid and tongue-tied. They were ten-year-old Jordans, not exactly the nicest shoes in the world, at least by modern shoe technology standards.

"I'm glad you kept them," Charlie replied. His eyes crinkled even more at the corners. He pressed his hands into his knees, rising to his feet in a far wearier motion than Liza would have ever expected of him.

Her cheeks burned again, this time in shame. She knew that her actions and her own stupidity must have contributed to the aging of this great man.

Charlie held out his hand and Liza took it, letting him pull her to her feet and taking the hair tie that he pulled from his pocket and offered without comment. Nancy's hair was short now, so Liza had no idea why he still kept a bag of them in his pocket at all times. She put her hair up and followed him out of the locker room wordlessly, tie dangling from her mouth as she gathered her thick blonde locks into some semblance of a ponytail.

"You had so much potential..." Charlie stood in the doorway and sighed, one hand resting on the worn door that Liza had been though more times than she cared to remember. His other hand was clenched in a fist. Looking down at the floor and at his own sneakers he said, "You had so much to offer the world—this *town*—and you threw it all away, Liza."

The urge to defend herself was so strong that she was halfway towards beginning a rant about how she could not and would not be held responsible for the actions of another. She was left holding the bag, as the saying went, nothing more than that. Jared had tricked her when he knew that the cops were on to him. He had done it three more times before the dumbass cops figured out his pattern.

It had still been her fault, in the end. She was the one that who had trusted Jared not to screw her over, knowing his past as well as she did at the time. Shame burned Liza's cheeks and she turned away, looking from Charlie back into the locker room. She had no answer to what he was saying, because she knew as well as he did that it was all true. She was no better than Jared, when all was said and done.

The door opened and closed with a loud bang as Charlie left the locker room, and Liza was left alone with her shame and her failure. It burned her chest and welled up in her throat like a laugh at something that truly wasn't funny. The harsh sob that echoed out of her chest was like a death rattle, and with it died the last of her dignity.

Liza clenched her hands into fists and squared her jaw. She would not let this beat her; she couldn't. She'd done a stupid thing, but she'd done her time and had paid a far larger price than most for her mistake. Now she was just one person again, standing in a locker room, knowing full well that if she didn't impress her coach, and the others watching her, this was the end of the line again. She would go back to being the orphan nobody, stuck in this place until she died.

There were kids in the gym when Liza managed to pull herself together and venture back into the large, echoing space. They were divided into three groups: red shirts for elementary school kids, blue shirts for the middle school, and black shirts for the handful of high school kids. Liza took the whistle that Ted shoved into her hands and put it around her neck shakily. She had been on the other side of a whistle so many times now that it felt odd to hold the power of it now.

Ted muttered to her out of the corner of his mouth, "Charlie says to take the elementary school kids and do warm-ups; he'll come tell you what drills to do with them afterwards." Then he marched off with a determined look on his face, heading towards the kids wearing blue.

Liza wanted to laugh, but she remembered flashes of Ted in middle school and knew that it had not been an easy time for him. Some wounds just didn't heal.

There were ten kids in red, and she gathered them all in a circle and got their names and ages. The little boy that had insulted her shoes—Nathan–*Nate*–Milton-Hall—was standing right in the middle of the group with a curious expression on his face. He gave his name and smiled politely when Liza told him her own in reply. Nate was ten years old, which meant that he was born not long after she had left town. It was strange, really, because Liza was sure that she would have heard about Sofia Milton being pregnant before she left. In a small town like Near Haven, rumors like *that* spread like wildfire. She resolved to ask Nancy when, exactly, Nathan came into being and when, exactly, David Hall had died. She wondered if Nathan was a bit like her, even though he still had his mother. To lose a parent at such a young age was a great trauma.

Liza led them through a few quick laps around the court and then fell into the timeless monotony of stretching and warming up. It had been a few years, but she found that it was a lot like riding a bicycle. She was never going to forget how to stretch her arms and legs so she wouldn't pull something important during practice or a game. As they stretched and held, stretched and held, Liza told them a little bit about the basics of basketball.

At some point Charlie came over to tell her that the first thing they were going to do was work on passing and then practice layups, until each kid could do five in a row perfectly. He always had exacting standards, especially when the kids in question were fairly young still.

She spent the afternoon correcting shots and standing under the basket, catching balls and passing them to the next kid in line. They were all pretty decent, as Liza reasoned most kids who went to basketball camp would be. Nathan Milton-Hall wasn't great, but there was definitely some talent there, and he was able to make it all the way around the world at the end before any of the other kids were even past the third stop.

They were sweaty and gross by the end of it, and Liza passed around her water bottle and the Gatorade that Charlie had left for them as they sat out in the sun, shoes kicked off, waiting for their parents. The kids left in little groups: older brothers and sisters picked up some and a few of the high school kids collected others, mumbling about promising to drive them home.

Nathan Milton sat on a basketball by himself, a little ways off from the crowd. He was rocking back and forth, rolling just far enough to nearly lose his balance before correcting it once more.

Liza slowly got to her feet and made her way over to him, wincing as her bare feet moved gingerly on the sun-warmed asphalt. "Is your mom coming to get you, kid?" she asked. She'd been watching him slowly braid some pulled up grass stalks together and then attempting to wrap the braid around his wrist.

He looked up, clearly startled. "She had a city council meeting until four. She told me I might have to wait a few minutes because people won't leave her alone once the meetings are over." He wrinkled his nose after he said that and tilted his head, looking at Liza curiously. "Is it true you've been to jail?" he asked. His face was a picture of childish innocence.

"Who told you that?" She folded her arms across her chest and found herself trying hard not to look embarrassed. It was always the hardest with kids for some reason. Maybe it was because they saw what they saw and made blanket judgments, no matter what the story was and no matter the circumstances. She remembered from her psychology class during freshman year in college that kids tended to see things as black and white. She hoped that Nate could look past the record that was forever stamped next to her name and see her for who she truly was. He was a good kid, and she was already catching herself sort of liking him.

Her smile must have looked more like an annoyed grimace, as the kid threw his hands up in the air and went back to rolling around on his basketball.

Liza could see his mother everywhere in him, but his thick mop of hair was all Dave's, and Liza wished that she had known him better. She knew what it was like to grow up not knowing anything about the people you came from. She would have been more than willing to answer Nathan's questions, if he'd had any.

"My mom was talking on the phone." Nathan shrugged. "I think it was to Coach White, but I don't know."

Liza's eyebrows shot up, and she glanced back towards the open gym door where Ted and Charlie were supervising a shoot-around with the remaining older kids. Charlie's disappointment in her had been so blatantly obvious that Liza could not help but wonder *what* exactly they talked about during that phone call, if it had been indeed with Charlie in the first place.

Still, it wasn't as if she could ask Sofia. Liza would be glared at, shut down, and told that she should take her delinquent ass and leave town. Liza knew how people here were about criminals. The worst things that happened in town weren't talked about. They were dirty little secrets that were swept under rugs and preserved for the sake of the name of the town and its great leaders.

She tapped the ball that Nathan sat on with her foot. When he turned to look up at her again, Liza pointed to the netless hoop that hung gaunt over in the far corner of the parking lot. "Wanna play one-on-one?" she asked. He scowled up at her. Liza hurriedly added, "Just 'til your mom comes, okay? It's something to do, at least."

Nathan's eyes narrowed. "You played in *college*," he said, almost accusingly. "I'm just a kid. You just want to beat up on someone."

Liza rolled her eyes. "I *wanted* to give you something to do while you wait for your mom, kid, but if you'd rather just sit and roll the air outta your ball instead of shooting around, it's your call." Liza turned back towards the door and jerked her chin towards Ted, "Besides, I'd beat up on Ted before I beat up on you."

He seemed to contemplate this for a moment before he scrambled to his feet and kicked the basketball up and into his hands. When Liza let out a low, impressed whistle, he smiled sheepishly. "I play soccer in the fall."

"Ah," Liza replied. As they walked towards the hoop, she debated whether to play him hard or just mess around because he was a kid. Little boys were competitive. When Kevin was younger, she remembered how angry he'd get because she was better at shooting hoops than he was. She got it, she understood, and she let Nathan have the ball first.

It wasn't until he had scored on her twice that Liza began coaching his footwork, telling him that he was too short to dribble through his legs when he lost the ball off the back of his knee and had to chase it off the court and onto the half-dead grass beside it. The salt air was cooler than it had been in the gym. Liza took the opportunity to give him pointers about how he was moving and backing up, as she held the ball in one hand.

"Watch me," she said. He nodded, still on defense.

He was playing her close, his hand in her face as best as he could get it, as Liza crossed over and then reversed, spinning away from him and up into a jump shot that rattled home.

She chased down her rebound and passed it back to Nathan at the top of the key. "You try it now." She pulled up her shorts and got down low so she was on his level. "And don't travel this time."

He nodded, his tongue poking out of his mouth in determination, spinning away from Liza's hands and dribbling around into a three-step layup. His feet fell and he heaved the ball up to bounce against the backboard and just off the rim.

Just like Mike, Liza thought with a smirk and wondered if he had seen that movie.

The black Mercedes pulled into the parking lot just then, and Nathan stood, ball resting against his hip, looking nervously at Liza for a moment.

She gave him a small smile and held out her hand. "Let's get you home then." She wasn't sure that he was going to take her hand. He was ten after all; he might be too old and too cool for that.

His hand was sweaty as he pressed it into Liza's and she smiled, thinking that maybe, just maybe, he was a little bit sweet. They walked slowly, as he dribbled the ball with his free hand, to where his mother's car was parked.

Gigantic bug sunglasses perched on top of her head, Sofia was getting out of her car. She was dressed in a pencil skirt and sensible flats. A pair of heels lay in the back seat next to her briefcase.

Liza resisted the urge to crack a smile at the level of practicality. Driving would be next to impossible in *those* after all.

"Ms. Hawke," Sofia said, crossing her arms over her chest and scowling.

Nathan handed Liza the basketball and she held it against her chest like a shield, desperate to escape whatever ire Sofia might be about to direct her way.

"Nathan." Sofia turned her attention to her son. "Hop in the car, dear."

"Bye, Liza," Nathan said, opening the car door.

"See you, Nathan." Liza smiled and gave him a one-handed wave as he closed the door behind him and reached for his seatbelt. She watched him until she was certain he'd strapped himself in properly, before she dared to glance at Sofia once more. "He's pretty good," she offered lamely as a way of starting the conversation.

Sofia's hand was resting on her hip, fingers tapping against the crisp fabric of her skirt. Her nails were manicured and Liza couldn't look away from them.

There was something about her that sent Liza back twenty years in time to another woman who used to do that same exact thing; her other hand was always clenched into an angry fist, though. Liza tried to keep her emotions under control, but her heart was hammering in her chest and she felt as though she might throw up at any given moment. She supposed she was lucky, Sofia's hand was merely resting on the roof of the car.

Sofia's expression softened and she nearly smiled at Liza before glancing over to Nathan. "He prefers soccer," she said, shaking her head.

There was something that was completely and utterly beautiful about Sofia in that moment. Liza's breath caught in her throat and she found herself unable to look away from the scar on Sofia's upper lip and the way her bangs fell into her eyes. She had aged beautifully and Liza feared that she still had the same crush on her that she'd had since forever.

"Thank you," Sofia added after a moment, as if she had remembered who she was talking to. "For entertaining him until I could get here."

Liza shrugged off the gratitude, feeling as though it was unwarranted. "Don't worry about it," she said. "Nathan's a good kid. I don't mind shooting around with him after camp."

Sofia said nothing for a long moment before she let out a quiet sigh and stepped closer. Her eyes were fierce now, flashing dangerously in the late afternoon sunlight.

It took all of Liza's willpower and self-control not to take a step backwards.

"Do not grow too attached, Ms. Hawke." Sofia hissed at her darkly. "We both know that you'll be gone again before the summer's out, and his heart will break when he learns that his new favorite person cares so little for him that she can't even be bothered to say good-bye."

Puffing out her cheeks and exhaling Liza clung to the basketball in her hands and retorted, forgetting herself completely in the heat of the moment, "It's not my fault that you weren't around. You were getting married in two months, for Christ's sake!" Liza sighed loudly and brushed at the loose strands of the bangs that had escaped from her ponytail back behind her ears. "Kevin told me about David. Sofia, I am *so* sorry."

To reach forward to touch Sofia's shoulder was probably one of the worst decisions in Liza's short life.

Sofia pulled away from her touch, grasped her keys tightly, and spun on the spot. "You overstep your bounds," she said. Her voice was a low hiss, and she turned back to face Liza with eyes so cold that Liza could *swear* she felt the temperature drop by degrees around them.

They glared at each other for a moment before Sofia turned and marched around to the other side of the car and climbed inside.

Liza watched them go, her shoulders slumped. A hollow feeling ached in her chest. Her eyes were trained on the black Mercedes as it pulled out of the parking lot and she hoped to God that Nathan would be at camp the next afternoon. She would apologize and apologize, but she had never thought that *Sofia* of all people would care about the fact that she'd left without saying good-bye. She was lying to herself, always thinking that they'd never been that close. Liza knew, she just knew, that Sofia probably blamed her for the scandal and the quiet revoking of the foster parent credentials that Sofia's mother had held.

Shaking her head, Liza turned and headed back into the gym to put the basketball away.

Charlie was standing in the doorway, his expression closed off and unreadable. "Sad business that," was all he said. He took the ball from Liza's hands and put it back on the rack.

The gym was mostly empty now; the few high school kids that remained were standing around Ted, discussing something in low voices among themselves.

Liza shifted uncomfortably under Charlie's gaze. "Kevin told me what happened," she said quietly, not wanting Ted or the kids to overhear. She didn't know why she was curious, or why she was even asking. She had been up since five that morning and desperately wanted a shower before she took her turn at cooking dinner for Kevin and Billy. Since she was skiving off the boat after the lunch hour, making them take her back to town and disrupting the usual route, she'd offered to cook until she could become full time again. "Is it true that some people think Dave got pushed off the boat?"

Liza felt, rather than saw, Charlie go rigid beside her. He shook his head violently and pressed his finger to his lips, pulling Liza out of the gym once more. "You need to be careful who you say that around, Liza," he whispered urgently. "I know that you've never really cared for the rules here, but this is one of those things that is better left *unsaid.*"

Swallowing hotly, Liza nodded her comprehension. She was already wondering if she could go to the town library and use the Internet to look into the death and see if there were any news articles about what happened that weren't local and therefore probably biased. "Got it," she lied.

"Good." Charlie clapped her on the shoulder. "You did good today kid."

And Liza's heart soared.

CHAPTER FOUR

Blueberry Sal (15 August, 2012)

When August came, Liza went back to working on Kevin's boat full time, but she missed Ted and Charlie and the constant, easy feeling of companionship that came from basketball drills and pickup games. She knew, going in, that the camp would only last a few weeks and that she had no real future in coaching with her record. She hated that she couldn't help but miss it. A small, almost childish part of Liza wished that she could apply to coaching positions, but she knew that someone with felony record would never be allowed to work with children. The exception that Charlie was able to get to allow her to work at the summer camp was one thing, but something more permanent and serious? It would never fly. Becoming a coach was a fool's dream, though; she knew that. There was no money in coaching.

Kevin's boat, at least, was steady income. It wasn't as much as Liza would have liked, but she was starting to feel almost comfortable. She had no idea what she was going to do when Kevin pulled the boat from the water and dry-docked it in November. His operation wasn't big enough to keep up through the winter. Deep-sea fishing off of the Grand Banks of Newfoundland was dangerous work, even during the summer, and when you added the freezing cold temperatures of Maine water in the winter, it wasn't something that Liza—or Kevin—wanted any part of. She just had not been able to find a way to ask him what exactly he did during the winter.

She fell into a pattern of eating brunch with Ted on Saturday mornings, watching him watch a woman and her husband across the diner with interest. Liza knew better than to say anything to Ted about it, for she knew that the husband and wife had been married since they left high school the year before Liza graduated. The husband was the part-time deputy sheriff and a vet tech at the animal hospital the next town over, and the wife was one of the town's three lawyers.

It was with a sick, twisting feeling in her throat, that Liza realized that Ted was in love with another man's wife one afternoon in early August. It was as obvious as the sky was blue. Liza had never actually seen them talk or interact, but after two weeks of lunches, she realized that their lunch time and table were very carefully chosen. Rachel must have noticed it too. She had taken to shooting dirty and exceedingly disapproving looks in Ted's direction whenever she thought she could get away with it. Liza was glad that she didn't have to play the disapproving friend, this time around. Rachel had it covered and Liza could simply sit back and not stick her nose into other people's business, where it clearly didn't belong.

Still, Liza tried with all her might not to get caught in the middle. She didn't ask Ted about it because she didn't want to know anything about it. Sometimes, mostly to herself, Liza liked to joke that Near Haven's town motto should really have been "Don't ask questions"; the answers were never worth the trouble. Liza chewed them over slowly in her mind, working them through and through. She never voiced her questions, for fear of destroying the easy peace of these mid-morning brunches. Ted was a good friend, and she didn't want to ruin the easily rekindled friendship that they'd forged over four weeks of summer camp. Instead, she retreated to the woods with Nancy, baskets slung over their arms, hunting for wild blueberries and blackberries.

Nancy's new apartment was part of the old grain foundry building. The company had closed its doors years before Liza was even born, and the building had been converted into apartments in the time since she had left. Despite her best efforts not to, Liza understood why someone with Nancy's taste would fall in love with the loft-style apartments that had been installed in the old foundry building. The apartments were all a mess of chipping paint and crumbling brick, with whitewashed kitchens and large, almost floor-to-ceiling windows along one side of the building. Ever practical, Liza couldn't help but think of the cost of heating the place once winter set it—she wasn't sure that the heating bill was going to be worth the comparatively low rent. Still, she had her own space in Nancy's new loft, and a bed and a bookshelf with exactly three books in it.

At the library she'd had to use Kevin's credit card and the public computer to order the third in the Bounty series; the book shop didn't have it in their catalogue at all, and the Barnes and Noble in Bangor didn't have it in stock. She had finished the entire series now, and was spending most of her nights lying awake, trying to figure out how she felt about the events that had transpired therein. At night, she sat up in her bedroom and stared at the exposed dark wood of the ceiling beams, wondering what she would have done in that impossible situation.

She understood the plight of the sailors on the Bounty, but she knew where the officers were coming from as well. Liza found herself caught, stuck in the middle of the conflict, not really sure that she wanted to think too hard about what she would have done, had she been in the officers' shoes. Maybe, she thought darkly, she was in the hell that Fletcher Christian, the mutinous master's mate on Lieutenant Bligh's ship in the story, had described; it had simply taken a different form.

Boats had been a part of her life since before she could remember. Liza had always been fascinated with them and how they worked. She was fostered with two fishermen when she was a child, both of whom had noticed her affinity for the sea and had welcomed her onto their boats. Sometimes Liza wished that she hadn't been so good at basketball. Maybe it would have been enough to settle for a place like Near Haven and a career as a fisherwoman—to have her own boat, her own lobster pots, and maybe a side business of cod fishing in the winter. It would have been so easy compared to her life as it was now.

The ocean was in her blood, basketball too. She knew she could not ever choose one over the other.

Liza followed Nancy into the woods on the weekends like a lost dog who craved the routine more than needing something to do. Nancy had been picking berries in the woods for years now, making homemade jam to sell at the Harvest and Hay celebration in October. She had never specifically planned for a particular yield or volume of jars, but she usually could get a good twenty or so large jars of jam out of the blueberries and blackberries that grew wild on the craggy hills above the town.

"You know..." Nancy said, reaching for a particular fat blackberry near Liza's knee. She was taking care of the lower branches as Liza tackled the top of the bush. Nancy inspected the berry carefully for worms and mold before putting it into her basket gently. Liza knew that one had to be gentle with blackberries. If they were handled roughly, they got bruised and apparently, it did something to the jam flavor. "You never told me how Sofia took you teaching Nathan basketball last month."

Liza bit her lip, setting a few berries into her basket and blinking up into the bright, mid-afternoon sun that was streaming through the tall pines above them. She wasn't really sure that she knew how to articulate how effectively she had been shut down by Sofia Milton. Nathan was a great kid, and Liza had gotten to know him pretty well over the past few weeks. He was even and steady, smart as all get out for a kid just going into the fourth grade. Liza missed him when he was not around, and the idea scared her half to death. She'd never cared for children at all before she'd met Nathan.

"I said I was sorry about Dave," she explained. She chose her words carefully. She had spent the better part of a Saturday, not long after Charlie told her to mind her own business, holed up in the library's basement archives.

The librarian (some flatlander import from Connecticut) was very helpful in providing her with all the old copies of the local paper and the Kennebec Journal that they had on microfiche. Liza had slogged back through time, reading about the special election for Sofia's horrible mother a year and a half after her husband's death. The governor had appointed her without questioning her character, which Liza thought was hilarious, considering how horrible that woman was.

Piecing together the investigation and circumstances surrounding the death of Sofia's husband had taken most of the afternoon. Liza could barely remember him outside of her memories of Sofia. The newspapers wrote that he was a fisherman's son who had liked horses more than people. Working as a pool boy and then on the docks as a skipper for the out-of-town crowd, he had hung out with the vacationers, taking them around the islands off the coast and out into the open water to fish. He had an oceanfront lifeguard certification and swam competitively for Near Haven High while he was at school there. The idea of him drowning, even in stormy seas, seemed unlikely to Liza. The fact that he wasn't even wearing a life vest stood out to her as the most telling fact of all. In weather like that, the first thing that any sailor worth his salt would do would be to throw on a life vest. It just didn't sit right with her.

"Ah." Nancy replied. She set her basket down and pushed herself up and onto to her feet.

Her voice pulled Liza out of her thoughts and she nodded slowly. The investigation had just stopped after the coast guard ruled it an accident, even if the facts didn't add up to even the most casual observer.

"I take it she shut you down?"

Liza nodded slowly and jammed her hands into the pockets of her cut-off jeans. Nancy's hair was frizzing slightly in the August heat and it almost looked like she had a halo in the sunlight. It was a strange look on her, especially since she hardly looked the picture of innocence, given her obsession with shabby chic and her tendency to dress as if she fell out of the sixties. "She doesn't like to talk about it, does she?"

"Dad says that she took it really hard." Nancy reached her hand back into the bush, plucked a berry from it, and inspected it carefully before popping it into her mouth. "I was at school when it happened. I have no idea what they were doing out in weather like that. Dave, at least, should have known better. The senator too."

Liza helped herself to a particularly fat berry, enjoying the tartness and then the sweet flavor on her tongue, before she swallowed and sighed almost regretfully. "Boys and their boats, huh?"

"I hate to think that ego caused that to happen," Nancy said. Her nose wrinkled in disgust.

They had four quarts of berries when all was said and done. Wild blueberries were a lot smaller than their commercially cultivated and farm-grown counterparts, and Liza was secretly impressed that they'd managed to find enough of them for Nancy to immediately start washing and laying them flat on a towel across the countertop. She explained that they had to be made into jam right away, or else they'd lose their flavor.

Liza hadn't made jam since she was probably ten or so—far too young to recall the exact process or to handle a steaming copper pot full of boiling fruit and sugar at any rate. She did what Nancy told her to do, half paying attention as Nancy threw jam jars and a fresh pack of sealing caps into a frying pan to boil everything so that it would be sterile. Liza was put in charge of stirring the blueberry and sugar mixture. Once it boiled they would have very little time to compete the next step.

"Why are we making it with pectin?" Liza asked, as Nancy pulled the package of white powder from the cupboard and read the instructions carefully. Liza knew she had done this so many times that she didn't need to check, but it was Nancy's ritual of the process that drew Liza in and held her attention. Everything in Near Haven was ritual and practice, performed over and over until it was perfect—somehow this helped mask the weariness and ugly cracks in the underbelly of the town. All Liza could see was a town struggling desperately to keep its head above water, but she knew that wasn't how outsiders saw things there. To them, Near Haven was a quaint little town full of vacation homes and fishermen who sold their catch at the docks at the end of the day. This was a place where there could be no secrets.

And yet all Near Haven had, it seemed, were secrets.

The last time Liza made jam was with the foster family that had kept her for nearly two years, before they'd had to move to Portland. Liza had never wanted in that house, and she counted that place as one of the few where she had ever felt truly loved. She remembered the jam taking hours to cook then, slowly stirring it in a copper-bottomed pan until it was thick and ready to be put into jars.

Nancy raised her eyebrows and squinted over at all the blackberries sitting in their baskets on the kitchen island counter. "We have a lot of jam to make, Liza. Forgive me if I cut a corner to save on cooking time."

Liza stuck her tongue out and, at Nancy's instruction, counted one Mississippi, two Mississippi as she stirred in the pectin that would help their jam to set nicely. It started to thicken almost instantly, and Liza stirred and counted steadily. Making jam was an exact science, hidden in the guise of something so practiced that it almost felt like habit. When she reached sixty, she cut off the heat and stepped back, letting a bright yellow glove-wearing Nancy pour the jam into little decorative jars one after another, putting the caps on them and tightening them in one fluid motion. Liza flipped them upside down after they had the caps put on, running a wet cloth over them to catch any drips and to ensure that they wouldn't be sticky when she and Liza turned them over in a few days. She set them on a high shelf to keep them out of the way and undisturbed until they'd fully set.

There were seventeen little jars of jam on the shelf by the time they finished. Nancy decided to start on the first batch of blackberry jam just as soon as Liza had scrubbed out the pot. The process started again and Liza found herself moving in tandem with Nancy around the apartment's small kitchen, making jam and washing dishes with the practiced ease of having done this for years.

Later that night, Nancy wrote out labels for the jam while Liza cooked dinner for the pair of them. She was making pesto with the basil that Nancy had been growing in a window box on Charlie's back porch; they'd relocated it when they moved in. It was now nestled in the bathroom window. Despite everything, the motions of cooking were so practiced by now that she almost lost herself in her thoughts, moving around the kitchen on autopilot.

Nancy set down her pen on a completed sheet of labels, now covered in her elementary school teacher handwriting and reached for her half-finished mug of tea. "Why didn't you come home when Kevin's father died?"

That...was not an easy question.

Liza, rummaging for the cheese grater, looked up. She stood, grater in one hand, and set about grating as much Parmesan as she thought should go into the food processor. The steady, up and down motion and the barrier of the kitchen island between the two of them was like a shield against all that Liza didn't want to think or talk about.

The problem was that Nancy had never judged Liza for anything she had ever done in her life, save for this. Not being there for Kevin, when he had needed her desperately, was the ultimate betrayal in her eyes, and even though he had long since forgiven her for it, Nancy apparently had not.

"When you called, I was in Montana." Liza told her. She gripped the top of the cheese grater so hard her knuckles were white. "I was about to start—it was the first game of conference play. I was broke, living on the charity of my teammates and coach. Do you know how hard it is for a coach to provide assistance to a player without the school or the NC-double-A coming down on their heads?" She set the wedge of cheese aside, on top of the Ziploc bag it had been stored in. "I didn't know how I was going to get home over the summer. And to ask for help with another plane ticket... I couldn't do it."

"He was your best friend, Liza," Nancy replied. Her lips were pulled into a scowl and she was glaring at the mug in her hands. "And you didn't even call..."

Liza ran a worried and distracted hand through her hair, forgetting that there was basil and cheese all over it, and cursed quietly. She moved over to the sink to rinse the food out of her hair. She stood there, with her shoulders slumped and her hands resting on the sides of the sink, almost shaking with fear and desperation. Nancy of all people should understand.

No one seemed to understand.

"I couldn't do it," Liza said. Her voice was shaking and she felt far smaller than she had in years. There was no gigantic, terrifying lesbian in her face this time, daring her to act out like the Barbie doll that they had all thought she was in prison. No, there was just a friend from home who had always seen straight through her bullshit. "I couldn't. Kevin's dad was like a father to me, same as your dad. I couldn't handle it. I went out and played my best for him. That was probably my best game in college, Nancy."

"And after?"

Liza sighed, her resolve crumbling away into nothingness. "After..." She let out a small-sounding bark of laughter that held no mirth. "After I didn't know what to say. I didn't even know he was struggling." She shook her head and tucked the wet strands that she'd rinsed out behind her ear. They were cool, and the wet, slightly clammy sensation of them against her skin was enough to keep her grounded, the dampness reminding her that she was alive. "It was a shit thing to do, I know that now. It took me a long time to figure that out, but I get it now."

"Is that why you came back?" The question was so innocent.

Liza didn't have the heart to tell her that this idyllic life in this dying town was really not her scene at all. She liked the smaller, less famous cities: St. Paul, Raleigh, Boston. They were big enough to be a city, but not big enough to overwhelm her. Chicago had been utterly mind-blowing in its size, and Liza had lost herself there for weeks before she'd felt comfortable enough to move around through life. She'd worked in a bakery there and had moved on to waiting tables and tending bar at a trendy nightclub.

It, like all opportunities offered to her, fell apart, though, like everything she had ever touched. Someone had googled her and she'd been fired on the spot.

She couldn't tell Nancy that she came back because she was too broke to go anywhere else or that she needed to lean on the kindness of others until she could get back on her feet. She couldn't very well tell Nancy the truth: that she couldn't apply for any meaningful job with her record and that she was going to be pulled back into the world that she had just barely brushed against when she'd first left this peaceful seaside haven, if she wasn't careful. "I came back because I needed to figure myself out," she said truthfully. She had been struggling to keep her head above water for so long now that being here and not needing to work so hard for it had left her desperate for things to occupy her mind. She was reading again now that she was back in Near Haven. She was drawn to books about betrayal, but that had always been a theme in her life.

Nancy smiled at her and it seemed real and genuine. Liza was grateful that Nancy had always been the forgive-and-forget type.

They ate in a comfortable silence, and afterwards Nancy did the dishes. Liza carefully wiped the jam jars clean for a second time with a soapy sponge and then dried them with a dishcloth before putting the labels on them.

"There's an odd number this year," Nancy said. She contemplated their batch of "Maine Wild Blueberry Jam 2012" with a finger to her lips and a towel over her shoulder. Reaching for the odd jar, she handed it to Liza. "You should find a home for this one. I don't like odd numbers."

Liza rolled her eyes and took the jar, holding it clutched in her hands like some sort of childish security blanket. The jam was an olive branch in the form of bizarre OCD and they both knew it. "I will," she promised.

The jar was placed on Liza's bookshelf, next to her three books and a nearly perfect urchin shell that she'd found out on the rocks one afternoon not too long ago. She stared at the little jar of jam every night for nearly a week as she fell asleep, before she figured out what to do with it.

Nathan Milton came around the harbor one afternoon, staying respectfully away from the edge of the docks as Liza, Billy, and Kevin unloaded the day's catch. They had gone to some of the pots that were further out, and the catch was very good. Liza was pretty sure that she was going to walk away from today with at least a hundred bucks in her pocket off of just one lobster and she was excited because that was half the rent right there. She could probably save at least half of it for the winter and the sure-to-be astronomical heating bill.

"Hey Nate," Kevin called, saluting him with his hook and smiling brightly.

Nancy once joked that Kevin was so good with kids because he would probably never have any of his own. Liza thought that it was something different though. Kevin was a true testament to the adage that it took a village to raise a child. He could, and did, play a father figure to Nathan same as Charlie or Ted did.

Nathan bit his lip and waved back and Liza had an idea. "Are you guys good for a few?" Most of the catch was unloaded now, and it was just a matter of wrestling it all into the back of Kevin's truck and taking it to the market.

"Sure," Billy said. Kevin smirked wickedly at her, wiggling his eyebrows.

Liza felt a wave of irritation well up inside her, twisting in her gut and making her see red. What the hell did he think she was up to? She just liked Nathan; she totally didn't have a thing for his mom. He was a good kid who was sort of like her. He shared the same sort of loneliness.

Liza shucked off her overalls and stood in cut-off jean shorts and rain boots. She had lobster ick in her hair and probably needed suspenders or a belt to help her pants stay up—the jeans that had been sacrificed to make these cut offs had been Kevin's, after all. She didn't care though, because Nathan's face lit up when Liza trotted up the dock to greet him.

"What're you doing down here?" Liza asked. She gave him what she hoped was a friendly and encouraging smile, but she wasn't sure how nice it actually looked. She felt like a total head case, standing there with her hands jammed into her back pockets and ridiculous rain boots on her feet, grinning like an idiot. It was the end of a long work day, and there was actually traffic around. Liza had no idea what Nathan did with his time when Sofia was working. She didn't think Charlie was running any more camps this summer. Liza hoped that Nathan wasn't left to his own devices all day, but it would explain why he was down here. It must have been lonely, rattling around in that big house on High Pine Street all day.

Nathan hitched his backpack up on his shoulders and shrugged. "I got bored at the library and they're about to close anyway. Mom said it was okay to come and see you since she's got stuff to do at the office still." He bit his lip again, very pointedly not looking Liza in the eye, before adding, "She's having a bad day. My grandma called this morning."

Oh Sofia, Liza thought. She could not imagine a conversation like that doing anything but absolutely ruining a day. Nathan was just so frank about it, like it really wasn't that big a deal that his mother was sending him into the care of the town's librarian and then potentially to see a known criminal. Liza's brow furrowed. "Why would she say something like that? I'm probably one of her least favorite people, kid."

"She said to come find you because you'd understand, whatever that means." Nathan stuck his lip out and eyed Kevin and Billy and the day's catch.

Liza was willing to bet a lot that he was going to ask if he could go to the market in Bangor with them. There were enough seats in the truck if Billy stayed behind (which he usually did since he had a girlfriend and all).

Oh. Swallowing hotly, Liza nodded once and held out her hand to Nathan. "You want to come to the market with us?"

She was throwing out a lifeline to a kid that didn't know he was drowning. She didn't even know if he was struggling. The guilt of not noticing before, when she was practically living with Kevin and his father was so like what she saw in Nathan now. The guilt of not realizing how much he had been struggling haunted Liza to this day.

Kevin came up the dock to stand beside them, his boots treading wet and heavy on the worn grey wood and concrete. "Best not take him out of town." He winked conspiratorially at Nathan. "Why don't you two hose down the boat while Billy and I go?" He looked Nathan up and down, appraisingly rubbing his unshaven chin. "You're a bit small for a cabin boy, but you'll have to do."

Nathan, to his credit, stuck his tongue out at Kevin and pulled his backpack off his shoulders. Fifteen comic books and a lunch box were jammed inside of the bag, as well as a beat-up pair of rubber boots. He kicked off his expensive-looking sandals and pulled on the boots. Gathering up his things and shoving the sandals back into the black backpack, he leaned it up against the far end of the dock where he was pretty sure it would not fall into the water. "I can do it," he assured Kevin with a smart salute.

Looking at his serious expression, Liza just smiled and shook her head.

"I'll bring you your pay later tonight." Kevin patted Liza on the shoulder, saluting with his prosthetic and winking lewdly at her.

Liza hoped it jabbed in him in his lewdly winking eye. Kevin was a terrible flirt, after all. "Leave it with Nancy if I'm not back yet," Liza replied.

He looked at her oddly for a moment, before he glanced down at Nathan.

Liza gave a small nod and his eyes widened before he stepped aside and moved back down the dock to help Billy lug the catch up to where his truck was waiting.

"Tell me how much you get for that big one!" Liza called as they drove away, hose slung over her shoulder. They had caught a *monster* of a lobster, with claws easily the size of Liza's hand. They had spent most of the day after they'd hauled it in speculating on how much it would sell for. The thing had to be at least seven pounds, maybe more.

"Will do!" Billy called back. The old Isuzu drove through the parking lot and towards the state road that would take them up to Bangor.

They washed the boat down quickly. It was low tide, and the waves were calm. The sun was not yet setting. They walked down the docks and towards the exposed, rocky outcropping that jutted out into the harbor, creating the gentle curl of the cove that housed the harbor.

Liza wasn't sure how comfortable Nathan was with the water. He kept a respectful distance as she picked her way down to one of the shallower pools and pulled the small bucket that she had brought down into the water with her. Harvesting mussels like this was hugely illegal, but she had never been caught before. Liza inspected the little blue shells and kept one eye on Nathan as he selected a rock that was barnacle and seagull shit free and settled himself onto it, eyes ever watchful.

"Does your mom have bad days a lot?" Liza asked. She should have had a tool to do this, pulling the suckers off the rocks was hard to do barehanded and she was a little worried that she was going to cut herself. She braced her feet in the shallow pool she was standing in, selected a section towards the bottom of the rock, and began to pluck the mussels off one by one. She dropped them into her bucket, which was in serious danger of floating away towards the deeper part of the tide pool.

She didn't want to look at Nathan when she asked. She wasn't sure if she could control the emotion on her face; the memories of his grandmother and how horrible she was were still fresh enough in her mind.

"Not as much as before," Nathan said. He picked at what Liza hoped wasn't bird shit on the rock next to his leg. "She used to be sad all the time, until Leslie and Grandma told her that she should run for mayor when Mr. Spencer retired."

Liza remembered Alan Spencer vaguely. He was always up for reelection when she was a kid. She had made a habit of stealing his signs and putting them all on his front lawn during the election her junior year of high school. She had never gotten caught doing it, but after that she'd noticed that when she was walking around town, everyone watched her a lot more closely. Alan Spencer was a decent mayor, neither good nor bad, really. Just *there*.

"I'm sorry about your dad, Nathan," Liza said. She tugged at a stubborn mussel for a minute before giving up and leaning over to retrieve her bucket from where it was attempting to float away. A crab scuttled across her shadow, pinchers raised in defense as Liza disturbed the peaceful surface of his tide pool. Shaking her head, Liza glanced up to see Nathan staring down at her. "He was a good guy."

"I don't remember him," Nathan said. He tilted his chin up defiantly and looking almost exactly like his mother. Haughty and unapologetic, he refused to admit emotion just like she did. "And Grandma threw out all the pictures..."

Liza dropped a mussel into the bucket, horrified. She had briefly borne the brunt of that hatred and need for control, but she never would have imagined that that awful woman would destroy all evidence of her daughter's momentary happiness. Liza's hands shook as she steadied herself, trying not to look too shocked as she clambered out of the pool and up to where Nathan was still picking at, yup, that was bird shit. *Gross.*

There were a good thirty mussels in the bucket, and Liza reasoned that it should be enough for two people. She held out her hand to Nathan, bucket banging against her calf as it dangled loosely from her other hand.

He took it and pulled himself to his feet.

"Your grandma was wrong to do that," Liza said. She looked him directly in the eyes. "I don't have any parents, Nathan, and even I know that's wrong."

He chewed his lip and didn't say anything. His hand was sweaty in Liza's and they walked back to the end of the dock to collect his backpack. Liza was not thinking about anything having to do with Nathan's family, because she thought she would hitch her way down to Washington and punch Constance Milton in the face if she did. Honestly, she could not believe the gall of that woman.

They walked through town, the criminal and the mayor's son—the senator's grandson. People looked at them curiously. Liza thought that it might have more to do with the bucket that she carried. "I want to change before I take you to meet your mom, okay?" Liza asked.

Nathan nodded and glanced towards the clock on top of the library, reading the time. It wasn't that late yet. "I think we have time," he said. He followed Liza up the steps into the old foundry building.

The clock over the stove read six thirty as Liza poured the mussels into the sink and filled it with cold water to soak the sand and salt out of them so she could cook them for dinner later. Nathan inspected the kitchen with interest and hopped up onto a stool when Liza told him to sit tight as she ran upstairs to change.

She threw on jeans and a tank top, and then pulled on an old flannel on top of it. She looked like a total dyke in this getup, but Liza had spent time in a women's prison and you gotta do what you gotta do. It wasn't like she was fooling anyone palling around with Kevin Jaspen anyway. The man was more flamboyant than most of the drag queens that Liza had met in her travels.

Liza was in the process of pulling her hair back into a ponytail, tie hanging from her mouth, when she saw the little jar of jam, sitting on top of her bookshelf with her hairbrush and her three books. She picked it up and stared at it for a long moment, before she tucked it into her pocket and headed back downstairs.

The walk to Sofia's office at city hall was surprisingly short, and Liza couldn't help but think of all the other times that she had been in this building. This was where the town clerk's office was, where she had to go every time she changed foster homes, so that the municipality could make sure she was properly accounted for. She had spent more time in this building than she cared to acknowledge, but she had never been to the third floor before. She couldn't shake the feeling of dread as her flip-flops smacked against the floor.

Nathan was still in his rain boots and was stomping around like he owned the place. He paused at a fairly nondescript door and waited for Liza to catch up before he pulled it open.

The mayor's office was decorated in black and white. Liza wondered if Sofia had missed her calling in life as an interior designer. The place was so very Sofia, while still being tasteful and professional. Liza could have done without the weird wallpaper that made the room look like a prison, however. She stood in the doorway as Nathan stomped his way over to where his mother was sitting behind a large and imposing-looking desk. Sofia's hair was looking slightly disheveled and she had a pair of glasses perched on the end of her nose. A stack of papers lay in front of her with various sticky notes and flags sticking out of it that reminded Liza a little too keenly of school.

"Nathan." Sofia honestly sounded surprised. Her eyes flicked to the watch on her wrist and she looked dismayed.

Liza wondered how common an occurrence this was, Sofia completely losing track of the time.

"Is it that late already?"

He nodded, his eyes solemn. "Kevin let me wash out his boat. And I read that book you told me about at the library."

"Did you now?" she murmured as he came around the desk to stand in front of her. She pressed a kiss to his forehead and glanced over to where Liza was still trying to decide if she would be intruding if she came completely into the office.

Nathan swiped at his forehead, trying to rub the kiss away, but Sofia caught his wrist with practiced fingers and kissed his palm. He scowled at her and she raised an eyebrow at him before asking, "Ms. Hawke helped with the boat washing, I hope?"

Liza shoved her hands in her pants pockets. "Nah, he was appointed cabin boy, I just supervised."

"And got the high spots and the coolers," Nathan added helpfully. He had explained to Liza that his mother didn't let him clamber around on the gunnels of boats without a life vest and that Kevin's boat didn't have any that would fit him. The harbor was deep, he explained, and while he could swim, he didn't think he could make it all the way over to the ladder on the other side of the docks without needing to be rescued. Liza had seen his point and did the hard-to-reach areas and the coolers for him.

"And those," Liza said. She was still hesitant to step into the room, but did so and closed the door behind her. "Thanks for sending along reinforcements."

Nathan crossed the room to sit on the couch and pulled off his rain boots before putting his sandals back on. He stood there, hands on his hips, surveying them for a moment before announcing that he was going to get a drink from the water fountain.

Liza watched him go and realized that he didn't really need one. Back on the docks he'd had water and drank some more at Nancy's. The kid was just stupidly perceptive and was giving them a chance to talk.

Pulling the jam jar from her pocket, Liza crossed the office and set it neatly before Sofia, right smack dab in the middle of a pile of what looked like budgets. Liza didn't envy her, having to deal with that.

"First batch of the year," she said.

Sofia picked up the jar and inspected it, holding it up in the setting sunlight through the large window behind her desk.

"We made it last weekend."

"I never realized she started so early." Setting the jar down Sofia rested two fingers on top of it thoughtfully. She looked up at Liza, who could see that beyond the strained corners of those eyes was a little redness, the remnants of tears that couldn't quite be disguised with makeup.

"Nancy's always been one for preparedness." Liza shrugged.

They lapsed into silence once again, and Liza chewed over what she could possibly say to Sofia. She didn't want to bring up Dave again, or even how terrible Sofia's mother could be. All she could think of was that she was sorry over and over again.

"I'm sorry I left." She pulled at a fraying piece of string that was coming off her jeans. "Both times." She looked up and met Sofia's eyes, steady and strong.

"You were a child," Sofia said wearily. She picked up the jam jar and reached for her purse, tucking it carefully inside. "You should have never been subjected to that in the first place."

Liza shook her head violently. "How can you say that? You…" She couldn't bring herself to say how guilty she felt that her placement with the senator's *kind* wife and young daughter all those years ago had been only temporary until a more permanent place could be found. She had gotten to leave, and she knew that it probably got worse for Sofia in that awful house. "You didn't get to leave…"

"What happened in that house when you were not there is none of your business, Ms. Hawke."

There was a softness at the corners of Sofia's eyes that caught Liza's interest. Maybe she just needed to keep trying and Sofia would eventually open up. Maybe she just had to find the right words.

"And besides, don't you have enough problems being a known felon in a town like this?" Sofia crossed her arms across her chest. "I don't see why you came back; you can't ride on Jaspen's kindness forever."

"I can't get the record expunged." Liza retorted with a scowl pulling at the corner of her mouth. "I've tried, trust me. They tell me that no matter how obviously a patsy I was, I was still holding the bag full of stolen watches at the end of the day. I did my time, but fuck… I can't even vote anymore, let alone get a job."

"Have you talked to Leslie Burke?" Sofia asked. Her kind tone surprised Liza, as Sofia didn't seem particularly moved by Liza whining about how she was disenfranchised, miserable, and broke.

Liza supposed that Sofia had never been particularly moved by her complaints, given how much Liza had enjoyed complaining about the summer work she'd been assigned for chemistry class back when Sofia tutored her in high school.

"She's quite good."

"I have no money," Liza said sadly. She had thought about it, fantasized really. Back then she was too young and too stupid to realize that the settlement she'd gotten from the government at her release was meant to cover the cost of expunging the record. Now, she regretted zigzagging across the country, trying to find a place where she could belong. She was back where she started, and this was the only place that truly felt like home. Liza shrugged. "I don't even know what I'm going to do come November when Kevin takes his boat out of the water for the winter."

"Talk to Leslie. Like Mr. White, you'll find that there are many people in this town who are willing to help, if you ask nicely." There was an almost knowing look on Sofia's face as she leaned back in her chair, fingers on one hand fiddling with a ring around her right ring finger. She looked like the cat who'd eaten the canary. There was something about the way she said it that made Liza's eyes widen in surprise. She remembered Nathan mentioning something about Sofia talking to Charlie back on his first day of basketball camp. She didn't know how to ask if it was Sofia who had put the coaching idea into Charlie's head. He and Ted would have had the camp covered, but they somehow had a place for Liza without even questioning her record. It all made a lot of sense, given that the school board had been willing to allow Liza the opportunity to work for the rec department-run camp despite her record.

The mayor calling in favors seemed a lot more probable than the high school girls' basketball coach.

Sofia stood, tugging her purse over her shoulder and stared down at the papers on the desk for a long time before reaching for her keys and jacket. She gave Liza a pointed look, plucked the glasses off of her nose, and put them away in a case that Liza thought said *Gucci*—but she couldn't be sure because Sofia's hand was partially covering the logo and she slipped the case back into her purse before Liza could get a better look.

"Are you willing to help?" Liza asked quietly, almost under her breath. "Because I'm willing to help you."

"I don't think you can help me, dear." Sofia said loftily. She swept over to collect Nathan's backpack and rain boots. She held them up gingerly, inspecting them. Judging by the way her nose wrinkled in disgust, she had obviously found the bird shit they'd walked through on their way out to the tide pool. "And I'll thank you to not take my son too close to the water again."

Liza bristled. Sofia had been the one who had sent Nathan down to the docks in the first place. Grouchy, moody woman that she was, she probably didn't even remember doing it. Liza scowled. "It was just the tide pool on the finger," she said. "Cove side, he wasn't even near the water. I was—"

"Gathering something illegal no doubt." Sofia glared at her and Liza folded her arms over her chest. "I could have the sheriff write you a ticket."

"I'd thank you to *not*," Liza retorted. Her tone was mocking, echoing Sofia's previous words. Sofia glared right back at her, and Liza raised an eyebrow in challenge.

"Then keep my son away from the ocean, Ms. Hawke," Sofia said. "It's bad enough that he's still so taken with you." She folded her coat over her arm and slung Nathan's backpack over her shoulder.

It was hilarious, almost, how *mom* she looked, despite the power suit and towering heels. It was a good look on her, and Liza found that she couldn't look away.

"And if you're serious about helping anyone, go see Leslie Burke."

Liza trailed after her and out of the office, watching as Sofia set the alarm and shut off the lights. It seemed as though they'd had their first productive conversation since Liza was seventeen and they were discussing molar mass and the periodic table. This was worlds away from that now, and Liza felt hopelessly out of her depth. "You'll be okay, though?" She knew that she was pushing it; she knew she should stop, but she couldn't. She had to make sure. "Nathan said you were having a bad day."

"It's a council meeting day, dear; they're always bad." Sofia brushed past her, smelling of Chanel and sunlight. Liza couldn't help herself, reaching out and touching her. She had to know she was real. Her fingers brushed against the silky material of Sofia's shirt and she snatched her hand back, her ears burning at her audacity.

Sofia said nothing, and the faint pink on the mayor's cheeks as she bustled down the hallway, calling for her son, was entirely worth the death glare that Liza received for her trouble. She stood there, hands in her pockets, smirking.

She was going to call Leslie Burke.

CHAPTER FIVE

Lobsters & Lawyers (3 September, 2012)

LABOR DAY WAS AWASH WITH colors, reds and blues and the beginnings of cooler nights that would set the trees in the woods above town ablaze with autumn's brilliant palate. Kevin, Billy, and Liza let the traps go longer and spent the last days of summer in the sunlight, sitting on Kevin's porch and drinking beer that Nancy's friend Chet made in his basement. It was delicious stuff and Liza told him so with a wide, slightly drunk smile as he leaned over the railing that wrapped around Kevin's porch and chatted with Billy. Chet was an older guy who worked down in the historic garnet and quartz mines during the summer, giving tours and speaking at length about the interesting local history and color that they provided Near Haven.

The homebrew was a weekend gig for him, apparently, and he had to be careful about how much he brewed in his basement. Liza was curious about how homebrew worked. She didn't know anything about beer making, but there was an actual brewery in Near Haven and two more in Bangor. She wondered, out loud to Chet, but mostly to herself, if she could get a job doing that once the winter set in. He'd shaken his head, and told her that there was no way; the people that worked at those places were lifers—they loved it as much as he did.

On Labor Day, Kevin had called Sofia, asking after Nathan and promising a lobster bake once it started to get dark. They had gathered all of the necessary supplies, including an obscene amount of seaweed to pile over the fire pit, which Liza and Billy had spent most of the night before digging out. The pit was down on the lone little patch of sand and shells amid the rocks that formed the shoreline. Liza was pretty good at preparing for these bakes; they used to have them at the beginning of every basketball season to raise money for the team, usually to great success and with most of the town turning out.

Sofia was coming to Kevin's house, which was beyond strange and the subject of much-whispered speculation between Liza and Nancy as they got things ready to start the lobster bake in the kitchen. She was the mayor and this was a holiday weekend.

"She'll have other things to do," Liza said. She took a long pull on her beer and leaned against the kitchen counter. "It's not like she'd grace us lowly peasants with her presence just because we asked. She's probably been asked to like ten of these things."

Nancy shook her head, pulling a pound of butter from the refrigerator and passing it to Liza. "This is where Nathan wants to be, trust me. And if he wants to be here, then this is where they will both be. He's a total mama's boy, and she dotes on him." She sighed, pressing her hands against the counter and pushing herself forward and up onto her tiptoes. "Besides," she added, handing Liza a saucepan from the top of the fridge, "School starts up again on Tuesday and that's the age that kids really start to pull away from their mothers. Boys especially. She's probably clinging to him for all she's worth." Nancy mused, sipping on her beer and prodding at a particularly enterprising lobster who was attempting to make a run for it out of the side of the plastic bucket they'd put it in. "Just be nice."

Liza rolled her eyes. "Of course I will." She would, too, provided Sofia was nice to her.

Billy's wheelbarrow was loaded with found driftwood and the remains of last year's firewood from four different households, apparently. He grunted as he picked it up, muscles straining through the back of his thin T-shirt as he pushed the whole thing forward across the road and towards the fire pit.

Liza followed him, halfway to waddling between an old canvas L.L. Bean bag full of kindling and pine needles under one arm and three days' worth of newspapers under the other. "You sure you can get this started?"

Billy turned to her with his silly knit cap half sliding off of his sweaty forehead, a wide grin on his face. He motioned for her to help, and together they started to unload the wood. "Of course I can." He flashed another, slightly darker look at Liza that told that he didn't appreciate her doubting his fire starting abilities. Liza grinned right back at him, because if he couldn't do it, she certainly could.

The pile of seaweed was jumping with small shrimp and flies, having attracted both while sitting out in the hot, mid-afternoon sun. That was to be expected, however. They'd wanted the seaweed to be a little dry before they started cooking. Liza poked it with her foot, grateful that she was wearing sneakers. A small cloud of sea and land creatures temporarily rose up off of the mound of seaweed before settling once more. "Gross," she muttered. She wrinkled her nose getting a whiff of warm salt and slightly putrefied compost.

Liza set down her newspaper and kindling on top of the sawed-in-half barrel that was going to serve as their steamer-come-smoker and got to work building a fire in the pit beneath it with pieces of firewood that Billy passed her, one by one, from the back of the wheelbarrow. The trick with lobster bakes, Liza knew from years of experience, was to put fresh, wet seaweed into the bottom of the steamer and to season that, rather than the food itself. She had always loved doing this. Kevin's dad used to do bakes like this one for the whole town on Labor Day to raise money for the orphanage, the school, or Make-a-Wish. It was something different every year, but Liza and Kevin were always in charge of helping with the fire and managing the steamer once the fire was lit.

Tonight they got the fire going pretty easily—the wood was dry and it was low tide so the sand was relatively dry around the steamer. As the flames roared to life within the smoke-blackened metal of the barrel, Nancy started the process of ferrying the food that they were going to cook down to the grill. She'd put lobsters, clams, and mussels in the bottom of the steamer on top of the bed of fresh seaweed pulled from the sea just moments before. She followed it with corn on the cob that had been soaking, husk still on, overnight in water. Corn was tricky, and Liza had never quite gotten the hang of it. In with the corn went onions and eggs, which would cook like they had been hard-boiled before the night was out.

Liza pulled out the tin of Old Bay that had been jammed into her pocket since she came down with the kindling and sprinkled it on everything, before shoving more seaweed from their pile on top of the food and stepping back, careful not to catch her jeans on fire.

The smell of warm, salty, and smoky seaweed filled the air as they backed away from the grill and retreated to the safety of Kevin's porch. It was going to take an hour or two for everything to be ready, and they were content to wait.

Liza had a second of Chet's basement brew. It was good; he told Liza that it was made with the blackberries that grew behind his house. She wondered if that was how he and Nancy had gotten to be such good friends, seeing as Nancy knew all the good berry spots around town and exploited them expertly in her Harvest and Hay Festival jam-making adventures.

Kevin came down to sit beside Liza on the porch steps. He wasn't wearing his usual prosthetic today, and the empty void where his hand had once been was strange to look at.

Catching herself staring at it, she wanted to reach out and grasp the empty space and reassure herself that it had all been a bad dream. "Have you ever thought about getting a hand-shaped one?" Liza asked, pointing with the neck of her beer bottle to the stump of his arm where it ended at what was once his wrist.

He shrugged and pulled his sleeve back with his remaining hand, beer carefully tucked between his booted feet.

The scarring ran all the way up his arm and Liza wondered just how bad of an accident he'd been in. He never spoke of the accident, except in the broadest of terms. It was always the sort of thing that he avoided mentioning altogether, and as much as Liza wanted to know the details, she knew that she could never stomach them.

"It was nasty at the time, but now it's just sort of there," Kevin said. "I still feel it sometimes, phantom limb and all that."

"I—" There was an apology on the tip of Liza's tongue. Ever since she had come back to Near Haven, there always seemed to be an apology spilling forth from her lips. She was constantly saying that she was sorry for something, apologizing her way through life because she had been nothing but a failure and a disappointment since birth. Rationally, she knew that such thoughts were completely unfounded, and that they weren't true. It was hard to look past those feelings of inadequacy, to look past them and see what was truly bothering her. "I know that I should have called or come home or something when your dad died."

Kevin pulled his shirt sleeve back down and reached for his beer. His expression was unreadable, a blank mask of half-shaven features. "I knew that you wouldn't, even after Nancy said that she'd spoken to you."

"How?"

"Because I wouldn't have known what to say either, Liza." He smiled sadly at her and touched her cheek with his weathered fingers. "You're like me. You say things when you can, but a lot of the time you don't." Staring out over the road to the cove and the gently lapping waves against the rocks, he sighed. It was mid-tide, and the tide pools were starting to disappear, one by one, as the water level rose. "My dad was like that too."

Liza ran a hand through her hair, biting at her lip. She didn't know what to say. She understood, she really did. Kevin's dad had been strong and silent, an unwavering man of the sea. He had longed for a peace that he'd never found and a love that he'd never had. Liza didn't know how he'd done it, all those years, when he was so obviously falling apart inside. "We should try and be better about it, for his memory," she said, taking a long pull on her beer.

Kevin nodded, but there was a twinkle in his eye that screamed "Danger Will Robinson," as loudly as the sky was blue. He winked at her and leaned in to whisper in her ear. "You should start by admitting to yourself that you nearly broke up the most beautiful marriage-to-be that Near Haven has ever seen with your devilish charm."

Planting her hand firmly on his face, Liza pushed him away. Her cheeks were burning scarlet and she was very pointedly looking at her feet, clutching her nondescript beer bottle like it was a shield. "I did nothing of the sort," she retorted. There was no feeling behind her words. She had done exactly what he'd said, which made the situation—and his joking about it—even worse.

"Tell that to the girl I found crying on my doorstep, demanding to know what airport you were flying out of." Kevin crossed his arms and grinned broadly at her.

Liza's ears burned and she bit her lip, looking away from his knowing gaze and out over the ocean once more. The ocean was simple. It had its moods, it ebbed and it flowed with the tide. The shorelines may change, but the ocean itself was constant. It was what Liza wished her life could be—steady and with none of the heartache of homecoming and return.

"She was getting married, Kevin." Liza all but spat out. She almost winced at the pain of remembering how it all had nearly been thrown away, had she simply asked. Liza couldn't steal a future like that, not when her own had been right before her. She'd left with Charlie and Nancy and had resolved to never come back for both their sakes. "She was happier that way."

Kevin scratched his chin with his lone hand and gave her a little shrug.

The smell of burning seaweed drifted over them now, along with the warm and fragrant tinge of roasting onions. Liza inhaled deeply and wondered if maybe they should check on the clams and mussels. The lobsters, by her estimation, needed about another fifteen minutes.

"She did love him," Kevin said. He watched as Nancy and Billy hurried across the street to pull aside the seaweed and open up the steamer. Ted, who apparently had arrived while Kevin and Liza were talking, was standing ready with a long stick to poke at the steamy mess of seaweed inside. "You confused her."

Liza groaned. Kevin was the last person she wanted to know that it had gone far deeper than a simple teenage sexuality crisis...that the confusion had passed to leave only desperate want and unending longing. It had left Liza running scared. "I confuse me," she mumbled darkly.

Some five minutes later, as Nancy and Billy finished checking on the steamer, Sofia arrived with a fresh green salad in hand. When Liza raised a skeptical eyebrow at it, she was greeted with a curt, "Corn does not count as a vegetable, Ms. Hawke," and a small, almost shy smile. It wasn't meant to be biting or harsh, just a playful reminder of the relationship they once had. Liza smiled back, a little uncertain. She had done what Sofia asked of her, but she wasn't sure that it was enough to say that she'd gone to see Leslie Burke earlier in the week.

Tuesday morning, Kevin had needed to get his boat's license renewed and had to go to Augusta to do it, giving Liza an unexpected day to herself in town. Leslie Burke was expecting her, a stack of papers on her desk and her eyes determined as she shook Liza's hand. She'd listened as Liza described the details of the case, the ones that she hadn't shared with Kevin or Nancy.

Liza talked for what seemed like hours, telling Leslie about how the judge believed that restitution was in order for wrongful imprisonment, but would not wipe her record clean. Leslie asked if Liza had thought to use the money she'd been granted to clear her name, but Liza sheepishly shook her head.

"I was too young," Liza said. "I just wanted to get as far away from that place as I could, before they tried to put me back there."

"Then where did you go?"

"Vegas, and then St. Paul. I was in Chicago for a while, and then Knoxville." Liza ticked them off on her fingers, one by one—the places that were never truly home. "I think I was in Chicago when I finally realized that I couldn't get a job without my record coming up."

She knew that more and more employers were starting to Google search potential employee names these days, and she could not escape that; but, if the record wasn't there,

Liza figured she had more of a chance of actually getting a job. She could be hired by someone who wasn't already a friend and wouldn't have to worry about the conviction causing her to be turned away.

Leslie Burke had sad eyes and dirty blonde hair that was thrown up into a messy ponytail. She took precise notes the whole time that Liza talked, but when Liza said that, she'd laid her pen down and bridged her fingers together. "What sort of work would you want, if you could do anything?"

She didn't really have an answer for that. She'd never had enough time to think about it. Her college education had been cut short and she'd only managed the general education classes through sheer stubbornness. No one ever told her that she'd be expected to practice all day, every day, with little time to do much other than go to class and scramble to complete her assignments.

"I…" She began, thinking about how she loved spending time on the boat with Kevin, but how it wasn't practical or sustainable in the long run. "I like kids?" she had ventured finally. She'd enjoyed coaching the elementary school kids a great deal in July and had found herself actively carving out time to spend with Nathan, regardless of Sofia's subtle disapproval.

And Liza understood why Sofia didn't approve, really she did. Sofia had been burned by Liza once already, and she had every right to be cautious with her fatherless son's affections.

"That's a decent start." Leslie pursed her lips and made a note. "Have you ever tried to work with children with this conviction?"

She'd never worked with children except at Charlie's camp. She hated that she'd spent nearly five years without any ambition at all, moving with the speed of molasses across the country, blowing through what little cash she had in stupid ways. "I never tried," Liza explained. "I knew what was going to be said, regardless of my qualifications."

Leslie hummed her agreement and tapped her pen against her pad pensively. "You've been five years without any criminal record, right?"

"Yeah," Liza replied.

Leslie smiled at her. "I think I can help you."

Liza didn't remember Leslie from school. They were five years apart, so they were always missing each other in school by a year. She was a good person, though, and Liza had desperately spent the entire meeting trying not to think about the lingering looks that Ted gave Leslie during their shared lunches at the diner in town. The lingering looks that Leslie had most certainly returned.

After the initial meeting, they met once more on Friday afternoon, before Leslie disappeared off to wherever it was that she was spending the holiday weekend. Liza had found Ted leaning over the L-corner of the counter at the diner, his face close to Leslie's with a smile pulling at the corners of his lips. Liza stood there in the doorway and watched as Leslie leaned in to whisper something in his ear. Her behavior was so brazen, so obvious, that Liza just about turned around and left in that moment. She wanted no part of whatever it was they were doing; it simply wasn't right.

In the end, she had stayed though, and slid onto the stool next to Leslie, accepting the cup of coffee that a disapproving-looking Rachel put in front of her with some trepidation. Liza didn't have the money to buy frivolous coffees.

"It's on the house." Rachel winked, and Liza tipped the mug to her and drained it gratefully. The sort of genuine friendliness that Rachel exuded on a daily basis was fascinating. Liza so rarely met genuinely nice people in her life, and Rachel's grandmother sure wasn't the nicest person she'd ever met. However, Rachel was just kind and quietly disapproving of what Leslie and Ted were doing, same as the rest of them.

Ted had left a few minutes earlier and Leslie had the good sense to look guilty as she turned her attention to Liza once more. She looked out of place in her smart suit and pumps in a diner that largely catered to local fishermen looking for a cheap dinner after a long day at sea.

"I talked to a former classmate of mine, out in Oregon," Leslie said. She pulled a notepad from her purse and set it on her knee. The other knee had been bouncing a mile a minute and she kept flashing Liza nervous looks.

Liza tried to smile and absolve her then. "I'm not much for judging." She shrugged. The coffee burned the back of her throat as she drank deeply, trying to avoid feeling anything at all, when Leslie flashed a grateful look in her direction before going back to her notes.

"The policy there's pretty much the same as it is here. Five years clean and you can petition to have the verdict changed." Leslie flipped to another page, reading quickly down the page, using a pen she'd pulled from the loose bun in her hair to tick down the page. "I was told that if you could get the guy who framed you to exonerate you through testimony—"

"He did," Liza answered quickly. "That's why they let me out, I think."

Leslie's lips pursed into a thin line and her whole body seemed to sag.

Liza had been afraid of this. Defeat came so easily to a place like this.

"I think I need to make some more calls."

"Okay," Liza replied. She drained the rest of her coffee and set the mug back down on the counter with a smile at Rachel. "I um… I don't have a phone."

"I'll tell Sofia," Leslie's eyes grew warm once more after she said it.

Liza grinned right back at her, until Leslie's expression became pensive once more.

"I… I hate to put you in the middle of this mess, but please try to not say anything to anyone about Ted. Sofia knows, but she's the only one."

Much later in the evening, Liza realized that Leslie had been pushing her towards Sofia. It had been a subtle push, one worthy of the skilled lawyer that she was. Liza sighed and flopped back onto her bed. She was reading Moby Dick now, having never quite managed to get through it in high school. Melville's prose was something she liked a lot, and she found herself lying awake wondering if she was chasing a white whale by coming back to this town.

Maybe they're all just looking for things they could not have, Liza mused, watching as Sofia stood in her jeans and crisp white shirt, looking out of place and a little uncomfortable as Liza bustled the salad over to the picnic table. It was strange to see Sofia among their motley group, but she cheered when Sofia settled herself down next to Kevin on the porch steps and refused the beer he offered her in favor of a ginger ale from the cooler.

From her place by the picnic table, Liza watched Kevin and Sofia speak quietly for a moment before Kevin rose to his feet and headed across the street, Nathan in tow, to help Ted and Billy as they unearthed eggs and onions and steamer clams from the pile of seaweed that had now gathered at their feet. Liza took a deep breath, then, and moved to the porch steps beside Sofia. From her vantage point, she could see Kevin eyeing her from across the street and tipped her beer to him, daring him to say something.

"I hear you're to thank for the fire." There was a hint of amusement in Sofia's eyes, warm, brown, and inviting.

Liza had fallen into them on more than one occasion, and this didn't seem much different.

Kevin, across the street, let out a yelp and jerked Nathan back from a waft of steam that billowed from the fire pit. Nathan glanced across the road towards Sofia, who made no move to run to protect him, and then turned back to his task of helping remove piping hot lobsters and ears of corn from the steamy mess over the fire that Liza had indeed built.

They were alone in the world, two people sitting next to each other, all hostility set aside for the time being. Liza knew why Sofia was angry with her, but she stood by her decision to this day. It had been the right thing for both of them at the time, and she couldn't look back now.

Liza grinned. "Aren't I always?"

Sofia let out a quiet snort of laughter and pensively sipped on her ginger ale. Liza watched as her eyes scanned the road for cars every so often, most of her attention on Nathan. After watching Kevin and Billy have at tense conversation about the state of the lobsters, Sofia turned to face Liza. Her eyes were alight with questions that Liza was sure weren't being asked and she had the look of someone about to demand answers clearly written on her face. "Leslie said that you went to see her."

"Yeah," Liza replied. She felt sheepish, knowing that Sofia was behind this good turn. She didn't know how to thank her for it. "I um...she likes Ted?" It wasn't what she wanted to say, and from the thin line of Sofia's lips, Liza knew that she was about to strike out big time. Liza backpedaled, picking at some dirt on her jeans. "I...oh fuck it. I know she's your friend."

"And Ted is yours. This isn't news, dear," Sofia said. She stared at Ted with narrowed eyes as he tugged on a pair of fisherman's gloves and reached into the steamer to unearth the lobsters. Nathan held a plate and looked up at him with adoring eyes.

Liza wondered if Sofia hated the example that was being set for Nathan, with all these less-than-perfect people surrounding him. She knew the Milton family way; they wanted the best out of everyone, even if it meant resorting to less-than-pleasant means to get it. Liza had experienced that fear and that power firsthand—as Sofia had as well. Liza's heart hammered in her chest, knowing she could do little more than stand idly by, even all these years later, as the pressure of being a Milton overwhelmed Sofia.

"She and Noah haven't been happy for quite some time."

Biting at her lip, Liza nodded. Marriage was one of those things that she'd never really understood. She'd lived long enough to know that sometimes people forged connections that were stronger than others, but she didn't understand how it happened. All she had ever known was impermanence. Relationships to Liza were too deep…too intense, and she was scared of them. They scared away the sense of safety and contentment that she was afraid to articulate, for fear of breaking the peace she'd finally found.

And somehow, it was never enough. Kevin, Charlie, Nancy, they were all friends. They were the sorts of people that Liza could breathe easily around, and she knew that she would not be judged. Liza understood friendship, but she dropped it easily, like the families of her childhood. Coming back here, and having to rely on people who would have stood by her had she simply reached out to them, was almost too much. She couldn't stomach that it was only her failure that had gotten her here, and she hated that she woke up every morning with it staring her in the face.

"I had wondered," Liza said.

The food was ready, or close to it. Nathan was ferrying the platter full of bright red lobsters across the street on slow and sure feet. He didn't look as he crossed, but the road had been dead for hours now and no one said anything. They didn't want to have to rinse the lobsters off if he dropped them.

Liza pushed herself to her feet and offered Sofia her hand. They were both in jeans and Sofia was in a nice white blouse that was going to get lobster all over it if she wasn't careful. "I'll flip you for dibs on not cutting up Kevin's lobster for him."

"That, my dear, is a deal."

Liza had been all over the country in her short life. She was twenty-eight now and she couldn't quite figure out why lobster was considered such a big deal in the Midwest. Along the coasts it was just another thing that could be eaten, but in Chicago and St. Paul, people would go nuts for the things like they were going out of style. She sat at the table that had been crudely constructed out of stacked lobster traps and a piece of plywood that was purportedly going to be cut up and used to repair Kevin's porch railing. Nancy had put a red and white checkered tablecloth over it and they drew up benches and chairs, talking, laughing, and enjoying the last hurrah of summer.

Everything was salty and tasted slightly of Old Bay seasoning. Liza shucked her corn as she waited for the lobster on her plate to cool enough to touch. Nathan ate with gusto across from her, not seeming to care that everything was too hot to touch. Kevin had, very nicely, asked Nancy to bust open his lobster and it was just the sort of meal that Liza had always found herself wanting.

Lobster bakes were a thing of her past, an entity that had taken on a feeling larger than life. Liza stared down at the sea creature that was waiting for her to take sheers to it and cut it open. It smelled heavenly, like the summer corn that fell off the ear as she bit into it. Lobsters were a way of life; they grew with the ocean and the fishermen around them. Lobsters brought people together.

They were a sort of family, or almost. Charlie was off fishing with some of his old man friends and Rachel was at someone else's lobster bake. This evening would have been perfect if they were here too, but the atmosphere wouldn't change. Liza liked it this way, easy and full of the companionship that she'd always longed for.

As night fell around them, Liza taught Nathan how to play poker with Kevin, Ted, and Chet while Sofia and Billy discussed the upcoming winter. Billy went up to Newfoundland and worked off one of the boats there during the winter, earning more money than God for what was apparently two months of straight hell in the northern Atlantic. Liza wondered if that was the sort of thing that she could handle, but she knew that that sort of work was a boy's club and the last thing she wanted to do was get trapped on a boat with a bunch of men for weeks at a time. Who knew what might happen.

A sick feeling of dread welled up in Liza's stomach as she thought about the winter. She knew that she would figure something out, but Leslie Burke was her best bet at getting a job. There was no kindness in the world that would keep her paying rent if she wouldn't be able to find herself a job come November. Liza pushed the emotion aside, not wanting to dwell on it, and flipped the last card in the river, her face perfectly neutral as she found herself sitting on two pair, aces high.

They threw out the remains of their lobsters for the gulls to find, scattering them into the tide where they were sure to be devoured come morning. Liza jammed her hands into her back pockets and turned to Sofia. "Do you hate me for what I did?"

Sofia tossed the last of the remnants of their meal into the ocean and shrugged.

She was remarkably clean for one who had just eaten a lobster, but Liza'd watched her do it with awe. Sofia was a fucking expert with a pair of shears and a fork. She had done Nathan's for him as well, dismantling the whole lobster in less than five minutes and with minimal mess. Liza, to her credit, was also fairly clean, but only because she'd tucked a napkin into her shirt and didn't much care what Chet or Kevin had to say about it.

"How can I hate you for doing the right thing?" she answered evenly.

It was a question to answer a question, but it intrigued Liza nonetheless.

"David and I were in love, we were getting married..."

Liza reached out for Sofia, taking her hand and holding it tightly, afraid that it would be yanked away.

Sofia met her gaze evenly and did not pull her hand away.

"I am really sorry about what happened. All of it."

"I know." Sofia's eyes fluttered shut. "I am too."

They stood there for a long time. Liza was just barely pushing back her fear and clinging to Sofia's hand. She didn't know what was happening, and she was not sure that she wanted to know. It felt good and right to stand there together, no matter the baggage and the damage and whatever else had transpired between them. There was peace in the moment, and Liza was grateful for it.

CHAPTER SIX

The Harvest and Hay Festival (5 October, 2012)

Noah Burke moved out of the house he shared with his estranged wife in the middle of September, taking a room at Rachel's grandmother's bed and breakfast. It came as no surprise to Liza, but it was still a little bit shocking to see Noah sitting by himself, in scrubs and crocs, drinking coffee at four in the morning when she stopped by the back of the diner to pick up the sandwiches that Rachel had left for them. "Can't sleep?" Her tone was mild as she tugged at her hoodie and checked that her T-shirt was tucked into her pants.

He looked up at her with weary eyes. Noah worked two jobs, just as Liza would if she had the ability to do so. One day, not too long ago, Noah confessed to Liza, over their bizarrely opposite breakfast and dinner schedules, that he'd picked up the part-time sheriff gig to supplement his income and to provide him with a little more excitement during the week. His normal job was at the vet clinic that was attached to the animal shelter. According to Nancy, Noah was a die-hard animal lover. Between his two jobs, he saw the worst of Near Haven. Liza wondered if that was what drove a wedge between him and Leslie.

"I suppose," he replied. He slumped back against the steps, looking defeated.

Liza left him to his coffee and headed down the road and out to the boat.

The days were cooler now, but it was the mornings that were the worst. Kevin had taken to steering the boat as the water grew ever-colder, letting Billy and Liza be the ones to hang over the sides with hooks on poles to try to catch buoys as they floated by. It was safer this way, they all reasoned, and Liza was happy that Kevin wasn't taking unnecessary risks.

Liza saw Leslie Burke once more as September faded into a brilliant October. The leaves were just starting to go, and it was beautiful to behold and absolutely wonderful to be outside to witness the hillsides by the sea stained crimson and yellow, aflame with nature's delight.

Nancy dragged her out to hike on the weekends and Nathan started to play youth-league soccer. Liza made a point to go to as many of his games as she could. She missed him now that he was back at school and didn't have whole days free to laze around with her on the weekends.

She missed Sofia too, but that was a slightly more complicated sort of relationship that was filled with an acute sense of longing. Sofia was buried under work with the city council, coordinating the Harvest and Hay Festival celebrations and getting the town ready for the winter. On one of their afternoons together, Nathan had whispered that his mother was always working after dinner, probably going long into the night after he was finished with his homework and had gone to bed.

It made Liza's heart ache, wishing that there was something that she could do to help. She knew better than to offer, because it would only be rebuffed with sad eyes and the terrible truth that she could do nothing. Not right now. She had to prove that she could fix her problems on her own, to show Sofia that she was trying. She was certain that it would be enough to make Sofia see. Liza was working with Leslie for a reason, and the reason was growing more and more clear to her with each passing day.

At their twice-weekly meetings, Leslie Burke had red eyes all the time, like she had been crying and was desperate for something that no one could give her. She'd thrown herself fully into Liza's case, even though she had no money to pay the bill. She sold Leslie's stupidly high allotment of harvest candles with Chet as a way of saying "thank you" when Leslie told her that she managed to get a copy of the testimony that Jared fucking Dickens (may he rot in jail forever) had given in his grand jury trial.

They were close to having everything they needed to file a motion, Leslie had promised Liza with a weary smile. It was late that night, and Liza had come by to bring her the money she'd made on candle sales. Leslie was still wide awake, sleepily typing on her laptop, as Liza stuck the money she'd collected into the envelope Leslie shoved in her direction. Liza's heart was lighter than it had been in weeks. Finally, they were getting somewhere. There was even a chance that this could be resolved, and soon.

"Do you have work lined up after Kevin winters the boat?" Leslie asked. Liza zipped up her jacket and pulled her scarf more tightly around her neck. Soon it would be too cold to go out in just this jacket alone.

Liza shook her head. "Just the library job, but..." The only solid lead that she'd had was that the librarian was embarking on some sort of archiving project and needed someone to do the heavy lifting down in the library's basement. Liza was still debating if she wanted to put in an application, since it was sure to lead to a background check, and she didn't want to bring that sort of headache onto the poor girl. The few times that they'd spoken, she seemed to be very nice and undeserving of *that* pain in Liza's collective ass. Despite all this, Liza knew that she couldn't be employed by the town government with her record. She'd never pass the background check and wasn't sure that she wanted to work for the city at all, especially if things with Sofia did continue to progress the way they'd been going.

"Well, if that doesn't pan out, let me know. I might be able to find you something." Leslie gave her a kind smile.

Liza swallowed the lump in her throat to smile back. It wasn't easy, to take advantage of kindness that was offered so freely. Liza was so used to fighting for everything she had that she could barely stomach the idea of someone helping her out of the goodness of her heart.

When she got home that evening, Charlie was sitting at the kitchen island. He looked older than Liza ever remembered, his grey hair frizzing at the temples and his beard far more unkempt than usual. He had a pile of colorful, checkered fabric swatches and rubber bands in front of him and was putting them on top of Nancy's jam jars in preparation for the Harvest and Hay Festival, while Nancy cooked dinner in the kitchen. Liza had had a similar chore that morning.

"Hey." Liza unwrapped her scarf from around her neck and smiled brightly at the pair. Her boots came off next, set beside Nancy's in a neat little row that made Liza feel like she was in a college dorm again, not in Near Haven, Maine. Near Haven: where absolutely nothing was easy or simple. "Can I help?"

Nancy passed her a knife and a bag of potatoes.

Liza stood over the sink and peeled them methodically into the dispose-all side, only half listening as Nancy chattered on about her day, mostly to her father.

Liza was exhausted, and listening to Nancy speak only made her feel more tired. The ocean had been rough that day, and they only made it two-thirds of the way through their route before they heard a small craft advisory over the radio and headed back to port. She was still cold, the dampness of the sea had crept its way under her clothes and wrapped her skin in a blanket of ice that not even a hot shower could seem to shake. She was going to get sick.

Maybe it was just the change in the weather. She had gone south after a winter in St. Paul and then a spring in Chicago. Liza had never really been much for the cold.

"Actually, Liza..." Charlie said. Liza's knife paused, her attention drawn. "I've been wanting to talk to you about something." Charlie faltered, his eyes crinkling at the corners as he snapped a rubber band around a fabric square over the cap of the jam jar in his hand. "You haven't got a phone though."

"I'm thinking about getting a pay-as-you-go next time someone's heading up towards Wal-Mart," Liza replied. "What's up, coach?" Keeping her tone neutral and easy was harder than Liza thought it would be initially. She recognized the little digs about her financial situation for what they were. With Charlie, things weren't ever just statements of the obvious. He was a good man, but he struggled to look past her failure. That much had become blatantly obvious during her stint teaching camp with him over the summer.

Charlie sat with his hands on the table. His knuckles were swollen, arthritic-looking, even, and he looked so impossibly old in that moment that Liza's breath caught in her throat. When the hell had that happened? "I want you to assist me with the team this season." He scratched at his beard, his eyes sharp under his bushy eyebrows. "I know that you need something to do once that boy puts his boat up for the winter."

Liza inclined her head, the only thing she was willing to concede to his point. "I've been thinking about options, yes. It's a little hard right now. I was thinking about putting in for the library job."

He shook his head. "You don't want to work for the town."

Nancy's eyebrows shot up.

Liza knew exactly what Nancy was thinking, and she couldn't help herself; if Charlie'd seen it like he did before…it was too late to attempt to hide the budding… whatever it was between herself and Sofia, then. The entire town would soon know and there was nothing she could do about it. News traveled fast in places where very little ever happened.

"I'm sure that Ms. Burke will come through for you, Liza, but you have to be realistic. The town can't hire you with your record."

Shame flooded Liza and she dropped her gaze down to the potato in her hands. She had learned so many things in her time away from this place: how to cook, how to live, how to be a functional adult member of society. But somehow, Charlie could still reduce her to nothing with a few harsh words. She hated that she cared so much. She hated how cruel he could be without seeming to care. "I know," she said. Her voice was quiet, barely audible over the sound of dinner cooking on the stove.

"Thanks to the senator's generosity, the schools here are always significantly under budget," Charlie added in an almost off-hand way. He had a rubber band around his fingers and a blue and white checkered patch in his hand, but his tone was severe. "I've already spoken to the school board and they'd be willing to take you on for the season, provided you can demonstrate to them that you're working towards some sort of an education for yourself. It's probationary, and if you fuck up, it'll be the last time you work in this town. They're taking a *huge* risk, Liza, they know what you did and where you spent the time you should have been hoopin' for Portland State."

It sounded so much like the conversation that she had had with Leslie Burke back in August that she wondered if Charlie had spoken to her. She should have known better than to expect privacy in a place like this. "They're waiving the background check?" At Charlie's slow nod, Liza ran a hand through her hair and let out a quiet breath of whistled air though her teeth. "How much? I can talk to Kevin about staying off the boat when practice starts, but he usually doesn't bring it in until the first week of November."

"I think you'll be okay," Charlie said with a broad smile.

Nancy touched his shoulder and Liza watched the silent exchange between them. They were so close—Nancy's mother had been gone since she was very young, and Charlie and Nancy had always relied almost exclusively on each other. Liza didn't remember if she'd ever met Nancy's mother, but she thought she'd remember the woman that Charlie and Nancy both spoke so fondly of.

It was still working for the town's government, but it was separate from the municipal government—where Sofia would be her direct superior. At the high school, at least, there was a buffer, and she wouldn't have to feel quite so guilty about pursuing a relationship with her boss.

"The stipend is somewhere between six and eight thousand, depending on how long the season goes."

Liza's eyes widened and she set the potato down on top of the peelings in the sink. That was far more than she could have ever hoped for, and if she could find some sort of second, part-time morning position...she would be set. She could go back to the boat once the season was over. It could be perfect. "I'll do it." She tried to show the determination she felt in her voice. She knew that she should probably think about it some more, but it was so much money that she couldn't possibly say no to Charlie. It was also work that Liza thought she'd like.

She didn't say thank you to Charlie until they were seeing him down the stairs and out of the building. He'd parked his old Crown Vic under the awning that Liza was convinced was going to turn hazardous once the snow came. He was going to the festival site early the next morning, and Nancy had asked him to take along the first of what would have been two or three trips up and down the narrow stairs with a large box of jam. He was getting to the festival before them, anyway.

Liza had never been good with words. She knew that kindness such as this deserved thanks, but she wasn't entirely sure how to articulate that. Coupled with the grim realization that she could not speak what she truly meant in terms of gratitude, was the fact that she wasn't entirely sure she knew how to "improve" herself for the school board, but she knew she had to do *something* to prove that she was worth the chance they were taking. She didn't want to take the money that Senator Milton and his wife, Sofia's horrible mother, had surely funneled into the Near Haven school system through probably nefarious means.

Or at least, that was what Liza's fantastic tin foil hat-wearing, inner conspiracy theorist said to her on a regular basis. She knew that the former Senator Milton would never have done such a thing. He had been far too good a man to ever stoop so low. He'd let his wife manipulate things behind the scenes when such actions were needed. Sofia had once said as much at twenty-two, tutoring Liza over the summer.

God, Liza shook her head ruefully. She didn't want to think about that summer and the horrible pain that had come after. She had not set out to hurt anyone, but young love, as it always did, got in the way and they were still picking up the pieces, some eleven years later.

"Coach," Liza said. Charlie set the box full of decorated little jam jars onto the passenger seat of his car.

Nancy rose up on tip toes and kissed her father on the cheek before turning to hurry back inside. She wasn't wearing a coat, after all, and the night had turned positively frigid. In a simple flannel shirt, Liza felt the cold that'd driven Nancy indoors acutely; it cut through her shirt as if it wasn't even there. She resisted the urge to shiver or to rub at her upper arms; she had to say her piece. She had to be firm. "Thank you."

He looked at her for a long time, hands in his pockets and his jacket hanging open and loose around his waist. "You're a good kid, Liza," he said at length. "I don't know if doing this will make things better for you, but I hope it will."

"I won't let you down." Liza replied, and knew even then that it was a piecrust sort of a promise. She couldn't guarantee something like that—no one could. All she could do was her best and hope it was good enough.

Charlie nodded grimly. "See that you don't."

That night Liza's dreams took her to the basement of the library. She'd had this dream many times now, and it never got easier.

She was seventeen—all elbows and knees and so much unspent energy that she played three sports just to have an outlet for it all. She was sitting, slumped in a chair, flipping listlessly through one of the summer reading books she was assigned for her world history class. It was called *Things Fall Apart* and Liza remembered thinking at the time that the title was apt.

In the dream, Sofia arrived late, which she had never done in all the years that Liza'd known her. Liza suffered through the book without her, hating every moment if it. As the hours dragged on, she could feel the sweat trickle down her back as she read. It was hot outside and the basement was stuffy and not nearly cool enough to be conducive to concentration, let alone comprehension.

The door to the study room opened, and Liza lowered her book, staring out into the blackness that appeared before her. A dark entity with cruel eyes and a hateful expression stared out at her from the blackness of the doorway.

As always, Liza bolted to her feet, the book falling forgotten to the floor. Her hand always clenched into fists during this part of the dream, and she fought the urge to cry out, to scream all the words in the world at this shadow, this ghost upon her memory.

Liza had dreamt of this moment so many times that she didn't wake up anymore when the hand of the shadowy creature closed around her neck and she was slammed against the white, painted brick wall of the library basement. The hissing voice was there, plain as day, telling her that she was abnormal, that she was a corrupting waste of space, that she was the only reason that the marriage between Sofia and Dave had been given the family's blessing.

She woke up gasping for air; Nancy's hand was like a claw, clutching her shoulder.

Liza blinked, her eyes adjusting to the light streaming in from the windows. It was morning, yet she felt like she hadn't slept at all.

"You were screaming," Nancy said in a mild voice. Her eyebrows were raised up to hover somewhere around her hairline.

Liza rolled over hurriedly, her stomach rebelling and the urge to vomit so great that she found herself dry heaving over the side of the bed. It had been years since she'd had that dream with that sort of intensity. She'd had this same dream for years now, and had gotten rather adept at waking herself up before it got to this point. The terror was enough to make her want to dry heave again, even though she knew there was nothing inside to throw up. Liza twisted the blanket into her fist and slammed both down on the bed beside her. She hated this. "I'm okay," she said weakly. "Thanks for coming to wake me up."

Nancy sat on the end of the bed and took Liza's hand in hers. The contact wasn't welcome, and she didn't really know how to respond to it. Others had attempted to soothe her from these nightmares before, but it had never felt quite right having someone help her through them. Nancy was no different. Her fingers were warm and comforting, and Liza felt as though she could not possibly be deserving of such kindness.

"Do you want to talk about it?" Nancy asked.

Liza wondered if she still thought they were on opposite ends of high school and this was the easiest thing in the world. Liza was not nursing bruises on her neck with no good explanation for them this time though. And she wasn't struggling with a terrible decision and falling in love at seventeen. She wasn't anything right now. Liza felt as though she were a blank slate, slowly but surely starting to develop its own, unique character, with each opportunity afforded to it.

The exposed beams in the ceiling cast long shadows. Liza stared hard at her bookshelf, with its three books, collection of shells, and interesting pieces of driftwood. The fourth book was discarded on the bed beside her, Captain Ahab descending slowly into madness and obsession over his white whale. "It isn't easy." Liza sighed and flopped back onto her pillow. "I wouldn't even know where to begin."

Nancy shrugged. "The beginning works."

Liza let out a harsh, short bark of laughter. She didn't even know if this story had a start. It was timeless like the library's broken clock tower and the constant tides that rose and fell as the days passed steadily on. "When I was three, the foster family that I was living with had to move to Portland. I don't know why, but I was a part of this pilot program that the state was trying, keeping kids within the same community if at all possible. So I couldn't go with them. Instead I was placed with a temporary family until a more permanent solution could be found."

Everyone knew this story—keeping a kid in the same community was a problem in the foster care system. It took a village or whatever that initiative was called. "I met a girl there." The announcement was greeted with laughter and Liza let her head fall down to rest on her fingers, cradling it as she stared up at the long, strange shadows of the ceiling. "And I think I might like her more than I've ever..." Liza trailed off, sighing and closing her eyes. She couldn't say it. She knew that there was something there:

true, real, genuine feelings that she was almost desperate to have returned.

"You broke her heart when you left," Nancy said.

"Kevin said as much," Liza grumbled, "but it was the right thing to do."

"It doesn't make it any easier, does it?"

Liza rolled onto her side. "Not at all." Her voice was still half-caught in a grumble. "Not at all."

Nancy left a few minutes later, and Liza drifted back into an uneasy sleep. She was curled around her pillow, clutching it like it was a lifeline. That moment, the terrible memory that her dream so vividly recreated, that moment had been her downfall once. It would never be again. The last thought that Liza had before sleep claimed her once more was that she never signed up for all the guilt and worry that came with being back here. Worry for Nathan, for Sofia, for the future. She was plagued by it.

The morning dawned bright and sunny, the temperature touching sixty. It was warm enough for Liza to wear just a light sweater and pack her jacket up with Nancy's in the final box of jam. She tucked their lunch on top of the load. Nancy locked up behind them, and they headed silently down to the car.

The Harvest and Hay Festival had been a fixture in the town for as long as anyone could remember. It was part autumn festival and part fundraiser for the quasi-private elementary school, and it had always been a great deal of fun. Usually the festival was held on the town green, but there were events held all across town to celebrate the day.

Liza barely remembered the history of the day from school, or what it celebrated anymore. It had been stained into the wood of Near Haven's history for so long that it was but a blemish sanded smooth. If Liza recalled the story correctly, the nuns who ran the elementary school, back when it was still a strictly religious school, had traded homemade whale blubber candles to the local woodsmen and farmers for food and wood to heat their school and feed their students during the winter. Now it was just a fundraiser and a town celebration that drew people from all over New England to partake in the food and late-season harvest festival feel that it effortlessly possessed.

"Do you want to close down the stand for a little while and do the corn maze?" Nancy asked as they passed a sign for it.

Liza was half-asleep still, a battered travel mug of coffee clutched in her hands, as Nancy drove them over to the municipal lot behind city hall.

"Guess so," Liza said. She stared out the window bleary-eyed, as people slowly moved across the green, setting up tables and greeting friends and neighbors. "We could always grab someone and make them man the booth too."

"Like who?" Nancy glanced over at Liza as she checked to see if the space ahead of them was clear to park in. There was an old Subaru that'd pulled way forward. Nancy's lips turned downwards into a frown and she drove the car forward once more.

Liza shrugged. "Don't know. Maybe Noah Burke might want to help out? I think he's real down right now."

"I'm not taking sides in that, Liza. I know Ted's your friend, but…" Nancy whipped the car into a vacant space and shifted into park in one fluid motion. "I just… I don't want to get involved."

Sipping her coffee, Liza rolled her eyes. "I'm not asking you to take sides. Just be friendly. He's a good guy." Liza thought that really, this whole thing had taken Noah completely by surprise. She understood his wanting to try and make it right, but she'd seen how Leslie had been since she moved out of their shared house. It hasn't been easy on either of them.

Their booth was shoved off to one corner, next to one of the local craftswomen selling thick, hand-knit scarves that Liza was sure would be wonderful come winter. Charlie had set up their first box of jam jars in neat little pyramids and Liza thought that she could see him speaking to Mr. Spencer, the former mayor, down towards the end of the line of booths. Their hands were shoved in their pockets like old men are wont to do, but they were both smiling and laughing.

There was a stack of candles, a last ditch effort to offload the rest of them, on the end of the table, along with the jam, and Liza helped Nancy to arrange their remaining wares into neat little displays. They'd written out placards with ingredients and information about the locales where the blueberries and blackberries were sourced. It seemed almost easy then, to settle onto the fifteen-year-old lawn chair next to Nancy and wait for the festival to truly get going.

At around nine-thirty, just as the booths were starting to fill up, Rachel and Ashleigh Boyd came by to bring them breakfast. The festival was slated to come to order at ten o'clock with an address from the mayor, and they'd resolved to take the cashbox with them and go to watch it. Together, she and Nancy ate the warm, oatmeal-cranberry muffins that Rachel's grandmother had kindly sent down with her granddaughter. Between bites and sips of steaming coffee, they chatted with the pair about how Ashleigh's kid was doing and how Rachel was getting along at the diner after the last waitress had up and quit to move to Manchester. Nancy had some truly hilarious stories to tell about her students' antics and Liza tried not to act like a walking stereotype and confirmed the rumors that Ashleigh had apparently heard about them finding an old boot in one of their traps the other day. She had no idea how *that* had gotten there.

"I don't even know how that works." Liza laughed in between bites of muffin and sips of now lukewarm coffee. "I mean, we were using a net, it was in a lobster pot. I guarantee you that one of those little ones we throw back was trying to fuck with us." She shook her head as Rachel and Ashleigh dissolved into giggles and Nancy rolled her eyes at the pair of them. She'd heard the story from Kevin and Liza both now—with Billy's embellishments about how there was a severed foot inside the boot—and Liza didn't blame her for not wanting to hear it again. It was a little gross.

At a few minutes before ten they trooped over to the city hall steps, Nancy clutching the cashbox to her chest and Liza with her hands plunged into the back pockets of her jeans. This was the first time that she'd been present at a gathering of this many people from Near Haven since her return to town. Heading down to Sprat's for groceries or eating at the diner didn't really count as full-on exposure—not like this. She could feel their eyes on her, could feel them watching as she fiddled with her hair, and she wished that she'd kept a hair tie around her wrist. Liza had half a mind to ask Charlie for one, but she'd made up her mind to keep her distance from him today.

She'd accepted his offer, but was not sure that it would be enough to just do that. He, and with him the school board, wanted her to *better* herself as an incentive to taking the job and Liza wasn't sure how to do that. She was not even sure that she could get into a community college with a criminal record. It might have to wait until Leslie could expunge her record, and Liza didn't know how to tell Charlie that either.

She shook her head, trying to force the thought from her mind. It was just another in a long list of failings. She was pretty sure that they'd figure it out when the time came. It was already October, anyway. It wasn't as if she could start classes until January; the school board must've known that.

Sofia came to stand on the top-most step going into city hall, Nathan by her side. He was holding a candle that Liza could only assume meant to serve as some sort of prop. There was a microphone set up. Local musicians usually played live music during the festival to keep the people lively. Liza was secretly hoping that the sheriff would bring out his guitar. He had always been really good playing at the open mic nights at the Rusty Wheel, a local dive bar in the basement of the bookshop, when she was still in high school. She could only assume that he'd gotten better. Chet had said he was going to play his fiddle at some point as well. Truth be told, Liza was looking forward to the music far more than listening to Sofia speak—at least that was the lie that she told herself.

Sofia coughed once, and the crowd quieted almost instantly, a respectful murmur moving through them.

Liza stared. She'd never seen Sofia as the mayor before. A strange sort of emotion welled up within her, and she thought of all the times when Sofia had never just been Sofia. She had always been something else to all those around her. Now she was a leader, and her presence was as commanding as her mother's. Liza hated that this was all she could see, as Sofia took the candle from Nathan and told of the history of this day in Near Haven. She felt those fingers around her neck and the threat that came ever closer as hissed words and the promise of swift retribution for her transgressions, both real and imagined. Liza didn't know what to make of Sofia in the same light, a woman in the same mold as the monster that raised her.

Closing her eyes, Liza tried to keep herself grounded in the present. She hadn't ever done anything save steal a kiss once. She swallowed yet another thing to not think about. *Ever.*

"And with that," Sofia said, "I declare this Harvest and Hay Day officially open." Her eyes swept across the crowd of people and a smile played on her lips. "Ms. White's blueberry jam is exceptional this year."

It wasn't until the quiet lull of conversation began to gain in volume that Nancy turned to Liza, cash box still clutched to her chest. "You gave it to *her*?" she demanded. Her glare was accusatory, but there was no malice behind it.

Liza wondered if this was really behind her strange reaction yesterday to Charlie's comment about not wanting to work for the city.

Nancy lowered her voice to a hiss. "Why?"

"Peace offering?" Liza ventured.

Nancy shook her head and turned on her heel. She made a beeline for Noah Burke and demanded to know if he'd be willing to work with her in her booth for a little while. Liza smiled as the man blinked and took a hesitant sip of his coffee before nodding his consent. It was only when he took the cash box from Nancy and offered her his arm that Liza felt disappointed. What the fuck, she'd just been ditched, by Nancy White of all people. Who knew she'd had it in her?

"Buuuuurn girl," Rachel commented, sweeping by with Ashleigh and the baby. Sean, Ashleigh's husband, was waving at them at the edge of the green and Liza knew that she would be the odd man out on this. Shoulders slumping, she sighed as she waved Rachel and her evil waggling eyebrows off. She could make her own fun. She could.

Kevin avoided the festival like the plague. He'd never been much for crowds, and he'd gone off on a rant about how he hated people asking him how he was "coping" with his father's death ten years after the fact on at least three different occasions in the past week. Liza didn't really blame him. Suicide cut into a community like a cancer, no matter how much on the fringe of society the person who died was. She hated it for him, because coming to the festival used to be one of his favorite things in the world when he was younger.

Liza wandered through the stalls alone, trying to force herself to seem inconspicuous. She wished that she could just march up to Sofia and ask her if she wanted to take Nathan to the corn maze together, but it was not that simple. She wasn't even sure that Sofia would say yes, for one. Nagging doubt filled Liza and she bit her lip. There was a lady selling honey straws and beeswax candles in the stall before her, and her smile was warm and welcoming. Liza dug in her pocket for a quarter, purchasing a raspberry honey straw, and sucked on it moodily as she walked around the stalls.

The question came to her mind unbidden: how do you pursue someone who doesn't give any indication of wanting to be pursued? Sofia had given her leeway, sure. She had let Liza become close with Nathan, certainly. But it'd been so long since Labor Day, and the feel of Sofia's hand warm in her own, that Liza wondered if it was just a one-off, doomed to never happen again.

"You mope like it's your job, dear."

Liza jumped, completely startled, and turned to find Sofia standing behind her. Sofia's hand was on Nathan's shoulder. She was smiling wickedly, a gleam in her eyes that set Liza on edge. She was up to something, and Liza knew Sofia's playful side well enough to know that it was *far* too early and she hadn't had *nearly* enough coffee to handle this. "Jesus," Liza muttered. She pulled the honey straw from her mouth. "You scared me."

She was greeted with a raised eyebrow and an amused giggle from Nathan.

"Really?" Sofia sounded almost impressed. Her grin widened. "I would have thought you impossible of startling, Ms. Hawke."

Folding her arms across her chest, Liza cocked her head to one side. She had no idea why anyone would think that. She was the biggest coward in this town. She tried to look brave and met Sofia's gaze coolly. "Is that a challenge, Ms. Milton?"

"It might be." Ever the politician, Sofia kept her tone neutral. She brought her hand up to ruffle Nathan's hair. He was wearing a flannel shirt that looked brand new and was certainly in better condition than the one that Liza was wearing.

Liza wondered if Sofia had actually let him out of the house in jeans, or if he'd insisted since it was a festival day.

"Nathan wanted to go to the corn maze before it gets crowded and my duties will force me to be here."

It was not articulated as such, but Liza knew that it was an invitation. They were not exactly direct people, the pair of them, but Liza desperately wanted this and was willing to read into implication and body language to get what she wanted. She smiled at Sofia and put her hands in her pockets. Had she been braver, she would have offered Sofia her arm. She was not Noah Burke, however. She could not woo this woman with noble intentions, apparently. "Sounds fun," she said.

They fell into step together, walking to where a horse-drawn wagon was parked, waiting to be driven by a disinterested-looking high school kid who would take people over the hill to the maze. The ride up to the maze had always been part of the charm of the whole experience for Liza. She liked horses well enough, and found the gentle sway of the cart as it drew them towards the maze to be soothing.

A knot of anxiety formed in Liza's stomach when Sofia asked her if she'd heard anything from Leslie regarding her case. It was never easy to talk about this, especially to Sofia. Liza's case was like a mirror of all that she was going through now: stymied in not knowing and not quite understanding, Liza hated how out of the loop she felt.

"Charlie wants me to be an assistant coach this year," Liza said. She slumped back against the hay bale that served as a barrier to keep small children and grown-ups alike from falling out of the wagon. She watched Sofia carefully as she spoke, looking for a reaction of any kind. Sofia had always had a great poker face; Liza detested the cause of that more than anything, but at least Sofia's eyes were always telling.

Brown eyes narrowed, and then cleared easily, as if relief had flooded through them. "So you're not going to run?" Sofia's tone was tentative and full of unexpressed emotion.

Liza hated that she'd had to make that decision when she left Near Haven. She'd hurt so many people and hurt Sofia most of all. Liza shook her head. "Nope."

Nathan was sitting at the front of the cart, talking to the driver, but Liza could tell by the way he was sitting, his head half-cocked, that he was listening in. There was a smile on his face that he couldn't hide, and he kept shooting his mother victorious little eyebrow wiggles. Liza almost laughed. He really was his mother's son.

"Leslie's doing my case *pro bono* and Kevin's going to need a hand until Billy gets back from Canada in April."

And there's you, went unsaid, but Liza desperately hoped that Sofia heard her implication anyway. "It doesn't seem fair to anyone to come back only to leave again after the summer. I'm not eighteen and in college anymore."

"No," Sofia agreed. "You're not."

The rest of the ride was spent in silence. They were the only people on the cart, the first run of the day. Since Sofia was the mayor, Liza assumed that the kid driving didn't launch into the usual historical tour of Near Haven and the surrounding area spiel. He dropped them off at the top of the hill with a bright smile and a promise to be back in a bit.

"Let's go!" Nathan said, bouncing into the entrance of the maze. "Race you guys!"

Sofia opened her mouth to call him back, but Liza put a hand on her shoulder and shook her head when Sofia turned to look at her. "He'll be fine." The maze had never been hard, just challenging enough for a person to get lost for a few minutes before crashing out at the other end to freshly pressed cider and laughter.

"I worry," Sofia confessed. Liza couldn't quite bring herself to pull her fingers away from Sofia's shirt sleeve. Liza lingered, fingers caught on the soft fabric, marveling at how Sofia didn't seem to mind. "He's always running off."

Liza smiled, grateful that Sofia was not pulling away. She felt hopeful for the first time in what felt like forever. "He gets that from you, you know."

Scowling, Sofia huffed and crossed her arms. "I think he gets it from Kevin."

"Oh, *sure*." Liza rolled her eyes. Kevin'd told her about how he and Sofia had become friends—how it was largely

Liza's fault. Liza didn't really know what to say to that, knowing that her once best friend had been the shoulder that Sofia cried on when she'd left town. Dave hadn't really been an option, she supposed, and Sofia's mom was a piece of work to this day. They were just…an odd couple, really. It was like they shouldn't be friends because their stations in life were so completely different. Liza bit her lip, wondering if she should say anything else and knowing that she was stepping dangerously close to the edge. "He's a good influence." Liza met Sofia's gaze evenly.

"He thinks himself a pirate," Sofia said. But Liza started towards the maze entrance, a smile blossoming across her face. Pirate he was not, but a good friend, Kevin definitely was. They were all just along for the ride, it seemed.

It was only when they'd gotten themselves turned around a few times and Liza could hear Nathan shouting that they were too slow, that she looked down and saw that their fingers were laced together. They were standing at a dead end, nose to nose as they contemplated their next move, and Liza caught herself wanting to kiss Sofia in that moment.

The first time had been a mistake. An adolescent fumbling spent steadfastly ignoring the engagement ring on Sofia's finger and the fact that you're only supposed to fall in love with one person at a time. Sofia's hair had been longer then, and her eyes not quite so sad. Now she looked quietly amused—a bit flustered—and her cheeks were puffed out in annoyance as Nathan started to taunt them once more.

"He's competitive," Liza said. Reaching forward, she picked a bit of straw from the cart ride off of the lapel of

Sofia's smart jacket. The dead end was small and they were so impossibly close to each other that Liza knew that if she asked, Sofia would say yes. "I'll give him that."

"That is my influence," Sofia replied. She was smiling now, bright and radiant.

In that split second, Liza thought that all of Sofia's pain had simply melted away. It was the pain that intrigued Liza, knowing that she'd caused some of it. People had been hurting Sofia her whole life, and Liza felt like she should try to make what she did right. She couldn't destroy Sofia's life then, but maybe now that they were older, they could try for happiness once more.

"I'm sure." Liza lifted a tentative finger to brush Sofia's bangs out of her eyes. The stare she received in response was intense and not without the carefully guarded hurt that Liza knew was always there. "He's a good kid. You did good."

After, she was not sure who moved first. Sofia tilted her head and Liza's fingers came down to cup her cheek, and then they were kissing and it was good. Fuck, it was so good.

CHAPTER SEVEN

Storm (28 October—31 October, 2012)

THE WAVES WERE HIGH AND they were racing against the clock. The *Roger* was a small boat, it could only ferry about fifteen traps at a time if the coolers were empty. Kevin had at least a one hundred-trap operation. He was driving today, wearing neon orange instead of his usual black rain slicker.

Liza was leaning off the stern, a hot pink life jacket strapped on over her bright yellow rain jacket that she had borrowed from Billy. It was a little bulky about the middle, but they were about the same height, so it worked as well as could be expected. The main point was to be visible, nothing more.

There was a storm coming. It had been all over the news and had nothing to do with the Red Sox imploding to a truly historic level and missing the playoffs. So, naturally, it was the only thing that was being discussed on any of the local news channels. Reports had been trickling in all week that a hurricane was racing up the east coast and was set to collide with the nor'easter that'd been brewing off in the North Atlantic for the better part of a week now.

If the two systems merged, they were likely to take all of New York and New England out with a whopping one-two punch of high seas and torrential rain.

Kevin stood at the helm, his eyes half-shut as he squinted through the wind and the rain. He was driving mostly from memory now, and they'd made a point to set out at low tide so they could see the rocks as they left the harbor. The absolute last thing that they wanted to do was wreck the boat in this weather. The water temperature had dropped to the low forties and it was splashing up in Liza's face as she stared blankly out at the surging sea, eyes peeled for another pot. All anyone could hear was the wind and the crackling of the weather radio as it read and repeated the same warnings over and over again. "Small crafts are warned to return to port, there will be swells increasing in size as the day goes on. Fishermen are urged to return to the shore as well."

"You sure this isn't just a nor'easter?" Liza shouted to Billy as they leaned forward as one, boots jammed under the coolers, while she attempted to hook one of Kevin's black and white-striped buoys. The last time there was a storm this bad, Kevin's dad lost seventeen pots and the town had flooded. They couldn't risk that, since none of them had the money to replace them.

Billy's long wooden hook caught around the rope and they quickly moved to haul the buoy over the side and attach the rope to their crank. It moved slowly, reeling in greenish rope from the steely depths of the ocean. "Yeah, they're saying it'll be like ninety-two again," he shouted over the roar of the ocean. Liza cast a nervous glance over towards the shore of the small, uninhabited island that they were circling.

They had started at dawn, a red sun rising, casting the sky a dangerous color as they worked as quickly as possible to haul in as many pots as they could and then ferry them back to shore. They figured that they'd take a look at the catch once they were safely in the harbor, because at least then, it'd be safe.

"What's this one?" Kevin called. His eyes never left the horizon, as he kept watch over the black clouds that were hovering there, down off towards Boothbay and Boston beyond. The governor had declared a state of emergency for the entire region and all the local fishermen were out, desperately scrambling to gather their supplies before the storm hit.

There was a sandbagging effort going on in Near Haven; the kids had been pulled out of school to help with it. Charlie had called her on the pay-as-you-go phone that Liza'd picked up a week ago and told her not to worry about practice until after the storm passed. Their first game wasn't for another two weeks anyway, an exhibition against the kids in Bangor to kick off the season. They all had time to volunteer to make sure that Near Haven could weather this storm.

Billy flipped the buoy over and squinted at the faded marks on the top. "Sixty-eight!" Kevin took the oil pencil that they had been using to draw a crude grid onto the navigation board, making a check mark under the appropriate square.

Over the course of the day, they'd brought in about forty pots, starting from the farthest away from shore and slowly working their way inland—making several trips back to port to leave the pots on the dock where a friend of Billy's was tying them down to the bulkhead.

Rain lashed against them as they made their way through the choppy sea, cutting through rain slickers and life vests and settling, cold and clammy, onto skin that could not be warmed, no matter how much they were moving around. Liza had on a sweatshirt and a thermal base layer underneath it, but she was soaked to the bone, each gust of wind cutting into her and stealing her breath away. The cold sapped her energy, making it near-impossible to move, and she felt sluggish. It was a struggle just to keep her mind focused, but she knew that if Kevin lost any pots, it would be financially devastating for the entire operation. She gritted her teeth and when Kevin spun the wheel and headed towards the next pot, she didn't complain and bit at the inside of her lip to keep her teeth from chattering in the cold.

The day dragged on and on. It had been getting dark close to five thirty these days, and there were still pots that had to be brought in as the light from the sun—hidden though it was by clouds—started to fade. *There aren't that many left*, Liza thought, *maybe only five more before we can go back to port and regroup for a few minutes.*

The sea was not agreeing with them. The wind was howling now, and water lashed against them as they stood and peered off into the growing darkness, trying to spot a black and white buoy amid the frosty grey sea. Liza felt like she was slogging through wet cement, each step growing more and more challenging as she tried to stay awake and alert, looking for another pot. She saw one, tossed about in the churning sea, and leaned over to collect the bobbing float.

Her wrist twisted around her hook, hitching around the buoy. A wave rocked against the gunnels of the boat, tipping it first left and then right. Time seemed to freeze as the wave rocked the boat out from underneath her feet. She pitched forward into the water, hand still half-holding onto her hook, the buoy whizzing by her head, the boat falling away behind her. The air was ripped from her lungs in a desperate choking sound as she landed flat on her stomach in the icy waves. She coughed and spluttered, struggling to right herself. The life vest was keeping her afloat and she could scarcely hear Billy and Kevin's shouts over the roar of the ocean in her ears.

The water was cold, so cold that Liza couldn't really feel it at first, as it flowed into her rain boots and soaked through to her skin. It pierced through what little warmth she still had under her rain-wet clothes with the twist of a knife in her back and steadied there, numbing her before she even had a chance to truly be shocked at how absolutely freezing the water was.

She had to get out, but she could barely see the lights from the boat now. Her feet were clumsy in her boots. She knew better than to try to kick them off in this water. She'd lose a toe to frostbite before she was rescued, probably, and she didn't want that. She flailed, struggling to hear, to see, and the boat seemed to drift further away.

Her mind was sluggish, addled by the cold. She didn't know how long she was in the water. Time seemed to blur into a complicated mess of gasping for air and flailing towards the bobbing light of the boat, never really moving anywhere at all. She was going to die in this water. She was going to die and so much had gone unsaid between her and this fucking place that she'd come back to. She was a fool to think she could do this, she was a fool—

A wave crashed over her head and the world went salty-dark for terrifying moments before hands landed on Liza's back. She wanted to fight against them, but as Kevin and Billy hauled her shaking and coughing body over the side of the boat all she felt was the stiffening and oppressive weight of the cold.

"Shit, Liz." Kevin pressed a trembling hand to her cheek and peered at her chattering teeth and soaked clothes. "We gotta get you to a hospital."

Billy steered the boat back into the harbor. The last pots that they'd have to bring in where there, in the protective cove where the waves shouldn't be so bad. They should be okay until... She let out a grunt, unable to articulate anything more than that. Her mind felt like it was moving through molasses, every thought taking a Herculean effort to process. She was so cold, and the icy cut of the rain against her skin was enough to make her want to stop violently shaking altogether and tip backwards off of the gunnels and into the icy warmth of the water that churned just beyond the relative safety of the *Roger*.

"Liza," Kevin said urgently. "Liza, I need you to stay awake." He bit his lower lip, nervous fingers tugging at her arm.

She blinked wearily at him. She could see how afraid he was, how absolutely terrified and she wanted to say, "Look, I'm here, alive, freezing my tits off, but I'm okay."

Billy barked into the radio, demanding an ambulance down by the docks and adding that he didn't care that the whole street was already sandbagged.

The world was starting to get fuzzy and Liza's breath came more slowly. How long had she been in the water? How cold...? The edges of everything blurred into one amorphous blob and Liza knew that that was very, very bad. She had to stay awake. She shook herself violently, desperate to stay awake as Billy let out a stream of curses.

"How long was she in, you think?" Kevin asked. He was half-shouting over the wind. They had pulled a shiny, silver space blanket from the first aid kit, but she was still in her wet clothes. He used his one hand to rub her back as roughly as he could, trying to keep her awake. They all knew better than to take off her clothes in this weather, whatever heat the wet fabric had, it was probably more than what they had without it. They had to keep the heat in now.

"I don't know...maybe five minutes?" Billy sounded panicked.

Liza sluggishly blinked her eyes, crusty though they were with salt. She could hardly keep her eyes open, but she knew that she needed to stay awake, to stay shivering. Shivering would keep her warm until they could get her to the ambulance and the hospital.

"They're going to send an ambulance."

"Good." Kevin's voice was tense as he kept rubbing Liza's back.

Liza drifted, in and out and across the sea. Her mind was in a million places, and she could scarcely concentrate on the fact that she'd spent five minutes in forty-degree water. She could have died.

When they pulled into port all she saw were the red and white flashing lights of the ambulance that Billy had called before her world went blank, fuzzy, and then dark once more.

She dreamt of the wind and the rain, of floating across the surface of a still pond. She was eleven and desperate to understand herself. She had let the water take her, allowing herself to fall down and under the water. She was only eleven; it should not have been this easy.

No one would care if she was gone.

She was eleven and trying to learn her place. She didn't understand the family that gave her back, or the family that had hurt her so badly and then sent her away. All she knew was that she had to stay here in this town, bounced around from place to place. A pillow for her head, but for how long would it last?

To sink down to the bottom of this lake would be easier. The new family that she had been given to was one that she'd never heard of before. No mom. A boy and his father. He was a lobster man.

Maybe it would be good this time.

The water rippled as Liza slowly pushed herself back towards the light.

Dawn broke overhead and she found herself wearing hospital scrubs and wrapped under three blankets. The light that had punched through her dream of cold, murky, underwater death was a dim table lamp, the only light in the otherwise dark room. A hand was clutched around her own, and a dark mop of hair splayed out across the pristine white of the bed sheets.

Somewhere, a monitor beeped quietly, the constant, steady sound barely audible over the sound of her own breathing. Liza stared down at the hand in her own. She'd never—not like this. Not even when she had sprained her ankle in seventh grade. No one had ever cared enough to sit with her before.

She was in the hospital; she knew that from the monitor and the scrubs. Outside, the wind howled angrily, the lights already flickering low. Liza wondered if the storm had fully hit now. If she listened closely, she was pretty sure that she could hear a generator roaring in the distance over the wind and rain. That was a bad sign. If the power was out then there was no telling when it would come back on. Liza remembered the storm in '92; they all did. That flood was like a scar across the collective memories of the town. They did not have power for two weeks then—two weeks at the end of October—and it had all started just like this.

"Sophie," Liza mumbled. She squeezed the hand in her own gently. Sofia hated the nickname, but Liza couldn't really help herself. It was one of those things that slipped out of a sleep-numbed mind and she couldn't very well take it back now that she'd said it. "Hey."

Sofia stirred, fingers curling up and into Liza's hand.

Liza held fast, a tired smile tugging at her lips. They felt horribly chapped, like they were cracking as she smiled. She licked them and tasted salt and shivered despite herself. She didn't know how much of the ocean she had managed to take back with her before Billy and Kevin had pulled her out.

"What time is it?" Sofia asked. She wiped the corner of her mouth with her free hand and then let it run tiredly through her hair.

Squinting to read the monitor that was keeping track of her vitals, Liza saw that it was close to two in the morning. Groaning, she struggled to sit up. "Two…" Liza stared down at their hands. "What the hell happened?"

All she remembered was the flashing lights and the freezing cold. After that there was nothing—a void as black as the ocean at night. Liza bit her lip and wondered why Sofia was even there.

"Kevin called me and said that you'd fallen in." Sofia's voice was scratchy with sleep and there were black circles under her eyes.

Her mascara had run and Liza wondered if it was because it was pouring sheets of rain outside or if she had been crying. She didn't know how to ask, and her mind was still sluggish with sleep and the cold.

"How could you be so stupid, going out in that weather?"

Blinking, Liza caught herself making a face; she looked offended. Her eyebrows knit together and she scowled. "I didn't mean to fall in." She understood why, especially to Sofia, this was a big deal. But she was also here; she was alive. She wasn't going to wash up some fifteen miles away, body battered and broken among the rocks. She was not Dave.

Liza hated that she could see the tears coming almost before they began to glisten at the corners of Sofia's eyes.

She shook her head and pushed herself into a more fully sitting-up position. "Hey," she said. Her fingers caught Sofia's cheek and brushed away the wetness there. It was a murky black; Sofia's makeup had started to run. "I'm okay," she said. "Promise. I just got too cold. I'm not going anywhere." This was the sort of a promise that she knew she could keep. She had sworn to herself that she wouldn't do that to Sofia, not ever again.

Sofia chuckled, her voice cracking quietly. "Piecrust."

Liza frowned. "What?"

"That's a piecrust promise," Sofia said. She wiped her eyes and pulled away from Liza.

She was beautiful like this, sad and oh so broken. Liza wondered if Sofia could ever be whole, and whether *she* could ever be whole as well. "You're always making them."

"I wasn't aware I had to take life lessons from *Mary Poppins*," Liza retorted. She folded her arms across her chest, defiant and refusing to let Sofia's scowl get to her. "I meant it. I don't want to go anywhere."

"You suffer from delusions as well as wanderlust, apparently." Sofia got to her feet and reached for her coat, still damp-looking, and slung it over the back of the spare chair.

Her hand was gone, and the warmth of Sofia's body against Liza's leg was gone. Liza missed her so desperately that her heart ached. "Why are you here?" she asked.

Sofia had one hand shoved down into her coat sleeve. Her scarf was hanging out the end of the other and she looked ridiculous in her anger.

Liza knew that she had no answer, because to say it would mean admitting that there was something between them. She swallowed, that something that could have as much potential as there'd been before. There was no answer to this predicament that they found themselves in, because to confess such a thing was surely too much for this fragile peace.

"Kevin called me," Sofia said shortly. She yanked her scarf out from the arm of her jacket and draped it around her neck before shrugging into the coat. The scarf was a deep red; it cut a bloody stripe down Sofia's black-clad middle. It was a reminder of everything that Liza could not have, shackled away in a prison that even stolen kisses and intense gazes could not infiltrate. "I don't abandon my friends."

Liza wanted to retort that they were never merely *friends*, but thought better of it. She let the warmth of Sofia's mistake wash over her instead. "Okay." A goofy smile drifted across her face.

"I'll send Doctor Howard in." With that, Sofia was gone. The wind whistled outside and the room felt suddenly mammoth.

Liza wondered just how bad the storm was outside, and if Sofia would come back in, looking like a drowned rat in a few minutes and asking to stay the night. She'd say yes, because she was a pushover. The minutes ticked by though, and there was no sign of Sofia's return. When the doctor came in, Liza answered his questions and soon found herself drifting back into an uneasy sleep.

This time, she didn't dream.

Liza woke up to a pale dawn and a flooded town. The bulkhead that wrapped around the harbor had failed in a few places, and the tide had washed over the street by the harbor. Liza knew that she was pushing it, but she called Nancy and demanded that she come down and argue with the doctor and insist that she be discharged so that she could help with the cleanup.

Nancy came to get her some twenty minutes later with coffee and warm clothes. The temperature was hovering at fifty degrees outside, Nancy warned her, and Liza couldn't help but wonder if she'd even truly warmed up from her icy swim the night before. She followed Nancy and Noah Burke as they picked their way after Rachel and Ashleigh down Main Street. They'd been tasked by the sheriff to take Noah's chain saw and cut up a few of the trees that had fallen into the road just past Sprat's grocery store.

"Hey," Noah said. He led them to the back of a forest green Subaru and waved enthusiastically at Leslie as she and Ted clambered out of the car. "I sent them back to the house to pick up all of the supplies we'll need," he added, mostly for Liza's benefit as a late-arriving volunteer.

There were work gloves, hatchets, and the chain saw itself. Liza stayed well away from it, taking a hand saw and moving to trot along beside Ted. Leslie lingered, her head bowed close to Noah, speaking in a low, urgent voice.

Their divorce was close to being finalized now, if Liza was remembering correctly. Leslie mentioned it during one of their seemingly constant meetings.

"Do you think it's weird that they can still be at least somewhat okay with each other?" Liza looked at Ted as he shouldered the axe in his hand like a professional lumberjack, not a gym teacher.

He shrugged. "I dunno, I've always been of the severing mindset, but that's kinda hard in a place like this."

"Tell me about it," Liza agreed. She thought of all the high school breakups and makeups that she'd witnessed.

There were five downed trees on Main Street alone and it was hard work to clear them. They worked through the morning, hacking, sawing, and loading logs onto the back of Ted's pickup truck. They had decided to save the wood, and were stacking it as best they could under a piece of plastic sheeting that they'd found under Ted's passenger seat. With no power, some people were going to need the wood to burn for heat.

At lunch time, Chet came by and told them that the bridge to the mainland was almost completely underwater at low tide, so they were probably not going to get any state aid until the water levels went down, and that the power would probably be off for a while.

Liza sighed. There was no power for half the town and without the bridge, the power companies couldn't get over to fix the downed lines.

They were onto the second tree, using the back of Ted's pickup to ferry the firewood to the town green, where they were stacking it under tarps for anyone who wanted to use it. It was hard work, and Liza knew by how exhausted she was that she was not fully recovered from her unexpected plunge into the ocean.

"I heard Sofia came to sit with you." Nancy said in a teasing undertone as they walked to the next downed tree. Everywhere was wet, covered in pine needles, small sticks, and fallen leaves. There were people raking out their lawns who raised their hands in greeting to Nancy and eyed Liza with some suspicion. "Last night, I mean," Nancy added.

Liza's cheeks burned at the mention of what had happened the night before. She knew that she was flushed so red she probably matched her jacket. She rubbed at her nose, wiping away snot and dirt and sniffed to avoid answering the question. Nancy was giving her that look that almost dared Liza to not answer. "I…" Liza started to explain, but noticed Leslie waving at them from where Ted was taking his turn with the chain saw. "Oh look, Leslie wants us."

Nancy grabbed Liza's arm and pulled her towards the leafy end of the tree, away from Ted, Leslie, and the noise of the chain saw. "Nice try, Liza." There was an almost motherly glint in her eye and Liza groaned long and loud.

"Worth a shot," Liza replied. She jammed her hands into the back pockets of her jeans, hand saw around one of her wrists like some sort of obscene, pointy bracelet. "Yeah," she added, feeling more than a little sheepish. "She was there until I woke up, about two or so this morning. And then she got all pissy that I was out on the ocean in that weather and stormed off in a huff because I told her I wasn't going anywhere."

"Huh." Nancy shook her head.

Her white coat was streaked with mud that Liza wasn't sure even Rachel's grandmother could get out, but Nancy didn't seem to care. She was here to help in whatever way she could, same as the rest of them. Sometimes, for the sake of the town, sacrifices had to be made.

There were reports on the radio that the entire coast from here to DC was decimated by the storm. Liza looked around and knew that they'd gotten off lucky. All that Near Haven had experienced was some relatively minor flooding and a ton of downed trees; it could be a whole hell of a lot worse.

Picking at a leaf from the downed tree beside them, Nancy sighed. "This is all because of David, you know."

"Oh, I know." Liza agreed. She wasn't stupid, and knew that Sofia had really good reason to want Liza as far away from the water as possible. Still, her hot and cold personality regarding Liza was enough to make her want to scream. She shouldn't have driven home in that storm, Liza knew it. "I just... I hate that I have to be in his shadow. I've always been there, and it's a shit place to be."

Nancy pulled Liza into a one-armed hug, their wood cutting tools held carefully away from their bodies. She smelled like the ocean and pine, clean and nice and comforting. Nancy had been a constant in Liza's life for longer than she cared to think about, no matter their age difference. "Maybe it'll just take some time? You left really abruptly back then. Maybe this is the price that you have to pay for that."

Liza shrugged, because Sofia Milton was an absolute mystery to her. "Who knows?"

They spent the rest of the day working to clear the third tree. In some parts of town, electricity had been restored, but the diner had had to cook through a lot of their perishables as their refrigerator had been off for most of the night. Rachel and her grandmother had thrown open their doors and offered to feed the town. Liza sat next to Ted and Leslie and they ate homemade mac and cheese. Liza's nose was still running like a sieve and she was trying to ignore the nagging sense of fear that was lingering in the back of her mind. She really should have stayed indoors today. She couldn't afford to get sick.

It was only when she started sneezing and couldn't stop that Nancy bustled her home and practically poured tea down her throat until Liza's breathing was relatively clear. "I don't want you getting pneumonia," Nancy grumbled. She handed Liza a bottle of cold medicine and pointed her in the general direction of her bed.

Liza sniffed at her in response and headed for the stairs, half-stumbling up them and finally falling onto her sun-bleached, hand-me-down sheets. They were in Charlie's guestroom before they'd been gifted to her. The bed was Nancy's when she was younger, and it'd been given to Liza without so much as a second thought. Everyone was showing her so much kindness and Liza didn't know how to handle it all. She was trying to earn her keep, working with Kevin, helping Nancy grade tests and homework assignments at night. Soon she was going to be helping Charlie too. It felt like penance for a mistake that was not wholly her own. Liza sniffed and rubbed her nose. She probably was getting sick, but she hated not being able to help a lot more than she hated being sick.

When sleep finally claimed her exhausted body, Liza dreamt of the mirror-calm lake once more. She didn't dare move for fear she'd make a ripple and ruin the serenity of this place.

She was eleven and she wanted to die. She was twenty-eight and she finally had something she wanted to fight for. The dichotomy was not lost on her, even in sleep.

Liza opened her eyes in the dream and stared at the single deer that was tentatively standing at the water's edge. Its eyes were wide and fearful even now, and Liza's body went completely still. The water was a glassy sheet, reflecting the sky above and the fear in the deer's eyes.

She didn't see the hunter until it was too late. An arrow pierced through the animal's side and Liza let out a shocked cry. A quiet ringing filled the silence of this beautiful place.

Liza, fumbling in her half-awake state, tried to find her phone. "Hello." She was still half-asleep; her mind wasn't fully processing.

"I need to talk to you; come let me in." The request was curt and to the point, but Sofia sounded troubled.

Liza blinked sleepily at the clock on top of her bedside table and realized that it was eleven thirty on a Wednesday and that she had better things to do than sleep the day away. Her head felt like there was wooly cotton stuffed into her ears and every time she moved, her jaw and ears popped almost painfully.

She stumbled down the stairs and padded across the ice-cold floor in bare feet. She'd been right—once it'd gotten cold, it was going to be an absolute bitch to heat this place. She opened the door and came face-to-face with a rather distraught-looking Sofia. Liza sniffed loudly, her head feeling clogged and foggy. "Hi," she said. Her voice sounded hoarse and disused, but she knew that she should sound better than this; she'd been sleeping for what felt like *days*.

"My mother is coming." Sofia pushed past Liza into the apartment. Her face was a contorted mixture of fear and worry and the dark circles under her eyes that Liza remembered from what felt like days ago were now more pronounced than ever.

Liza stood in the doorway, her heart pounding in her chest as she desperately tried to will her brain to *think* and to think faster.

Sofia had crossed the room, her hands now resting on the countertop over the sink. Her shoulders were shaking and her breath was coming in short, fearful gasps.

Liza pushed the door closed, locked it and reached for her slippers. She tugged them on with hesitant hands and turned to face Sofia. "Why?"

"Why?" Sofia whirled to face Liza, her eyes flashing danger and fear all in one desperate push of emotion.

Liza took one step forward, but then faltered.

"She's a senator, Liza. She took over my father's seat when she married him in all but name, and now one of the best pieces of political capital that she's stumbled upon in *years* has happened to her hometown." Sofia glanced down at her hands, her chest heaving underneath her jacket and that same blood-red scarf from before a slash of bloody promise across her chest. "She's coming here because it will win her support in Washington."

But it's Maine, Liza's brain wanted to protest. Maine was a tiny state with no political clout whatsoever. Everyone knew that. That was part of the problem with being from New England. Your vote (if you, unlike Liza, could actually vote) didn't mean much if you were voting for a sure thing. Liza took another step forward into the kitchen and reached for the kettle. It was heavy, clearly almost full. Nancy must have made tea this morning.

The burner clicked on and Liza turned to face Sofia. "New York, New Jersey, they were hit way worse than here, if the radio's to be believed." Liza took a deep breath, worried that what she was about to say was going to sound cold and insensitive to Near Haven's plight. "Won't people think she's taking advantage of the situation?"

"Probably." Sofia sounded disgusted.

Her hands were shaking and Liza reached for them, her fingers closing around icy and numb ones. Liza's head felt a little clearer now and she met Sofia's eyes steadily.

"She's coming *here*."

"You're an adult," Liza said quietly. She was overstepping, but she was desperate. She had to find a way to say this that would get through to Sofia. There had to be a way that would let Sofia know that all this panic was entirely unnecessary. "You're not a kid. She can't—"

"Don't." Sofia wrenched her hand away from Liza and brought it to rest against her own arm, squeezing tightly.

Liza wondered if she was using the pain of that gesture to keep herself grounded. She hoped not.

"Don't say it."

Liza opened her mouth to protest, but Sofia just shook her head. "You know as well as I do what she did, what she *does*. I want nothing to do with it, but I have no choice. Nathan has no choice. You can still escape this."

"How? How can I escape this when I'm stuck here? I don't know if you've noticed Sofia, but I'm broke. I have no car and no friends outside of this town!" Sofia looked away and Liza started again, desperate to say everything she wanted to say. Her head ached as she spoke, but she didn't care. It had to be said. "I fell into the ocean two days ago, Sofia. I'm no better than anyone else who's here. I'm one of you. One of us. This town is in my blood, as it's in yours."

"You can leave, Liza." Sofia's nostrils flared dangerously.

Liza took half a step back. Sofia looked so much like her mother in that moment that Liza wanted to turn and run. She didn't want to feel the powerlessness and terror that welled up within her. It was ingrained, settled from when she was very young, and then again when she understood far too well. Liza hated it, hated what Sofia had so easily become.

"You've always been able to leave." Sofia bit her lip and looked down at her hands, fidgeting with the place mat on the kitchen island before her. She had an air of utter resignation, and Liza's mouth was open to reply, but the shrill whistling of the kettle filled the silence between them instead.

Liza reached for two clean mugs from the dish rack beside the sink. She didn't respond, not at first. She didn't really know how to respond to what Sofia was accusing her of, because it had never been her choice to leave, not truly. It was always the same person, pushing her away before Liza could truly know the one thing in this town that she thought was worth knowing.

"I never wanted…" The teabag in Liza's hand slipped from her fingers as she spoke, its string fluttering as it fell to the floor like some sort of obscene tail. "Never."

"Everyone always leaves." Sofia was nearly shaking, as she wrapped her arms around herself.

Liza wanted to reach for her, but instead bent and picked up the teabag. She brushed past Sofia to run it under the cold water in the sink, before dropping it, unceremoniously into her mug.

"She's the only one who comes back."

"I did too," Liza said. She knew it sounded sad, pathetic even. She was just trying to make Sofia see that this wasn't a wholly bad thing. That maybe, just maybe, this was what they both needed. Liza bit her lip and poured the water into the mugs. She didn't know what to say to Sofia that would make this better. There were so many words that swam before her in her mind's eye, but none of them seemed *enough*. She was floundering.

Sofia's smile was full of heartbreak and pain, and Liza couldn't stand it any longer. She shoved the kettle back into the now-cold burner and crossed the tiny kitchen in three steps to pull Sofia into a hug. She didn't know why she did it, or what prompted the need to physically express everything that she couldn't say. She had never really understood the need for contact. Hugs got you hit, smiles got you slapped. It wasn't worth it, she'd learned, to put yourself out there like that.

And yet, as always, it was different with Sofia. Sofia was the one thing in Liza's life that she was okay with not making sense. She knew that she hadn't earned her right to be easy, not yet. That would come later, when Liza'd had more time to prove herself—to prove her worth. She was warm; her head was stuffed full of wooly incomprehension.

Sofia kissed her without care that Liza was sick, warm and sweet against Nancy's kitchen island.

Liza held her close and tried to use her lips to say everything that she couldn't articulate.

She was *here*; she was not going anywhere.

They'd figure this out.

They had to.

CHAPTER EIGHT

Mother (7-8 November, 2012)

IT BECAME A REGULAR THING, Liza finding Sofia at her doorstep as the days counted closer to her mother's arrival. Nancy kept her mouth shut after the first visit, smiling privately, her eyes sad and distant as she disappeared off into her bedroom and shut the door behind her.

"She doesn't approve of my being here?" Sofia asked. They made their way up to up Liza's bedroom.

"I don't know," Liza replied. Pulling up the covers on her unmade bed, she made a space for them both to sit. She'd spent the day outside helping with the cleanup effort, as the temperature had been hovering right at sixty degrees and Nancy had determined that it was warm enough for her to go outside without further aggravating her case of the sniffles. "I think she just wants me to concentrate on getting better for a while."

Sofia turned away then, her face in profile and her eyes downcast. "I should go."

Liza reached out and touched the sleeve of Sofia's blouse. It felt silky smooth under her fingers. "Don't!" she said. They needed each other, she knew that. She had to give Sofia what she needed; it was all that she could do to alleviate the anxiety of such a tense situation.

Kevin came by on Monday, announcing that he had successfully dry-docked the boat for the winter. "And... I am now unemployed!" He said with a flourish that spoke of years of playacting in the town's youth theatre.

Liza raised an eyebrow at him and he hurriedly continued, saying that he was going to be helping out the librarian with some of the youth programs that she ran during the snowy winter months to keep kids warm and indoors.

Liza smiled. Kevin had always been very good with kids, ever since they were teenagers. She was happy for him, but the urge to poke fun was something she couldn't quite suppress. "Better than collecting disability?" She cocked an eyebrow and a teasing smile played on her lips.

"Oh, definitely." Kevin agreed. He'd completely missed her joke.

Liza supposed that some things were simply not meant to be funny.

He'd brought over a gallon of cider pressed into an old milk jug. Liza, after some rummaging, had found mulling spices in the back of the pantry. They were sitting on the foundry's cold metal fire escape, drinking steaming mugs of warm, spicy cider and watching the sun set over the harbor. In the distance, as the evening mist started to roll in, the foghorn off the far end of Sawn Island sounded, low and mournful. Liza had to shake herself against the shiver that ran up her spine.

They sat in silence for a long time, Liza chewing on her lip and staring out at the setting sun. There were so many things that she wanted to ask Kevin about what had happened the first time she'd left Near Haven. Everything was so different now, and yet so many things were painfully the same.

"So the senator's coming back?" Kevin asked. Steam was curling around his head, like twin horns of the devil that his personality sometimes reminded her of. Liza scowled at him and he wiggled his eyebrows. "And a little birdy told me that it was *you* that our fearless leader came running to when she found out about it."

Liza picked a bit of clove out of her cider and flicked it out over the parking lot below her. She didn't understand why, but it was true. Sofia had come to see her and she'd lingered for far longer than she should have in Liza's arms. "She did," Liza replied. "Don't know why though."

When they were kids, there had been a potential for them to be closer, but Liza'd never let herself grow attached. There was the threat, and then the knowledge that Dave was always there, and he would always come first. Liza remembered hating it. Back then she took her emotions out on the court, playing physical and larger than she was. She'd wanted to start fights, to rage against the situation she'd found herself in. It had been two wonderful summers. Just two perfect summers of easy, nonjudgmental friendship.

The dark circles under Kevin's eyes made them look comically wide as he reached forward, hooked his prosthetic around Liza's arm, and turned her gently around to face him."Are you stupid?"

There was something about the way he was asking that made Liza wonder why he cared so much. She'd never meant that much to anyone—she'd known that since her eleventh birthday. No one cared if she was there or not, and she could slip away, underneath the water, and no one would be any the wiser. Time didn't change things like that, not when they'd been ingrained into the fabric of a town for twenty-eight odd years.

"No?" Liza ventured with an eyebrow raised in challenge to his remark. Kevin's hook was biting into her upper arm and the pain was a welcome reminder that she was still alive after her best efforts not to be.

He set his mug down and unhooked himself from her arm, his solitary hand coming to rest on her cheek. His nails were chipped and broken, gnarled by the sea.

Liza wanted to flinch away from his touch, because she'd been touched like that before, and it hadn't worked out well for her that time either. Jared had liked to play the kind-hearted, slightly older man. And Liza had fallen for it like a set of dominoes.

"Liza, why do you sell yourself so short?" Kevin's tone was serious and eyebrows dipped down low across his forehead. It gave him the severe look of a man twice his age, and Liza couldn't meet his gaze.

Liza had no answer for him.

"Sofia came to you because you are the one person who knows everything about the circumstances of her childhood, because you experienced them too. She came to you because she fell in love with you when she was twenty-two and engaged to marry another. She came to you because you came back and you haven't left." Kevin's eyes flickered downwards to make sure that they didn't have an audience down in the parking lot and he leaned in close. "And because she is still in love with you, despite her best efforts to push you away."

The statement was chilling, damning even. It made Liza's blood run cold. No one had ever loved her. Liza knew this. Love was a luxury children—*people*—like her did not deserve. It was a weakness to her now, something that she knew she could never have. Not after she'd stupidly risked it all with Jared and had gotten her heart dashed upon the concrete floor of the prison in Oregon.

Sipping her cider was easier than trying to answer Kevin's accusatory stare. Liza raised the mug to her lips and listened to the foghorn's call in the distance once more. The cider was cooling rapidly now, still spicy against her tongue, but now it was just warm enough for her to taste the apples and not just the heat of the drink. She inhaled quietly and shook her head, catching sight of herself in the reflection of the glass window on the fire escape door behind them. Her hair was spilling down like straw in a field right before the harvest against her black sweater. "She can't be in love with me," she said with a sad bark of self-deprecating laughter. The fake smile that Liza had put on left her face when she saw the look on Kevin's face. It was a betrayal and the truth in one anguished stare. "She can't be...."

Kevin picked up his mug and stared down at the homemade glaze job on it, tilting it this way and that in the growing evening light. "I think that you'd be surprised what people truly feel for you, Liza." He didn't meet her eyes when he added, half a second later, "You were never taught to love yourself in all those homes, and it's not really your fault."

"I was thrown away like trash," Liza retorted. "Over and over again. Your dad, at least, had the good grace to tell me why I had to go—because he was spiraling into a depression he was never going to come out of." She shook her head again, an unhappy little laugh bubbling out of her throat. "Don't you dare tell me that Sofia Milton is in love with me. She was never in love with me." Liza looked away from him and his sad expression, out across the harbor. "Love is a weakness people like us are not allowed to have."

"But you can't deny that you hold meaning to her," Kevin replied. His tone was quietly questioning. It was not threatening or combative, this was just a conversation. Liza could do conversations. "Because she obviously still cares for you."

"I guess," Liza said. She shrugged and went back to staring down into her cider. Fidgeting with her cup, Liza tried to convey how much she desperately wanted to change the subject. She didn't want to talk about this, or even think about it, because thinking about how she'd purposefully looked past something for this long was making her head hurt. She didn't know how to process such information. She'd gotten so good at ignoring it up until this point.

"Also, I think she taught you chemistry in more than one sense of the word." Kevin wiggled his eyebrows lewdly.

Liza shoved him playfully and he yelped, holding his mug out before him, trying desperately to keep it from sloshing all over his black jeans.

The realization that Kevin was another person she'd pushed away and ignored hit Liza all at once. He obviously cared for her a great deal, even now when she'd ignored him at the lowest point in his life. Liza hated that she was so broken that she didn't see these things. She hated a lot of things, and coming back here was only serving to pull them front and center.

In the growing night, she leaned back against Kevin, wiggling into his warmth and was grateful that he'd quit smoking. He smelled like the sea and now of cider as well. It was a comforting sort of a smell, one that Liza knew well. She was going to need all the comfort she could get, if she was going to have to deal with the aftermath of Sofia's mother coming to town.

Kevin went home after dinner and Liza waited until she was absolutely certain that Nancy didn't need her help grading papers before Liza slipped out into the chilly evening. Her breath fogged in the air, and she jammed her hands into her pockets, heading up towards Main Street with no real destination in mind. She'd wanted a walk ever since Kevin's departure, and had found that forced small talk with Nancy, when her feet were itching to move, simply didn't work.

Fear bubbled up unbidden within Liza with every second that counted down to the arrival of the good senator. Liza was still torn as to what she wanted to do about the woman's presence in Near Haven. She was of two minds about the whole thing: she could stay out of sight, or she could try to be there for Sofia. Both were terrible options, no matter how Liza tried to think about them.

She supposed that she couldn't completely disappear. The basketball team's practice started in earnest the next day after school. Charlie had dropped off a tape of the team from last year and asked Liza to watch it before the practice. She was nervous about that as well, unsure if she could take being around Charlie and his judgmental stares for as long as the lifeline he'd thrown her lasted. She had taken the position for the money, and for the chance to prove to him that she wasn't the fuck-up he thought her to be. She wasn't sure she even wanted to coach.

Just another dead-end girl from a dead-end town. Liza moodily kicked a rock through the scattered leaves that covered the sidewalk. Hands jammed into her jacket pockets, she wandered unabated down Main Street. It was cold, but the wind hadn't turned bitter yet. Winter was coming and soon it would be the worst time of the year. She hated it when it got that cold. In a sense, they were lucky that the storm came when it did. The end of October and the beginning of November were always a crapshoot, the weather oscillating between pleasant and fucking freezing at the drop of a hat.

It wasn't until Liza found herself standing at the base of the hill that went up to High Pine Street that she allowed herself to think about Sofia. Kevin had had a point earlier, one that Liza had been forcing herself to ignore for so long that it felt almost like second nature to her.

Maybe it hadn't been enough to be attracted to Sofia, maybe it had just been what she'd refused to see. The truth had been right in front of her all that time. Kevin had joked that she'd filled Sofia with confusion, but Liza had never been confused. She'd known full well that she could never have Sofia. That was Dave's place, no matter the consequences.

Now though, Liza could have what she'd denied herself for so long. She'd promised herself, sworn up and down that they hadn't been close because it'd been easier than feeling that pain all over again. To know...to know full well and to go in anyway, that was Liza's way.

It still was, Liza realized, picking her way through the remaining storm debris and scattered leaves from the half-starved trees overhead. Soon there would be no leaves on the trees, and they would be bare skeletons until spring.

The white house at the top of the hill was mostly dark, a single window was illuminated against the blackness of the night. Liza swallowed, recalling all that had transpired in that room, the first time she'd felt the full weight of how little she meant to that family. She wanted to forget that place, but there was something about seeing a room, *that* room, illuminated against the sea of black behind Sofia's home, that set Liza's teeth on edge. It was in there, after all, that Liza had first realized just how horrible a mother the senator's wife was.

Swallowing nervously, Liza tried to bury her nerves. She still wasn't entirely sure that she could go into Sofia's house without flashing back to that day—the day that she'd been taken away once more from a family that was supposed to love her. Those marks had never shown, but they'd been there, clear as day. No one had ever known. Liza had kept her mouth shut and her head down, shunted from house to house within this town, finally resting at Kevin's father's, and then at Charlie's in high school.

Fighting against the urge to turn around and leave, Liza stood at the edge of the property and looked up at the house. Nathan was in there, probably lying awake and thinking about what was slated to happen in the morning. He was a smart kid; he probably picked up on the fact that his mom and grandmother didn't get on very well.

There was a light on in the room that had once served as a den. Liza wondered if Sofia was there, sitting by herself, staring off into nothingness as Liza remembered her doing when they were children.

The latch on the gate went up soundlessly, and Liza pushed it open, one foot tentatively stepping onto the brick walkway that led to the door. The yard was the same; the rose bushes were bigger, shuttered already to protect against snow falling from the roof. Liza caught herself wanting to know how Sofia's beloved crabapple tree out in the backyard was doing. Given the area, it was probably flourishing.

It took no time at all to move up the walkway. This was not a good idea. All of Liza's better angels were screaming at her to turn around and leave. Her feet drew level with the base of the steps to the front door and she stood there, trapped awkwardly by indecision. She wanted to offer support on the eve of the second storm that Sofia would have to weather in a week. She wanted to see if maybe Kevin was right and Sofia truly did care. Her tongue felt like sandpaper in her mouth and she hated that she could not find the words to say hello, to ask what she knew she had to ask.

The door opened before she could knock, and Sofia was standing there in bare feet and an oversized sweater, which Liza was sure used to belong to Dave, draped over her shoulders. She wanted to step back, to recoil away, knowing that Sofia had turned to the memory of a dead lover for comfort.

"What are you doing here?" Sofia's voice was wary, but also full of the weariness that came from carrying the weight of the world on her shoulders.

Liza had seen the hours that Sofia worked, that they'd all worked, trying to clean up the town and waiting for the waters over the bridge to recede enough for the power companies to get across and fix the outages that dotted their semi-island. They were all exhausted from the cleanup effort and the very *thought* that there would soon be an interloper among them who claimed to represent them was almost too much for Liza. She was too tired to handle this, but she had to, for Sofia and for everyone else she'd hurt in this town. Liza stood with her hands shoved into her jacket pockets, twisting the quarter that her fingers found over and over between her slightly numb fingers. It was a nervous habit, but not one that she thought she could break easily. "I um…I thought you might want some company."

The gaze that Sofia fixed her with was curiosity, relief, and revulsion all rolled up into one.

Liza knew that Sofia hated having to rely on anyone and that asking for the help that Liza was offering was next to impossible for her to do. Liza had to give it freely or else it wouldn't be taken at all.

"Come in," Sofia said at length.

Relieved, Liza climbed the three steps in one, coming to stand in the doorway before Sofia, her breath fogging in the light from the foyer inside. "Hi," Liza said. She didn't lean in to kiss Sofia. Kissing was easy, it was about forgetting and not dealing with emotions. This, today, was about being supportive. Liza reached out a tentative hand and rested it on Sofia's arm. She looked so small, lost in the sweater that obviously didn't belong to her, and her arm was shaking as Liza touched it.

"Hello, Ms. Hawke," Sofia replied A smile flickered across her eyes, but not her lips. "Why have you come to darken my doorway?"

They stepped inside and Sofia pushed the door shut, closing and locking it in one fluid motion.

Liza leaned forward then, her lips brushing against Sofia's, her fingers lingering on Sofia's arm. There was warmth there, and the faintest hint of wine on Sofia's breath. Liza didn't blame her for *that* at all. "I came because I know what dread feels like."

"Do you now." Her breath was a whisper against Liza's lips, and her fingers were pulling at the zipper on Liza's jacket, tugging it slowly down and open, letting in the warmth of the house. "And you thought I might want what, a shoulder to cry on?" She pushed Liza's jacket off of her shoulders and backed away with it in hand, her expression unreadable.

Liza stood there in her tattered old sweater and boots, watching as Sofia turned and hung her jacket up in the closet. "Maybe just someone to stay with you tonight, to make sure that you get some sleep?" Liza ventured.

"Are you propositioning me?" Sofia's expression was not unkind, and there was a subtle hint of amusement half-hidden behind her eyes. "Because it will take far more than a few kisses to get me to bed."

They both knew that already, though.

"Not like that." Liza shook her head. "I just...I thought that maybe you'd actually get some rest." She stepped forward and traced her finger gently over the dark circles under Sofia's eyes. "Since you're obviously not getting any now."

Sofia's lips parted. She moved to speak, but her eyes flashed dangerously and her lips closed once more.

Liza pulled her hand away, not wanting to poke Sofia in the eye and took a half step back. She was pretty good at interpreting a screaming demand for personal space. Liza glanced around at the stark black and white foyer. When she'd lived here as a child it had all been warm reds and hardwood. Liza liked it more now. The blankness of the walls made the place seem cleaner, like the secrets hidden here had been brought out into the light and expunged.

"What are we doing, Liza?" The question was quiet, full of fear.

Liza bit at her lip and turned to look at Sofia. "Trying again," she offered, like it was all the explanation that was needed.

Sofia wrapped her arms around herself, the over-long sleeves of the sweater falling over her hands and masking her fingers. She wrapped herself in the straitjacket of a dead lover's warmth, as if it would somehow protect her from *feeling*, and Liza hated it. She hated how sad Sofia sounded when she sighed, her shoulders slumping.

"I don't know if I can do this," Sofia said.

It was then that Liza had her confirmation. She knew it with more certainty than she'd ever known anything. This was what she wanted, and she would fight for it, no matter what the cost. She stood tall, looking defiantly into the worry that was clearly written across Sofia's face. The worry that said that Sofia was not worthy of what was being so hesitantly offered to her. "That's okay," Liza promised. A smile ghosted across her lips. "I know that I...I should have said good-bye. That I should have fought for you."

"You're not supposed to fall in love with two people at the same time, you know?" Sofia let out a little laugh and Liza felt her heart break. "My mother liked to say that love was a luxury that couldn't be afforded, but I felt it so strongly that my heart was full to burst."

Liza sighed and shoved her hands back into her pockets. She wanted to pick at something to distract herself from how this conversation was going, and the only thing available was a thread that was pulling out of her cheap T-shirt. She didn't want to lose the hem of her shirt due to her nervous habit, so she put her hands in her pockets and left them there. "I'm sorry I confused you so much." It was all Liza could say, because she wouldn't apologize for anything else.

Shaking her head, Sofia glanced down at her feet. She was standing awkwardly in the middle of her foyer, barefoot in an oversized sweater. "You know," she said, "I spent so long trying to convince myself that I hated you, that I think I forgot everything else about you." She looked up then, bangs falling into her eyes and a pleasant smile dancing at her lips.

"I had myself just about convinced that you didn't matter," Liza said. "That we were never all that close."

Sofia stepped forward, fingers playing at the hem of Liza's tatty sweater. "Oh, I think that you will find that I want to be much *closer* to you now, my dear." Her fingers were hot when they dipped underneath the thin material of Liza's sweater and T-shirt to press against her stomach.

Liza swallowed and kept her hands in her pockets. She could barely think straight with Sofia's hand on her skin. Her mind was flashing through scenarios that would end in getting her laid. She wanted to shove Sofia up against a wall and make her feel everything that Liza had always wanted her to feel.

"Wouldn't you agree?" Sophia asked.

Desperate to push the lump that had welled up in her throat down so she could speak, Liza tried to keep her mind on the present and not running with her libido. Sleeping with Sofia when they were both so emotionally vulnerable would be a bad idea. "Yes." Liza leaned forward, her lips just next to Sofia's ear. She was not sure how to say that she wanted to wait until Sofia's mother was gone and they could actually be themselves around each other again. "But not tonight."

Sofia pulled back and looked at Liza harshly, hurt welling up in her eyes.

Liza quickly added, sensing disaster, "I don't want to rush this just because we're going through a bad time mentally."

Seeming to contemplate this for a minute, Sofia chewed on her lip in a gesture that settled between Liza's legs and pooled in the heat that was already there. She let out a shaky breath, trying to will herself calm once more.

"Okay." Sofia reached out and tugged Liza's hand from where she'd shoved it into her pocket. There were no more words, just Sofia leading Liza up the stairs and down the hall to the room that had always been Sofia's, even when they were children.

Inside of Liza there was fear; there would always be fear. No matter what Liza did, she would always be fueled by fear and anxiety. She didn't want to be chucked out like before. She wanted this to mean something and to matter. "What side?" she asked. Sofia simply pointed to the side of the bed opposite the door.

"You'll have to be out early. My mother is arriving at seven." Sofia's gaze turned dark as she stared at the alarm clock on her bedside table. "She wants to take Nathan to breakfast before school."

Liza stared up at the ceiling some twenty minutes later, thinking of that flat, quiet lake again. Slipping under the surface had been so easy then, back when nothing had mattered in the big scheme of things. Now she realized how foolish even thinking about something like that had been.

Sofia rolled closer, her back pressing up against Liza's side and Liza cautiously put an arm over her, pulling her tight and finally letting sleep claim her.

And she did not dream.

Liza got home the next morning at six-fifty, early enough to find Nancy fresh out of the shower and bustling around the kitchen. Liza pretended that she didn't notice her at first, but when Nancy headed for the door at exactly seven on the dot, she came out of her room to stand at the top of the stairs, "Might want to avoid the diner this morning."

"Who said I was going to the diner?" Nancy asked. Her fingers twisted into the fabric on her favorite knit cap. She was halfway to pulling it on, but now clutched it to her chest.

Sleepily, Liza padded in socked feet over to the top of the stairs, tugging a blanket around herself against the morning chill. "Sofia told me that her mother was taking Nathan to breakfast before school. Probably not a good idea to have a senator seeing you with a not-quite-divorced man."

The previous evening, Kevin had mentioned again how close Nancy and Noah Burke were growing. Ever since he'd mentioned it the first time some two weeks ago, Liza hadn't been able to not see it. It was everywhere, the way that Nancy smiled at texts or the way she disappeared every morning right about the time that the night shift at the sheriff's department ended. Noah would be getting dinner; Nancy got coffee and a muffin. They were not dates, but they could be, and Liza was trying not to get judgy about the fact that he wasn't quite divorced yet.

Nancy threw back her head and laughed loud and long. "I doubt she even knows who I am," she replied breezily.

"But you're welcome to come along if you want to make it look less date-like—which it isn't." She stressed the last word.

Liza just rolled her eyes and grinned down the stairs at her before glancing back towards the warmth of her bed and her discarded jeans and sweater that were lying on the bedroom floor. She stepped back into the bedroom and scooped them up, shoving them into her hamper, selecting a longer shirt and some leggings from the pile of clean laundry that Nancy had left on her bed sometime the previous night. Liza tugged them on over the thick, wooly socks she had on and pulled the shirt over her head, feeling world weary and exhausted.

Nancy humored her as she tugged on her jacket and braided her hair quickly into a lose plait. It hadn't been washed, so it hung limply into her eyes and Liza hated it like that. She wanted to look different, just in case she did see the senator. Liza didn't think that the woman would risk the bad press of denying Rachel's grandmother of a Thursday morning's business to close the restaurant to all but her family. Or at least she hoped she wouldn't.

"Are you really okay with my coming?" Liza asked. Despite this being a not-date, it was still a meeting of two people who probably liked each other. "I mean... I don't mind not going."

"You want to keep an eye on the mayor." Nancy laughed and clapped Liza on her shoulder. Her fingers were warm and comforting through Liza's thin jacket. "Don't think I don't know where you were last night."

Liza's cheeks burned, but she refused to dignify such teasing with a response. She trailed after Nancy, her shitty pay-as-you-go phone burning a hole in her pocket. She desperately wanted to text Sofia, to offer reassurances and kind words, but she knew that they'd fall onto the same deaf ears that she'd witnessed this morning before she left.

The diner was quiet for the breakfast hour. Liza slid into the booth across from Noah and smiled at him pleasantly as Nancy elbowed her from her place at the edge. Liza was grateful for the Nancy-shaped shield that allowed her to glance around the rest of the diner, eyes desperately searching for Sofia and the rest of her family.

"Liza thought she'd join us today." Nancy flipped open the menu and raising an amused eyebrow in Noah's direction. "As this is *just* a friendly breakfast." She put more emphasis on the qualifier than was strictly necessary, only adding to the overwhelming feeling of triumph that Liza felt watching the pair of them. This might not be a date, but it was getting damn close.

"Uh huh," Liza said with a roll of her eyes.

Noah snorted into his coffee cup and winked at her. He looked like he hadn't slept in a week, and Liza was sure she didn't look much better. She had never slept well in new places, not at first, anyway. Sleeping with someone else threw another monkey wrench into things, but that was the good kind, the kind that Liza liked. Sofia had been warm and pliant, and Liza hadn't felt awkward curling a protective arm around her and drifting off to sleep.

Rachel ambled up to their table a few minutes later, pad in hand. She was wearing obscenely short shorts for the forty degree weather outside and her hot pink tights clashed violently with the overall décor of the diner. She had her hip cocked in such a way that meant that she was putting on a show for someone behind her.

Liza had been a waitress; she knew what one looked like when they were trying to get laid or hoping for a really stellar tip.

"Coffee, cocoa?" Rachel pointed at Nancy and then Liza in turn.

"Coffee for me today, Rach," Liza replied. She was certain she looked like death warmed over and she didn't want to hear what Charlie was sure to say about it when she went to see him later that day. She needed to be awake and alert for the first practice that she was helping to coach.

"Gotcha," Rachel replied. She spun on her toes, pausing to check on Mr. Spencer and his wife at the counter before heading towards the kitchen.

Liza glanced over to see only Kevin's friend the librarian, absorbed in a book, behind where Rachel stood. Liza's eyebrows shot up. She didn't say anything though, as it seemed that Rachel's bid for the librarian's attention had gone largely unnoticed. Over the top of her coffee cup, she flashed a sympathetic smile at Rachel.

The chime on the door rang loudly across the quiet restaurant and Liza's eyes slid over to where Sofia and Nathan were standing behind the imposing form of Constance Milton, US Senator for the Great State of Maine. Liza's mind flashed backwards, tumbled really, to a time before she was old enough to understand what was happening to her. She had been a child, young and innocent. They'd all been younger then.

"Welcome." Rachel called from behind the counter. "I'll be with you in just a sec."

"That woman will always look imposing," Nancy muttered under her breath. Noah cracked a smile behind his coffee cup.

Liza bit her lip as Rachel swept over, two mugs in her hands and deposited them on the table. "There you are. I'll be back in a minute to get your orders."

"Take your time," Nancy replied.

There was a stiffness in Nancy's shoulders underneath the bulky sweater she was wearing. It was not a natural look on her. Nancy was at home with herself, no matter who she was around. Liza supposed that the senator was the one woman who would push that quiet self-assurance away to reveal all of Nancy's insecurities. The damn woman had a knack for doing just that.

Liza chewed on her lip and watched as Rachel seated Sofia and her family.

Nathan's eyes widened when he caught sight of Liza, half-hidden as she was behind a few other diners and a stack of menus. He knew that she wasn't supposed to be there and tried to cover for his apparently sharp intake of breath, if Sofia's concerned look was anything to go off of. He hurriedly turned back to his mother and grandmother, his attention, as Liza suspected, mostly focused on his grandmother. They were sitting close enough, just on the other side of the thin aisle between the booths and tables that dotted the middle of the restaurant between the door and the bar, that Liza could overhear their conversation over the quiet murmuring of Noah and Nancy. She was sitting with her back to Sofia, but all it would take to look at her was a quick glance over her shoulder. Rachel probably had done this on purpose, if her kind smile and nod were any indication when she came back. Liza mumbled out a request for toast and eggs since they were cheap and filling, her attention not really leaving the conversation she was in the process of trying to overhear.

"And how are his extracurriculars, Sofia, you know it's never too early to start thinking about preparatory schools," the senator said.

Liza's eyes narrowed—there was no way that Sofia would send Nathan away from her after Dave died. Surely Senator Milton would know that.

"I'd rather keep Nathan with me for the time being," Sofia replied. "He's doing very well, considering."

Liza swallowed and flicked her hair over her shoulder, using the motion to sneak a glance behind her.

"Yes, considering." The senator glanced around the diner before leaning in further, her voice dropping to the point where Liza could barely hear it over the din and Rachel's not-so-subtle flirting attempts with the librarian in the corner. "I received a rather interesting email from Mr. Sawyer at the newspaper a few weeks ago. It seems that Near Haven's greatest failure has returned to town."

White-hot anger rose up inside Liza, and there was a ringing in her ears that no amount of shaking her head seemed to clear. She reached blindly for her coffee and took a gulp of the steaming liquid, forcing herself to swallow even though it burned her throat.

"I wouldn't know." Sofia shrugged and met her mother's gaze evenly. "Things have been hectic here lately."

Liza wondered when Sofia had gotten to be such a good liar.

The senator inclined her head, tapping her chin thoughtfully as Rachel returned with mugs of coffee for them and cocoa for Nathan.

Nathan was steadfastly ignoring Liza and Nancy now, focusing on his cocoa and the conversation between his mother and grandmother.

"Then I needn't stress to you that getting involved with that woman would be your ruin, right dear?"

"Quite," Sofia said. The muscle in her jaw clenched tightly. She was probably speaking through gritted teeth, with her hand clenched into a fist in her lap.

Their food came not long after that and Liza ate her toast and eggs, trying not to listen in to the conversation at the table behind her. The pure anger of before only seemed to intensify. Liza sat and chewed on dry toast, stewing over what the senator had said. She was playing the conversation over and over in her mind, trying to figure out a way to shove her presence in the woman's face that didn't involve decking her.

Nancy got up ten minutes later and pulled Liza up with her right after Sofia and Nathan's pancakes were brought out from the kitchen. Liza was just a little bit startled. "I have to get to school, Liz." Nancy had a guilty look on her face. "I got your breakfast."

"Uh...thanks," Liza said. She wasn't bothered by the generosity, too distracted with what was happening at the table behind her as Nancy went up to the till to pay for their order. She could hear the conversation between the senator and Nathan about his soccer team quiet and she could actually feel the woman's eyes on her, calculating and predatory, as Liza straightened her scarf and offered her hand to Noah. "Good to see you again."

"You too." He munched on his hamburger and dipped a fry into the leftover syrup on Nancy's plate.

Gross, Liza wrinkled her nose and tried not to lose her breakfast all over him at the positively sickening combination of flavors.

"You doing that thing with Kevin this weekend?" Noah asked.

"Maybe." Liza honestly hadn't thought about it. She knew that she should consider the sheriff's department's offer to earn some good karma points and go with Kevin to re-blaze some of the hiking trails in the woods above the town. It had been hard to look past today since the middle of last week, though. She would have to cross that bridge when she came to it. "I'll let you know."

"Okay." Noah popped his gross-ass fry into his mouth and his eyes fluttered closed, savoring the taste. "Delicious."

"You're nasty." Liza stuck her tongue out at him. "See you around, Noah."

He waved his burger at her, obviously overtired from being up all night, and Liza took a deep breath and turned around. She knew what to expect, the accusatory and angry eyes of Constance Milton, looking at her as though she was less than dirt. Somehow, though, the expectation always paled in relation to the reality.

The senator was looking at her with a mixture of surprise and unadulterated loathing. She was glaring openly and Liza shifted uncomfortably under her gaze.

"Morning Nathan." Liza hedged, placing her hopes in the kid and tussling his hair as she walked by him. "Madam Mayor, Senator." She nodded and made a beeline to the door before they had a chance to say anything to her. She followed Nancy out and let the door bang shut behind her.

Nancy glanced towards the door when Liza rounded the gate in front of the diner. "You're either brave or foolish, I can't decide."

"That makes two of us." Liza replied with a bravado she didn't feel. She felt like a coward for bolting, but she didn't know what else she could have done or said. She was probably one of the last people the senator wanted to be seen with, horrible woman that she was.

It was easy to linger while Nancy hurried down the road towards the elementary school. Liza wondered if she should go back inside and keep an eye on the situation there. She had time before she had to start her tape review, anyway.

Liza wrapped her arms around herself and leaned against the wall of the building next to the diner, watching for a few moments before she finally decided to go back home. There was nothing she could do for Sofia now; she knew that. It was probably better to stay away.

The bell over the door rang and Liza turned to glance back, surprised to see the senator exiting alone. Liza watched with interest as she reached into her purse and pulled out a packet of Virginia Slims. She lit one expertly with a lighter produced from her jacket pocket. She looked around before taking a drag and Liza jammed her hands into her pockets and moved to walk away.

"Ms. Hawke," the senator called. She was exhaling smoke from her nose like some sort of terrifying nightmare from Liza's childhood. It curled around the Constance's head and lingered, casting her into shadow and secrets. "A word?"

Liza didn't want to talk to her, but she turned anyway, knowing that it was probably better to have this conversation now, rather than have things go unsaid. She was going to get warned away from Sofia, away from this town and everything else.

"Mrs. Milton." Liza tried to sound as polite as she could possibly fake. She put on what she hoped was a pleasant smile, and knew that it looked about as phony as the one she received in response. "I'm surprised they haven't got you traveling with Secret Service."

"I left them in Bangor. I have to head up to Augusta in the afternoon, and I didn't think I would find use for them here. Imagine my surprise." Liza stared at her, feeling a bit shell-shocked and wobbly in the knees, but the senator waved her off. She flicked her cigarette ash onto the ground and added, "Come now, dear, you don't honestly expect me to allow criminals to roam free in my home town, being friendly with my grandson, do you?"

"I think that's his mother's call." Liza's jaw was clenched so tightly she could barely speak around her gritted teeth.

"I'd say her judgment is clearly impaired in this particular situation," she replied. "But know this: I will not have you carrying on with my daughter. She is going places and I will not have trash like you dragging her down."

Liza watched as the senator flicked her cigarette butt onto the wet ground, not bothering to stub it out.

"Isn't that what you said about Dave?" Liza was used to verbal sparring. Sofia could give just as good as she got, but this was different. This conversation had venom and barely veiled threats carefully hidden inside it. Liza was worried that if she said the wrong thing, she would end up dead in a ditch somewhere. She steeled herself, teeth clenched, her jaw set in a resolute line, and added in a serious tone, "Shame about him. I know Sofia loved him dearly."

"Love is weakness." The senator stared hard at Liza with empty, black eyes that seemed devoid of any human decency. Her lip curled into an almost familiar sneer and the senator hitched her purse up on her shoulder and turned towards the door.

Liza could see Sofia and Nathan inside, putting on coats and heading towards the exit. Nathan must have had to use the bathroom or something.

"You of all people should know that."

Yes, Liza supposed that she should. She had had love ripped from her over and over again and yet she kept coming back for more, craving it like a glutton for punishment.

Still, it was not worth it to push and say anything more. "I guess I would know that better than most," Liza answered. It took all the courage she had to turn and walk away from Constance then. She didn't want Sofia to hear her threats. Liza was not afraid of her. The senator never came home, back to this place where nothing was as it seemed and everything stayed the same.

"Goodbye, Ms. Hawke."

Liza didn't dignify her with a response. The woman didn't deserve it.

CHAPTER NINE

Forty Minutes of Hell (December 7, 2012)

LIZA SAT ON A FRIGID bench down by the docks, staring out over the harbor. There were no boats docked here; only a few skiffs were tied to a portion of dock, in order to save the dock from stormy winter seas. She could count the number of buoys that still floated in the harbor on one hand. It was Kevin's side project, supervised by Isabelle de la Mount, his librarian friend, every day before they went off together to start the youth program for the afternoon. He sold the lobsters he caught to Sprat and Co. for a reasonable price, but no one in Near Haven really ate lobster, aside from those who could afford such a luxury. More often than not, the lobsters died in the store tank.

A newspaper was rolled up in Liza's lap, but she was hesitant to read it. Sam Sawyer at the paper had written an article about the first game of the season, slated for that afternoon. It was against the school just over the bridge on the mainland. He had titled the article "Forty Minutes of Hell," as if they were Arkansas back in the day or something. Sure, Charlie ran the full-court press, and the kids on the team could probably pull off something akin to the Arkansas defense if Charlie were to push them; but nothing like *that*. That team was just about as close to God status as the Fab Five at Michigan were.

"Are you actually going to read it?" Nathan demanded from where he was sitting at her side. He had a half-day at school today due to parent-teacher conferences, and had some time before he needed to drag his too-heavy backpack over to the library to help Kevin out with the holiday pageant. Even Liza had been roped into working on the project. Nathan looked down at his tightly done-up coat and picked at the fringe of his scarf. "I stole it from my mom's office just for you."

Liza sincerely doubted that he did anything of the sort. She could picture Sofia leaving the article out for him to read and could even imagine her telling him to take it along to his "top secret meeting" that she totally didn't know about. Still, Sofia humored Nathan like the best of 'em. "Well thanks." Liza flashed him what she hoped was a placating smile.

After her mother's visit, Sofia had been somewhat distant. Liza understood why she was staying away and she respected her for doing what she had to do. Sofia had retreated into herself; and Liza knew that being around a woman like Constance Milton could not be easy on anyone. Sofia had been right to back away, to keep herself locked up until she knew she could handle being around people without hurting them the way her mother did.

Following the Thanksgiving holiday, during which Liza'd sat with Nancy, Charlie, and Noah at the diner for the usual gathering of strays with nowhere else to go, Liza thought that maybe she could get Sofia to open up, just a little. She wanted to see her more than just in passing, with just a fleeting smile or a touch to the cheek. Their time spent together had all but evaporated with the coming holidays, the aftermath of the storm, and the senator's subsequent appearance in town.

Liza chewed on her lip for a moment, the newspaper heavy in her hands. She shivered and tucked the paper under her arm. The clock tower over the library was busted still, but a quick glance at her shitty pay-as-you-go phone told her that she was due to meet Leslie. They'd have their meeting and then Liza would head over to the diner were she was going to catch a ride with Charlie up to the school. "We gotta get going," she said, offering Nathan her hand.

Nathan's hand was small in hers. He was everything that she'd never been able to be. He was a good kid with a winning smile, an athlete (although in Liza's opinion, he was not as keen on basketball as he perhaps should be), and a beloved child. A wave of jealousy surged up in Liza like a storm cresting over a bulkhead. It was so overwhelming that she nearly dropped his hand from her own as she got to her feet. She didn't dare let go though, for he was an innocent. He had no idea what she had to go through as a child.

"When are you going to come 'round again?" Nathan asked. They walked past the cannery by the shore.

Liza eyed the building with interest; she'd never thought about applying to work there. The building was mostly dilapidated, the boards weathered a greyish slate that almost looked like the sea-beaten rocks that formed the harbor.

Nathan was looking up at her with wide, innocent eyes and Liza couldn't help but wonder if she was growing too close to this child. There was so little of his father in him that Liza thought that if she were to blink, she'd miss it altogether. All she could see in Nathan was Sofia and the child that she'd once been, all those frowns turned into happy smiles and carefree laughs.

"I don't know," Liza confessed. "Your mom wanted some space; I think your grandma coming freaked her out. She never comes home, right?"

Nathan shook his head. "Not even on Christmas. She likes to stay in Washington, or go see her cousins in New York. They're closer, she says, and if she needs to get back to Washington she can return in a hurry. We Skype at Christmas sometimes, but mostly it's just me and Mom." He was talking quickly as they walked up towards Main Street.

The library was already coming into view and Liza almost didn't want to let go of Nathan's hand, preferring to get more information out of him about what he usually did at Christmas.

"Christmas can be unfun, huh kid?" Liza caught the negative tone that he'd cast out so freely.

"Mom gets sad," Nathan gave a melancholy sort of nod. He used his free hand to wipe his nose and blinked up at Liza. "Maybe since you're here, she won't be sad?"

Lord, Liza hoped so. They were both finally free, not without baggage, but finally able to start over. The senator's threat had not fallen on deaf ears, but Liza's resolve was true. It was as Charlie was always saying: "Clear hearts, clear heads, can't lose." This was Liza's game, and she had to run the next play. "Maybe." She spoke in what she hoped was a reassuring voice. "I'm going to read this before I meet up with Ms. Leslie. You should tell your mom that you want to come to the game, okay?"

Nathan wrinkled his nose, "But it's far away."

Liza shrugged. "Just over the bridge. Bring your mom and your yelling voice. It's crappy opening on the road."

Nathan nodded and squeezed her hand. "I don't know if I can get her to come, but I'll try." Liza knew that his promise was made out of the same piecrust as her own promise to Sofia before. Easily made and broken, like so much else in her life.

"Don't stress it." Liza grinned as he scampered into warmth of the library, following a girl with blonde braids that were poking awkwardly out from under an oversized sheepskin hat. Liza waited until she knew Nathan was inside before turning on one booted foot and heading towards Leslie's office.

Her case was going well, or so Leslie thought. She had spoken to the state's attorney that had prosecuted both Liza's case and Jared's, explaining the situation and how Liza had returned home and was looking to start her life again. The guy had apparently been pretty chill about the whole thing. He'd been pushing for a more lenient sentence with the judge— especially since Liza was so young when she'd gotten caught with Jared's stupid stolen watches. They were now waiting to hear back from the judge in Oregon, to see if he'd be willing to sign off on an order to expunge or if they'd have to have a second hearing. They'd do it in a closed court, via Skype probably up in Bangor, Leslie had explained. Liza didn't have the resources to fly across the country to speak before a judge for less than an hour.

Still, Liza was worried. She hated the idea of having to speak to that same heartless bastard who had sent her away with no questions asked. It was easy to lose herself in the horror stories, Liza remembered the court case of that judge in Pennsylvania, the one who was getting kickbacks from the local private prison to send people away. She hoped that the judge wasn't like that guy.

Leslie's office was in one of the repurposed buildings that probably used to be part of the cannery back in the day. The building was made of brick and stood solid after storm water had pounded against it for nearly eighty years. It had a welcoming, friendly glow to it now, with warm lamps to light the front windows of shops that operated during off-season hours. It was only three-thirty and already two of the stores were closed. The bookstore was still open though; a small cart of books rolled out tentatively under the awning, as if tempting the dark and murderous clouds overhead to spit down rain or snow.

Liza inhaled deeply, pausing in front of large doors that opened onto a stairway leading to the offices on the second floor. There was a bitter bite to the air, and the smell of salty wood smoke filled her nose. It wasn't quite ready to snow, but it was coming.

Pushing her way into the warmth of Leslie's office building, Liza trotted up the stairs and hung a left, heading down the hall to the frosted glass door that had Leslie's name on it. Liza wondered if she'd ever change her name back from Burke, or if she even wanted to. She probably wouldn't ask about that though, since it didn't seem polite.

The door opened into a small reception area and Liza took a seat. Giving in to her curiosity, she unfolded the newspaper and read Mr. Sawyer's article about Charlie's team this year and their forty-minute full-court press. The truth was somewhere in between, really. They had a team of agile guards and forwards, and no true center to play the post. Charlie had hope for a girl that had been on the junior varsity squad last year, but her family had had to move to Boston over the summer and frankly, Liza was glad that someone had been able to get out of this town. The team meshed well as a group: two seniors, four sophomores, and three juniors. They had a good sub rotation and some of the newspaper guys who weren't Mr. Sawyer were picking Near Haven to make some noise this season. Briannan Montclair, the starting point guard, was already getting some long looks from out-of-state schools.

Liza stared down at the team picture; in it Liza was standing off to one side in a grey Near Haven High T-shirt and sweatpants and was named in the caption as the assistant coach.

"Liza?" Leslie's voice came from behind her half-closed office door. "You out there?"

"Yeah," Liza replied. She folded up the paper and tucked it into the back pocket of her jeans, trying to ignore how it dug into her back. She had left her supplies with Rachel at the diner earlier, before she met Nathan—a pair of nice slacks that still had the tags on them when she'd found them at the thrift store in Bangor and a blouse. As an assistant so she wouldn't need a blazer. Hopefully. "Should I come in?"

Leslie appeared in the door wearing an oversized and obviously hand-knit sweater over her blouse and jeans. It was a casual day at the office, then. It was a Friday, after all.

"Don't bother. I haven't heard much of anything yet. Your friend Kevin out there seems to think that this probably isn't going to go anywhere until after Christmas, anyway. The judge has something like ten grandkids." She flashed Liza a sympathetic smile and crossed the room to sit down next to her. "I think that we're in the clear, though." Leslie tucked a lock of straight blonde hair behind her ear and could feel Liza sigh from across the room. She didn't know how to thank Leslie for all that she'd done on this case. She didn't even know if she should be thankful. Liza was still so unaccustomed to people being nice to her without wanting something in return, that it felt odd to her, like she was waiting for the other shoe to drop.

Leslie had thrown herself into this case as her divorce was being finalized, and was probably using it as an excuse not to get too close to Ted just yet. He had bemoaned this to Liza over Chet's winter brew, as they sat sipping it on Kevin's porch after their Patriots watch parties a few times now, but Liza had just rolled her eyes at him.

"Thanks for calling him," Liza said. Fuck—she'd never been good at this. Accepting help, accepting praise, it all came so hard to her. She knew it was because of her childhood, because of the constant stream of faces that danced across her mind when she thought of growing up in this town. "I know that this isn't really how you want to spend your Friday afternoon."

Leslie shrugged. "I have three foreclosures, but there's a moratorium between now and the first, so I can't proceed on those right now. Other than that, it's the usual small claims and divorce stuff. You're really the most interesting thing I'm working on right now, Liz." She shook her head after she finished speaking and Liza grinned back at her. "I just want to help."

It was this part that Liza always found to be the hardest of them all. Gratitude, and the feeling of being completely unworthy of what was being offered to her without anything expected in return, were so completely and utterly alien to her. People always wanted something, and for Leslie to be offering this freely felt so strange. Her cheeks burned as she nodded resolutely. "Thank you, Leslie." Nudging Leslie with her shoulder she grinned broadly at her. "You're a saint."

"Hardly." Leslie laughed.

Liza could see the darkness in her eyes and knew that she was thinking of how her marriage had dissolved into divorce.

"Don't you have a game?" Leslie asked, glancing at the clock on the wall over her office door.

Liza's eyes shot to the clock on the wall and she hurriedly got to her feet, zipping up her jacket and jamming the newspaper back into her pocket from where it had slipped. "Shit, you're right." She had five minutes to get to the diner to meet Charlie or else she was going to be late. "Look, do you like fudge?"

"Uh…" Leslie trailed off and then nodded once.

Liza grinned at her and headed for the door, thinking that her brilliant Christmas present plan might pan out after all. Nancy was on board and Liza was already a fairly decent cook—but the discovery of a fully-copper saucepan for seven bucks at the thrift store in Bangor, where she'd gotten her grown-up dress pants, had pretty much solidified her plan. She was making candy for everyone and she didn't care who knew it.

"I'll see you later," Liza said. She closed the door behind her and took the stairs three at a time, until they started to get wet and she slowed, the faux-fur of her jacket's hood tickling the back of her neck. The diner was half a block away and Charlie's car was already there, but he wasn't leaning against the passenger's side scowling. Liza took that to be a good sign; it meant that he'd stepped in to get a coffee and to say hello to Rachel's grandmother. Liza cut down between the diner and the building next to it, dodging around trashcans and a few old wooden pallets. Her bag was sitting on top of the old coin-op washer in the back room of the diner. Liza scooped it up over her shoulder and pushed the door into the dining room open.

Charlie was standing at the register, talking to the proprietor, Rachel's grandmother, a to-go cup of coffee in his hands. "Ah," he said. Liza closed the door behind her. "I see that Ms. Hawke is here now, ma'am. I gotta go."

Rachel's grandmother nodded and flashed a small smile that made her usually severe face soften. She looked like someone's grandmother in that moment, rather than the fierce owner of the town's lone, year-round restaurant.

Charlie didn't say anything until they were nearly at the high school. The team was standing by the bus, backpacks at their feet and determined looks on their faces. He parked the old Vic and leaned over to pull an L.L. Bean canvas bag bearing Near Haven's mascot on the side from the backseat; he plopped it into his lap. It was stuffed with the playbook and first aid kit. "You've done a remarkable job at this, Liza."

Liza collected her own bag from the backseat, as well as the six-pack of water bottles that Charlie had already filled. "I get your system, coach."

He nodded, his grey beard frizzing slightly in the winter air. "Let's see how you do in a game." He said it like it was a challenge and Liza took it that way. Nothing was ever good enough for Charlie. Liza sometimes found herself thinking that he was impossible to please, not to mention a grouchy asshole when he wanted to be. Which was, naturally, most of the time.

Charlie would drive the bus and they made sure everyone was accounted for before heading off. It was four thirty now, and the game was at six. Liza sat towards the front, next to Jess and Briannan. They were still a little skeptical of her; everyone in Near Haven knew her story, and Jess had even gone so far as to accuse Liza of trying to relive her old glory.

It had been hard to explain why she was back in Near Haven, back *coaching*. They couldn't understand why she was getting back into the sport that had ultimately been her downfall. She'd talked to the team one afternoon in the locker room, explaining that she wanted to be there for them, and not for herself. "I'd take any job I could find," she'd explained, swallowing nervously as nine pairs of eyes stared her down with expectant gazes. "I can't get many of them right now and that's my fault. So when Charlie offered me something, I took it. I think that that's okay."

"So do you want to be here?" Briannan had folded her arms, a scowl on her lips.

Liza'd laughed. "There was a point in time, not too long ago, when I would have told you that no, being in Near Haven was probably the last thing on my mind, and do you want to know why? Because I always associated this place with my own shortcomings; but since I've come back here, I've realized that this place is where I am at my strongest. I have people who care for me, a team to rally behind, and a sense of purpose. I want to get you guys back to that championship game, and I think we can do it." She'd raised an eyebrow in defiance. "So are you with me?"

With that cocky challenge and her brazen defiance of traditional authority, Liza had won the team over.

The bus rocked over the bumpy, frost-heave-riddled road. Jess was bemoaning an English test in the morning, and Liza got her to talk about the book her class was reading. It was one that she had re-read down in Raleigh, while enjoying the mild winter and easy work she'd found. Liza talked about her favorite parts of the story, and the girls were all staring at her like she had three heads when she finished.

"How the hell were you ever a jock?" Meghan, one of the junior forwards, demanded. She looked incredulous at the very idea. "You're way too into books, Hawke."

Liza shrugged. She had always liked books.

The boys were playing after them, and as the bus rolled over the bridge, Liza could see the banner welcoming them to "dawg country." Liza scowled at it and the team booed loudly as they drove past.

There were already a good number of people milling around the outside of the school, and the parking lot was half full already. Liza wondered if it was because their opponent's boys' team was picked to finish first in their division, or if it was because it was the first conference game of the season. Her stomach twisted into knots as she grabbed her stuff and followed the team off the bus.

Liza hadn't been in a game day atmosphere for years now, and she stood with her blouse half buttoned, watching as the girls grew silent around her. They were ready for anything, and Liza knew it. She her fingers flew over the rest of her buttons and she left them to their pregame rituals.

When her breath caught at the announcement of her name as assistant coach, Charlie squeezed her shoulder comfortingly. She recognized some of the older fans, the ones who'd been around for a while. They craned their necks to get a good look at her. She was known here; even among rivals, she was known.

"Just ignore the crowd," Charlie whispered. He gathered the team in a huddle.

Liza leaned in and listened to his game plan and the pledge that he'd made before every game for what felt like years now.

"You will win," he promised them, "so long as you play with pure hearts and play your best. Do it for Near Haven."

The team's voice echoed the promise as one, and Liza put on her best determined face. She was not looking into the crowd, because she knew that if she looked, she would see Nathan and his mother. She would see the girl she had fallen in love with all those years ago—the girl she had left behind, who had grown into a woman and knew more sadness and heartbreak than anyone should have to stomach at her age. Sofia couldn't refuse Nathan anything, and Liza knew that they were out there, somewhere, watching.

Liza was absolutely determined to win for that alone, to give Sofia a reason to smile. She pulled Jess aside and gestured to the team's starting guard. "She doesn't go left very well—she'll always drive right—you and Bri, you work that."

Jess nodded and they lined up, hands over their hearts, and listened to some terrible singer botch the national anthem. Liza tried not to cringe during the octave change and the singer's awkward warbling, grateful when it was over. She stood tall and stretched her hands above her head, ready to get things started.

During the first two quarters, the game was fast-paced and chippy. Liza watched them play and realized that there was very little that she wouldn't give to suit up and get out on the court. She hated that she was stuck on the sideline, and she could see that Charlie was aware of her dilemma. They got a brief respite with a little under a minute left. The Bulldogs had taken a time-out and Charlie shoved the play board into her hands. "Call the final play," he said. His eyes were dark and intense.

Liza took a deep breath and opened her mouth to protest.

He silenced her with a stern look and a glance towards the officials' table, where the head ref was checking her watch.

There was a dry erase marker at the top of the play board and Liza closed her eyes. They had been shooting the three well, but it was stupid to rely on that with the Bulldog defense playing as well as they were. There was twenty seconds in the time-out, and the play that they had to run flew into Liza's mind almost instantly. "Bri." Liza drew her first x. "You take the inbound, pass it over the line, and then get it back. Meghan, you drive left and Jess you go sweep right down on the baseline. Marina, you stay at the top of the key and play D. Ash, I want you to run with twenty-five—the point guard—and make sure she doesn't get a steal. No fouls guys, we don't have any left to give."

They broke apart from their huddle with a pledge of "teamwork" and headed back onto the floor. Briannan took the ball from the ref and moved to pass it inbounds. Liza watched with rapt attention as the play evolved and the pieces began to fall into place. Jess passed to Meghan who bounced the ball over to a driving Briannan, and Liza whooped as their ace laid the ball up and into the net just as the clock buzzed the end of the second quarter. They were up by seven, but that didn't really mean anything. There was a whole second half to play.

Charlie led them into the locker room and pointed out things that Liza hadn't even noticed, laying out a sketch of a game plan for the second half that fell into perfect pieces as they bounded back onto the court.

This time Liza risked a look into the stands and saw Nathan Milton, a brown paper bag of concession-stand popcorn balanced on his knees, and his mother, halfway towards putting a piece in her mouth. He saw her looking and waved energetically. Sofia's eyes went soft as Liza met them, warmth pooling in the pit of Liza's stomach.

She'd make sure that they won for them. Just to see them smile.

The team started to run their press in the third quarter, trapping on every play, never letting the ball get out of one Bulldog's hands easily. Jess had two steals within the first three minutes off of the back-up guard and they quickly extended their lead to twelve points. Liza was chewing nervously on her lip though, when she noticed Briannan and Meghan had both started to look tired. Her worry grew when Ashleigh took an inbound pass to the chest and dropped it back out of bounds. Charlie was beside himself, yelling at her from the sidelines, but it was a lost cause. The press was what was killing them, but it was getting them points and letting them win.

Briannan stepped back and drained a perfect three over number twenty-five's head with four minutes gone in the fourth quarter. They were up big, but Charlie kept the press going. Liza wanted to tell him to stop as they reached the under-five-minute time-out, but he shook his head at the look she gave him. "We've got to keep them on their heels. We're better than this exhaustion. We can take 'em." He said it with such conviction that Liza could see the competitive gleam grow in the nine pairs of eyeballs that stared adoringly at him as he ran through a few plays on the board, shooting them out rapid-fire and then flipping the board over to diagram them out.

The game ended 67-48, and it really hadn't been much of a contest. Liza smiled and shook hands, pausing to speak to their opponent's head coach, telling him a little about what she'd been up to since her release from prison. The starkness of that phrase really was starting to get to her. Knowing that *everyone* they would play this year was aware of her past was enough to make her stomach turn and her head hurt. She hated that her failure was so public. "I've been living like a nomad." She smiled. "Seeing the country, you know?"

He nodded and clapped her on the back. "It's good to have you back, Hawke. You guys got one hell of a team this year."

Nathan had fought his way down from the stands, a half-eaten bag of popcorn clutched in one hand and his coat under the other. "Liza you won!" He launched himself at her and hugged her around the middle.

Briannan and some of the other players were talking with their parents before the postgame meeting and showers. They were looking at Liza as she smoothed down Nathan's hair, a small smile on her face.

Liza didn't care.

"Yeah kid. We did." She took a second to explain to Nathan that she would be back in a minute, but that she had to go back into the locker room and speak to the team.

He nodded earnestly and trotted over to where Liza saw Sofia chatting with some older-looking guy that Liza didn't recognize. Sofia had on her politician's smile and Liza wondered if maybe he was on the town council or something, either here or in Near Haven.

Rounding up the players and pulling them from their families was always rough. Charlie was a bit lax about postgame locker room meetings. With most teams, it was straight there after a game, but Charlie always liked to linger after the handshake. These kids had grown up twenty minutes from each other and they played on the same summer leagues, he'd explained to reporters time and time again. It was unfair to deny them a chance to socialize.

They were kids—this was just a game—friendship was always more important. His stance hadn't earned him many friends, but most opposing coaches that Liza remembered from her playing days had humored his odd coaching style.

Charlie stood in the locker room with his hands clasped behind his back. His face was drawn and Liza was struck, for what felt like the thousandth time since she'd come back, at how very old he looked. The wrinkles in his face were cut deep and drew shadows, making his expression look more serious. He looked like a villain from a science fiction movie, and Liza half expected him to start breathing like Darth Vader just for the effect.

They all sat, uniforms still on, and Charlie began to speak: "That was a promising opening to the season." He rocked forward on the balls of his feet, his expression growing more serious. "However it was a sloppy press. Mr. Sawyer wrote an article in the newspaper about you guys, and he said that you were running the Arkansas defense. What I saw out there today was *not* the Arkansas defense. You got tired—you let your tiredness show and they took advantage of that. We won big, and I'm proud of you for that, but we let them back into things when we started to get sloppy. Hands need to be up, eyes need to be focused. You're not tired, you're pushing through it." He folded his arms across his chest and a smile blossomed from behind his beard. "It was a wicked good show for the first conference game of the season. Congrats, ladies."

Liza started to clap and soon they all joined in. Meghan whistled and Ashleigh let out a whoop.

"Show of hands." The applause had died down. "How many of you are staying for the boy's game?" Charlie asked.

A few hands went up.

"How many of you have guaranteed rides home? Coach Swanson has told me that this season he won't be up to giving my players rides home on his bus just because they decide to stay and cheer."

"Why can't we just ride the same bus, coach?" Jess asked. She was one of the ones who had put her hand up. She was dating a boy on the team, a junior with a beat-up old Civic who usually provided rides home to a few of the girls after practice. "It'd be better for the environment; I know diesel isn't cheap."

Charlie shrugged. "This is the way that the school board wanted it done, guys. I can't help that it's a silly situation, but if you don't have a ride home from a parent," Jess opened her mouth to protest, but Charlie continued, "or a significant other, I can't let you stay."

There was some grumbling, but everyone knew that Coach Swanson was a bit of a hard-ass and no one wanted to tempt fate by asking him for a lift.

Liza took her bag and, with a nod to Charlie, slipped out of the locker room. Her cheeks burned a little as Charlie nodded in an somewhat approving fashion when she walked by him. He had seen the exchange between Liza and Nathan, obviously. She supposed that that meant he approved, and she was not sure how to deal with the emotion that lurched forward inside of her. It was almost like pride, mixed with affection. She wondered if this is what it was like to have parental approval to do something.

Sofia was waiting with Nathan in the school's lobby. Nathan had either finished or thrown away his popcorn and was sitting with a book open on his lap, studiously doing problems while Sofia messed around on her Blackberry. She looked up when she heard Liza's footsteps and smiled shyly.

Liza found herself smiling back.

"That was a very well-coached game, Ms. Hawke," Sofia said. She tucked her phone into her purse. Nathan closed his book and returned it to his backpack. "Congratulations on your first conference win."

"Thanks." Liza rubbed at the back of her neck, not entirely sure what to say next, but knowing that she had to say *something*. She settled on a polite inquiry as to how Sofia was doing after the holiday, and followed after Sofia and Nathan as they headed out to the car. There was an unspoken agreement that Liza was going back with them. It had been there since the first time Liza laid eyes on them, coming out after the half.

"Holidays are hard," Sofia said. The thirty-minute ride to the house on High Pine Street was passed in an uneasy silence.

Liza kept thinking of all the things she wanted to say, but the words didn't come. She wanted to tell Sofia that this was it, a final chance for them, because it was *Sofia* and not an obligation to Kevin or Charlie or Nancy that made her want to stay here.

Near Haven was a place that Liza had sworn she would never settle on, and still she found herself wanting it. She was no politician's girl, and she was not a member of the wealthy, New England elite. She was a nobody who had held the heart of Sofia Milton in her hands and felt the love that was contained within that brilliant soul.

When they arrived back to the house and were inside, Sofia sent Nathan upstairs to wash his hands and led Liza into the kitchen. She got down bowls and unearthed a Tupperware full of what looked like chili from the refrigerator. "I'm sorry I've been avoiding you," she said. She began emptying the container into a saucepan on the stove and adding a little bit of water to it before turning the heat on low.

"I understand," Liza said. She shifted awkwardly from foot to foot. "Your mom's a real piece of work."

"I know." Sofia sighed and hooked her ankle around one of the kitchen stools, collapsing down into it and resting her chin on her hand, elbow on the countertop. "She told me that I'm just looking to replace David, that he's the love of my life, and that I'll never love anyone like him again." She shook her head and looked up at Liza. "I don't..." Faltering, Sofia reached for Liza's hand. Her fingers were warm and comforting, intertwining with Liza's and staying there, fitting perfectly. "I don't want to replace him. I don't think I can."

"Love is different each time," Liza said. She thought about Jared and how it had felt so different from the stolen kiss and constant fear of discovery that had colored her teenage infatuation with this woman. Loving Jared had been so easy; he'd been easy in all the ways that Liza'd liked at the time. She'd looked past his faults then, and she was pretty sure she'd do it now. Great love was hard to come by.

Sofia nodded in agreement. "It is. I don't want to make you feel the way I did back then. He'd asked me to marry him before I came home, before, well, before *you*. And my mother hated the idea, absolutely hated it, until she saw us that one time."

Liza cringed, thinking of that moment under the apple tree out back and the near-kiss that had almost destroyed them both. "So we start over," she said. "I can't be Dave, and I don't want to replace him. You can't replace the asshole that I fell in love with either. We're just two people who happen to have liked each other for a long time."

The chili sizzled on the stove and Sofia pushed herself up to tend to it. She brushed past Liza, a smile curling at her lips. "I think we can work with that."

Yeah, Liza thought, *I can too.*

CHAPTER TEN

Coach (December 23—25, 2012)

THE FIRST SNOW OF THE season came two days before Christmas. Liza stood in the high school parking lot following a blowout 85-50 victory over one of the bottom dwellers in their conference, shivering as she watched it come down around her. Her bag was over one shoulder, her hands plunged deeply into her pockets, and she was staring up at the big, fat flakes as they silently fell to the ground.

Somewhere behind her, she could hear Bri and Jess let out excited whoops. Something cold and hard hit her squarely in the back and slid down her jacket. Liza turned, letting out a startled shriek as another snowball whizzed past her head. Jess and Bri were standing by Jess's boyfriend's truck, packing more snowballs. They were distracted from Liza quickly, though, their attention turned towards the other girls as they emerged from the gym. Liza shook her head at their antics, and turned away.

The smell of wood smoke, the crisp biting scent of the sea, and the cool feel of the snow as it gathered in her hair pulled Liza back to her childhood so utterly, it was almost alarming.

She had always loved the snow. It was the blanket that you pulled up over you, washing everything clean and white and pure once more. Snow hid the darkness in the world beneath a coating of wonderment that Liza couldn't shake, even well past the age when she was supposed to believe in such things.

They'd given her a Christmas present before the game. Apparently they all pitched in as a team to get her the beautifully wrapped box that Liza carefully placed in her bag so that it wouldn't get damaged. Liza hadn't known how to handle their expectant faces and stumbled her way through explaining that she wanted to open it on Christmas morning; she wasn't sure how much else she'd have to unwrap. They'd understood, sort of, and Liza'd left as soon as she could, coming out to stand in the snow and be alone with her almost overwhelming feelings.

There was an old poem that said that watching the woods fill up with snow was the best way to watch the snow fall, but Liza liked to watch the town fill up with snow instead. This town had so much more to mask behind the carefully blank veneer of snow than did the woods.

They'd won again, four times in a row now. They had lost an out-of-conference game against Portland, but out of the jaws of that defeat, they'd rattled off four wins in a row. Liza knew that she should feel happy, proud even, but all she could feel was that it wasn't going to be enough: not enough to sway her court case, not enough to prove to Sofia that this, what they had between them, was what she wanted, that *she* was who Liza wanted, and that the where of it didn't matter at all.

In the distance, Liza could see Sofia's car waiting. Nathan's breath and little stick figure drawings on the window seemed to dance from the dome light that was on inside the warm-looking car. Liza shivered, sneezed, and turned to face the girls, who were still shrieking, giggling, and throwing snowballs at each other.

"You guys all have rides, right?" Liza called over their shrieks. She watched as Charlie locked up the gym behind the last girl out of the locker room.

They all nodded and Liza waved to Charlie, who raised his arm in return. He moved to actually wave, only to let his arm fall and rest on his chest briefly, before shaking his head. Liza's eyes narrowed, watching as the snow fell around him and his rack of empty and rinsed-out water bottles. She had already put the L.L. Bean bag full of their playbook and Saturday's game tape into his car. There had never been a need to lock cars in Near Haven.

Liza glanced over towards Sofia's car once more, and then turned, hitching her bag up under her hood and headed over to Charlie. "Coach." She drew level with him as he held his keys up to the light over the door, hand shaking slightly as he tried to find his the car key. "Are you okay?"

Charlie's brow furrowed under his cap and he scowled at her. "Never better, Hawke." But there was a worried pull at the corners of his lips that made Liza want to make him sit down somewhere and maybe go see a doctor. "Your ride's waiting, kid." He glanced at Sofia's idling car. "Don't want to keep her waiting, do you?"

"No sir." Liza shook her head and smiled at him.

The worry was still there on his face, but his hands weren't shaking anymore and he seemed to grow and stand tall and proud before her.

"I'll see you Saturday for the pregame conference."

"All right." Charlie waved her off. His breath misted before him, making him look like a creature of Tolkien's or like Jack Frost himself. It wrapped him in mystery and filled Liza with the oddest sense of foreboding as she shifted uncomfortably from foot to foot. Charlie was almost smiling, and she was still not quite used to him doing that. He would always be her unsmiling, perfectionist coach, no matter how their relationship grew and changed. "Merry Christmas, if I don't see you."

"You too." Liza replied, with emotion that she didn't really feel. Christmas had always been just another day to her, a day of broken promises and disappointment.

She had a present though. And she'd given presents this year. They were all delivered, left in little packages with tinsel and ribbon tied around them. The copper pot she had found at that thrift shop had been clutch and Nancy kept eyeing it enviously when she thought Liza wasn't looking. She was maybe, just maybe chancing into new routines and traditions around the holiday.

Her boots splashed quietly on the snow-damp pavement. The only sounds that filled the night air now were Charlie and Sofia's engines idling, rattling out a metallic purr that disrupted the peaceful, silent sound of the snow. Glancing back at his car one last time, Liza sighed. She didn't know why she was so worried about Charlie. It was good that Nancy would be at home this week so there would be someone to watch him.

Inside the car, Nathan was hanging over the driver's seat, and Sofia was looking over a homework assignment, a pen in her hand and her lips pursed as she checked his math. Liza pulled the door open and leaned down to stick her head inside, her hand pressed against the damp roof of the car. "Mind if I join you guys?" she asked. Nathan's face brightened into a happy smile and the look of concentration on Sofia's face faded to one of quiet welcome as she handed the paper back to Nathan.

Sofia glanced back at Nathan with a small smile playing on her lips, "I think that the Lady Knights could go all the way again this year."

Liza swallowed. She'd been avoiding thinking about it because there was a potential for it to actually happen. The last time they'd done it they'd had a guard just like Bri, and had played this same style of offensive defense. Liza hated that she could see so much of her own championship-winning team in this one; it drove home her failure more and more. "Maybe," she said, glancing back at the door to the gym, caught in a moment of nostalgia. Liza shook herself and got into the car. It had become another routine that she had fallen into. Sofia came to the home games with Nathan, and Liza went home with her afterwards.

"Mom made lasagna because it's so close to Christmas." Nathan was speaking about a mile a minute from the backseat. He was practically vibrating with excitement, and Liza couldn't help but smile at him as Sofia put the Mercedes into drive and headed out of the snowy parking lot.

Charlie's car was still sitting in its parking space when they went around the bend, but the dome light was on and he was clearly on the phone. Liza hoped that she'd imagined the worry pulling at his lips and in his eyes. He was strong, but he wasn't stupid. If there was something wrong, she was pretty sure he'd ask for help.

"You're quiet tonight," Sofia said. They turned up the side street shortcut to High Pine Street.

Liza bit her lip and didn't point out that Sofia was quiet too, perhaps because she was driving in the snow; it was reasonable to expect concentration on slick roads. Still, Nathan was in the car and Liza wasn't really sure that she should say anything just yet. She swallowed the want to tell someone about what she'd seen, as she'd done so many times before, and to voice the other thing that was bothering her. "The girls..." She trailed off and shook her head. She didn't know why she was avoiding the discussion of Charlie and his potentially perceived illness, but she supposed that it was worth it to avoid upsetting Nathan. "They got me a Christmas present."

The corners of Sofia's eyes crinkled, crow's feet appearing as she smiled and turned onto High Pine Street. Theirs was the only car on the road, and the town was fast filling up with snow. Yellow light spilled from the windows around them as they drove slowly past. "I can imagine that that was weird for you."

"Why?" Nathan wanted to know from the back seat.

There was a moment then, when this careful peace could have snapped so easily. Liza hadn't really ever talked to Nathan about her childhood, and she was pretty sure Sofia hadn't mentioned it either. There was a silent understanding between them that it was never to be spoken of.

Liza was saved by the bell, or rather by the sudden turn into Sofia's driveway. Nathan scrambled from the car without an answer to his question and Liza allowed herself to take a hesitant, shaky breath. It rattled around in her chest, wings fluttering, a moth to the flame. It didn't make her feel any better. Rather, it just settled the dread and self-doubt more firmly in the pit of her stomach.

"How do you tell a kid that you've never really had a Christmas?" Liza asked. Sofia reached behind Liza to retrieve her purse and briefcase, set them on her lap, and stared down at the expensive leather and Coach logo. "How can I explain that to him and have him understand?"

"Try," Sofia suggested. Her fingers closed around the straps of her purse and briefcase. She slung them both over her shoulder and settled them there before taking the keys out of the ignition and switching off the lights. "And I understand, even if he doesn't."

Liza bit her lip and looked away. "I'm glad you do," she said. Everything had been so hectic since she'd taken this coaching position. She was spending more and more time holed up with Charlie in his office, watching game film and going over game plans and contingency plans to attach to their game plans. They planned every aspect of the game so completely that Liza thought she could do game prep in her sleep. She didn't get moments like this with Sofia unless she made sure that they happened, carving the time from the precious few hours she had to sleep. Still, it wasn't enough. Liza wanted to be with them constantly and hated that she couldn't.

Sofia flashed her a tight-lipped smile before getting out of the car. They trailed inside after Nathan, stomping the snow off of their boots and then peering out the windows of the darkened dining room, watching the yard fill up with snow. Sofia set about heating up the lasagna and Liza took the plates that Nathan handed her into the dining room. She set the table in the dark, grateful that the blackness of the room covered how her hands were shaking.

She hated Christmas, she always had. It was a day that meant more broken promises than her birthday, a month and a half ago. It was strange that one of her better Christmas memories came from this house, when Sofia's father had been home and everything had been so much simpler. She'd kept that stuffed bear until they'd taken all of her things from her at the prison in Oregon. Liza had no idea where it went. At least her baby blanket, the one thing she still had of the family that abandoned her to this village by the sea, had survived, tucked aside with her belongings in storage. She was thinking in circles.

"Are you okay?" Nathan asked. He was standing in the doorway, three glasses cradled against his chest, silverware poking out of the top of one.

Liza shook her head. "I don't know, Nate." she replied. She took the glasses he offered and set them around the table, plucking silverware out of the final glass and settling them around the plates. She had learned that here, she thought, before they took her away on a snowy day sort of like this one. "I was trying to figure out how to answer your question from earlier, honestly," she said.

Nathan climbed into the seat next to Liza, as she very carefully arranged forks and knives on top of neatly folded napkins. "How do you mean?" His eyes were wide and Liza knew that even though there were quiet bangs and the sounds of Sofia puttering around in the kitchen, that she was listening in. "Everyone likes Christmas."

"They like Christmas when they have families that love them and presents to unwrap. For kids who don't have that, it's just another day. A bad day." Liza did not dare to meet Nathan's eyes.

He was sitting with his hands in his lap, hanging his head and fidgeting. "That just means that you have to spend Christmas with us." Nathan bounced excitedly just as Sofia walked into the room, the pan of lasagna and a spatula in hand. She set it down on the trivet that Nathan had earlier produced from some drawer below the breakfast bar that Liza hadn't known existed. "Right Mom?"

Sofia was silent, slowly crossing over to switch on the light above the table. This game had had an early tip; it was only eight thirty. Already, with the snow, it looked like midnight outside. The snow was swirling down around them. Sofia lingered in shadow, even after Liza and Nathan were bathed in light, watching with solemn eyes from the darkness.

"Nathan…" Liza began, biting at the inside of her cheek to keep from protesting that she'd never wanted to spend the day with them anyway—because she really, really had.

She was cut off with a quiet cough as Sofia swept back into the light. Her eyes were bright now, glistening at the edges, and she shook her head firmly, just once, to silence Liza's protest. "If you are free, Liza, we'd love to have you. You know it's just Nathan and me…my mother prefers to avoid Maine in the winter."

Liza's heart felt full to bursting, and she couldn't even trust herself to speak. She nodded her agreement and helped to cut and serve the lasagna without comment, trying not to think of how this would probably only be her fifth true Christmas.

She recalled the times with Kevin's father, with Charlie and Nancy, with Sofia's family when she'd been scarcely old enough to remember, that first winter with Jared before everything had gone so horribly wrong; those were the good times. She could count the number of times that the holiday hadn't ended in frustrated tears and longing for something that she knew she could never have on one hand. Today, Sofia was offering her a chance to fill out that hand and branch on to the next. She would take it, yes, she would take it a thousand times over.

Nathan asked about the game as they ate and Liza finally, with food to talk around, found words enough to ask about his homework and if they still read *The Phantom Tollbooth* in the fourth grade. This led to a discussion of the finer aspects of Milo and Tock's exploits in the Kingdom of Wisdom. Nathan was convinced that there had to be more to the story, as it jumped to the end so quickly once Milo reached the Island of Conclusions. Liza, for her part, tried to explain to him that it was all a big joke for the grown-ups who read that book to their kids.

She showed him the jump to conclusions scene from *Office Space* on YouTube before he went to bed to prove her point, and he scowled at her and asked if she was going to be sleeping over.

"That depends on your mom," Liza said. She glanced over her shoulder to where Sofia lingered in the doorway.

"There's a lot of dishes though, and I'm pretty sure that she'll put me to work." She wrinkled her nose at this and Nathan laughed—it was his usual chore. Liza reached over and mussed up his hair. Tugging up his covers, she smiled down at him. "Night kid." She retreated into the hallway as Sofia said her goodnights and shut off the light. Together they headed back downstairs.

Outside, the snow was coming down harder than before. It looked like there would be a decent amount of accumulation on the roads now, and the posts of the fence were capped with little snow hats that looked to be about three inches tall.

"Dang." Liza peered out the window in the dining room. She had her hands full of plates, but it didn't take much to see how fast it was coming down now.

"You might have to stay here after all, dear," Sofia commented from where she was packing up the rest of the lasagna in a few Tupperware containers to be frozen and dispersed as lunches once the holidays were over. "I don't want you getting lost in the snow."

"I'm pretty sure that I'd be okay." Liza rinsed off the plates and loaded them into the dishwasher before going back into the dining room for the cutlery and glasses. Those, too, were rinsed out and loaded up before Sofia handed her the Pyrex dish that she'd used for baking the lasagna. It was an older model, white and printed with flowers on the inside—the sort of bakeware Liza would expect a grandmother to have, not someone like Sofia Milton, whose kitchen was decked out in all the latest kitchen gadgetry. She supposed that it could have been the senator's, but it was Sofia's father who had liked to cook, if she remembered correctly.

She set it to soak in warm soapy water up to her elbows, grateful that she rolled the sleeves of her dress shirt up. She felt silly and out of place in this kitchen, playing house with someone who had always seemed so completely and utterly unattainable to a person like Liza. "But I don't mind staying."

"Good," Sofia said. There was a hint of darkness in her tone that Liza found intriguing. She turned to look at her as she scrubbed off crusted cheese and tomato sauce from the sides of the dish with a bit of steel wool. "I hadn't intended on letting you leave."

Liza raised her eyebrows in silent challenge.

Sofia was sitting at the breakfast bar, a glass of something dark and amber resting on the table before her. She had one finger poised on the edge.

"Is that so?" Liza asked.

"Oh, I'm quite certain," Sofia said.

Liza knew that this was what she wanted more than anything else. This was the piece that had been missing… what she had run away from last time. She ran like a coward because it was the right thing to do. She wasn't there first, and she wasn't going to deny Sofia a chance at normalcy and at least tacit parental approval.

The dish went forgotten in the sink as Liza dried her hands and drew Sofia up the stairs and into her dark bedroom. The snow was falling heavily outside, casting fluffy shadows across Sofia's crisp white sheets as they stumbled forward and landed in a giggling heap. This was all so sudden, but it was what Liza'd wanted for years now.

She was tired of running from whatever this was between them, this love that was not quite yet love, but could be love in short order. She wanted it and Sofia wanted it and finally, finally, they both could have it.

Snow fell quietly outside and the flakes filled up the panes in the windows, impervious to the warmth inside. Liza found herself babbling, her forehead pressed into Sofia's shoulder, rocking back and forth, a rhythm they'd been building to for what felt like close to a decade. She talked about how this was what she'd always wanted, how she was done lying to herself about it. She came apart promising that it would not ever be forgotten, that Sofia was utterly unforgettable no matter how hard Liza had tried to forget her. Sofia looked at her so tenderly in that moment, with wide brown eyes and fingers curling, as Liza's fumbling hands found her and began to rock her towards her release. The feeling of Sofia's breath on her lips as her eyes went wide and then squeezed tightly shut was enough to melt even the darkest of hearts. She was so warm, so welcoming, and so clearly overjoyed at Liza's presence.

It was when they were dozing afterwards, sweat-sticky skin pressed against cool sheets, that Liza finally said what had been bothering her since she'd left the school after the game. "I think that Charlie's sick." Her forearm was flung over her forehead and the other was wrapped around Sofia, holding her close. "And that's why he's letting me coach. *I* wouldn't let me near corruptible kids. Nope. Not in a million years"

Sofia hummed at the back of her throat and twisted over to set an alarm. She fiddled with her phone for a few moments before settling back into the comfort of Liza's embrace. "I think you're better with kids than you give yourself credit for. Nathan adores you."

Liza sighed. "I just hate that everyone knows how badly I messed up. I could have been the one person in this town aside from your dad to make something of myself, but I threw it all away on a shit boyfriend who knew what to say to me when I was at my absolute worst."

"Yet you've come back with your head held high." Sofia prodded Liza in the cheek with her finger. "It's more than I could have done."

Liza was sleepy and Sofia's words were blending together like a river meeting the sea, swirls of two different bodies of water trying to blend and not quite managing it. She let her eyes flutter closed before she could tell Sofia that she was stronger, far stronger than Liza ever could be.

Liza would have never carried on.

And outside, the snow fell silently onto the sleeping town.

Liza dreamt of warmth and the comfort of a home, the end to a long journey. She was standing in the woods, watching them as they filled with silent fluffy flakes, plunging the world into crisp, clean white. She was not on a horse, not like in the poem; she was just standing by the side of the road, hands in her pockets, watching the snow fall around her.

It was starting over; the past was being washed anew.

Christmas Eve in Near Haven was something of a group affair. The diner hosted a pancake breakfast and then the entire town worked together, setting up a luminaire for the night.

Liza listened sleepily as Sofia dressed Nathan in more layers than were probably needed. She was explaining that the lights were a tradition started by the miners in response to the nuns who sold their candles for wood to heat the convent school during the winter back in the day. It was their way of honoring them, Sofia added, handing Liza a pair of ski gloves and a hat that probably belonged to Nathan, because of the obnoxiously red tassel and Patriots logo stitched into the side.

Liza crammed it on over her head and they all headed out to the garage.

"I usually just save my milk jugs for about a month or so," Sofia said. She collected a large storage bin full of washed clean and capped milk jugs, and set two aside by the door; they loaded the rest into the car. "Some people save them all year."

"That's a lot," Liza said, wide eyed. She knew how fast some families went through milk. When she and Kevin had been kids, they'd been notorious for finishing off a half-gallon in a day between glasses of the stuff at dinner and bowls of cereal for breakfast and after school.

They hadn't talked much, not really anyway. Sofia's alarm had gone off at stupid o'clock and Liza'd rolled out of bed and spent a few more cold hours on the couch until Nathan had prodded her awake and promised free pancakes. Never one to turn down a free meal, Liza had rolled over and had promptly fallen off the couch. Half an hour later her ass still hurt and Sofia kept shooting her amused little grins when she thought Liza wasn't looking.

After Nathan was safely in the car, Liza hissed over the roof to Sofia. "You know, this would have been a *lot* less painful for me if you'd just let me stay."

Sofia's lips had quirked downwards. She shook her head and spoke in a whisper. "He knows…" They were both well aware that Nathan was listening in. "But I want…" She trailed off, sighing a puff of foggy breath into the morning air. Liza could see the conflict in her eyes, two warring factions of herself. "I want to tell him about us before he wakes up to find us together. I don't want him to think I'm replacing David."

"Okay," Liza said. There was really no other response. She couldn't replace Nathan's father and she certainly was not going to try. Kevin hadn't attempted to replace David either and it was working out okay for the both of them, Liza thought. They were just positive influences in Nathan's life, no matter how ridiculous Kevin was most of the time. "You guys should have a talk soon though; your couch is too short and uncomfortable."

"Yes, dear," Sofia said dismissively.

Liza stuck her tongue out at her.

The diner was crowded and Liza was a little taken aback by how many people were still in town despite the holiday and the snow. Kevin slung his arm over her shoulder and sipped coffee expertly out of the mug that he had his hook neatly tangled around. Liza laughed at him and leaned in, grateful that he was there and that he didn't mind her presence. "I got your little care package." He spoke in a low tone. "Really good fudge."

Liza smiled easily at him, watching as his own smile returned in a cheerful quirk of eyebrows and twist of lips. "Please tell me you didn't eat it all at once."

"Might have had a few pieces..." Kevin mumbled, a guilty look in his eye.

Liza rolled her eyes. The fudge that she and Nancy had made was rather rich. They'd used the recipe off of the back of the jar of marshmallow fluff that Liza picked up at Sprat's earlier that day. They'd set the trays out to cool on the fire escape while attempting a marbled batch that tasted good, but looked a hot mess. Still, it was worth it to wrap the little bundles up and write notes to everyone who'd helped her since she returned to Near Haven. She'd borrowed Nancy's beat-up old Blazer to deliver the goods before the game, while most people were at work. That way, the packages would remain in mailboxes and on back porches until their recipients returned home.

Later, Liza and Kevin sat, drinking coffee outside the diner. They watched as their breath fogged up the morning and listened to the foghorn call mournfully in the distance. The snow had drifted up to Liza's knees in places; a true Christmas storm had blanketed the town into something almost picturesque. "Are you ready for tonight?" Liza asked.

"I am, if the kids are," Kevin replied. He smiled then, slow and easy, sipping at his coffee as Christmas Eve morning grew into what precious little warmth the day was going to offer.

Liza shivered and shuffled closer to Kevin. She was still wearing yesterday's clothes and she was absolutely certain he'd noticed. He hadn't said anything and Liza was grateful for that. She didn't think she could quite explain what had happened last night, or if she truly wanted to risk putting a label on what she and Sofia were tentatively exploring.

Every year, the children who were a part of the after-school program that Kevin helped run at the library put on a Christmas Eve play. It was always carefully planned in advance; any children who were going out of town were not involved in the actual production. Liza had been in it twice, once as a snowflake and then again as a reindeer. She had been quite the show stealer,. Clearly.

This year's play was an adaptation of some TV special that Liza hadn't heard of. It told the story of a little boy who had no parents and was trying to find a home at Christmas. Liza was pretty sure that Kevin adapted it himself and didn't say much of anything when he got this wistful, nostalgic look on his face while talking about the show. She was just glad he had found something to spend his off-season doing that didn't involve risking life and limb in a tiny rowboat out in the bay.

"Six in the pot by the dock today," Kevin commented. Liza's eyebrows shot up. "Not entirely sure why they're not hibernating."

"Probably because they've only just recently remembered it's winter." Liza shivered again and glanced back towards the diner door. She wondered how appropriate it was for her to spend time with Sofia at a public event like this. They had arrived together and it was obvious for anyone who could have possibly wanted to see; but after that, they had split off into their own little social circles. Liza gravitated towards Noah and Kevin, who were sitting near the back of the diner at one of the booths, racing each other through two copies of the newspaper's daily Sudoku.

"Could be that." Kevin sipped his coffee and nodded out at the misty morning.

Later that night, Liza found herself following Sofia back inside the house that held so many secrets. She lingered for a moment at the door, then settled in next to Nathan to read him *The Polar Express* and *The Littlest Angel*. Liza tried not to think too hard about what it must be like to be so loved as a child. She would have killed for such a feeling of love and happiness when she was the age of the children in these stories—when she was Nathan's age. But back then everything kept getting worse and worse.

Sofia found a third stocking somewhere in the attic and Liza very carefully hid the small collection of presents she'd brought with her for Nathan (and the one small box for Sofia) in the hall closet. She felt like she was imposing, but as Sofia carted a sleepy Nathan up to bed and put out milk and cookies for Santa, Liza wondered if this wasn't exactly where she was supposed to be. She stood in front of the merrily crackling fire that she had helped Nathan build after dinner, her fingers resting on the mantle. She could belong here, yes, she really, really could.

A quiet buzzing from her pocket pulled Liza from her thoughts and she absently fished the phone from her pocket. Nancy was calling her, which was strange, because she was usually in bed by ten o'clock, even on a vacation day. Liza flipped the phone open and pressed the receive button. "Hey, what's up?"

There was a scratchy sound on the other end, like the phone was being jostled, and Liza could hear voices. Her stomach clenched and she glanced down at the stockings that were dangling down over the fire, not low enough to catch fire, but low enough to be worrisome. "Nancy?" Liza tried again.

"Liza?" Her voice sounded distant. It was hoarse like she had been crying and there was the dry sniffle that said maybe she still was. "Liza where are you?"

Glancing around, Liza wondered if she should tell the truth or back away from the situation. She had no idea what was bothering Nancy, but the sick feeling in the pit of her stomach drew her back to the sight of Charlie clutching his chest last night after the game. *God*, Liza swallowed and steeled her nerves. "I'm at Sofia's. We went to see Kevin's play together." She paused for a half a beat before adding the more important question: "What's wrong?"

Nancy sniffed loudly and there was a pause before she said, her voice sounding broken and unhappy, "My dad's in the hospital, Liza. He had a heart attack. They've got him in surgery now."

There was a ringing in Liza's ears. It echoed louder and louder as she reached out blindly and grabbed hold of the mantle before her. Her grip was white-knuckled and she was shaking all over. She could scarcely hear Nancy's plea for a response; her mind was racing so fast.

Charlie was the closest thing Liza had ever had to a father. He'd been a coach and a mentor to her for as long as she could remember. He was a constant, a good-natured, grouchy old man who pushed Liza harder than anyone had ever pushed her before. He was supposed to be invincible.

"Liza." Nancy's voice was shaky, and the ringing grew louder still.

Liza was standing there, shell-shocked, staring with unseeing eyes into the merrily dancing flames on the eve of what was supposed to be the beginning of a happy memory.

"Liza, can you come?"

Shaking herself, Liza blinked rapidly. There were tears stinging at the corners of her eyes and she couldn't help but wince, trying to will them away into nothingness. She had to be strong, for Nancy and for Charlie. "Yeah, I'll come. Are you at the hospital in Bar Harbor?"

Nancy made an affirmative noise and sniffed loudly. "Our attending physician's name is Williams."

Liza tried to commit the name to memory. "Okay, I'll be there as soon as I can." She was going to have to drive around the park—and she didn't have a car. She hung up the phone and stared down at it in her hand. It seemed so insignificant now, and she wanted to hurl it out into the fire, to pretend that Charlie wasn't sick and that the sick feeling of dread that had welled up in the pit of her stomach was nothing but indigestion.

She could call Kevin, but he was probably off with his librarian friend, celebrating another year's successful performance. Liza sighed and ran a hand through her hair. She didn't want to ask Sofia, because this had nothing to do with her.

There was a quiet click behind her as Sofia pushed the study door closed against Nathan's prying ears and folded her arms across her chest.

Liza knew that she must look a wreck, that it would be so completely obvious she was upset and was on the verge of falling apart.

"You look like you've seen a ghost."

Though her tone was mild, Liza could see the concern in Sofia's eyes and it made her stomach hurt even more thinking about how she could possibly tell someone that an old family friend was in the hospital, probably about to die.

Liza stared down at her phone, willing it to ring and for Nancy to come on, howling with laughter, saying that she got Liza good. It wasn't going to happen and Liza was stuck trying to swallow all that had happened. She took a deep breath. "Charlie had a heart attack. I need to go to the hospital." She said it like she was trying to stay calm, which she desperately was. She was desperate to keep her breathing level and her voice calm. She didn't want to alarm Sofia by completely falling apart; she had done that before—when she was far younger—to disastrous results.

A dry, wretched sound escaped Liza's mouth then, and she raised a shaking hand to cover it. She was going to completely lose it. Her phone fell to the floor and the fire popped happily behind her. She couldn't handle this, not again. She had to get out of here. She was about to crumple, to fall to her knees, anxiety overcoming her, when Sofia's hands closed around her own and pulled her in as close as Liza dared get. She was sobbing into Sofia's expensive silk shirt, her tears blossoming wet flowers all over Sofia's shoulder.

"Do you need me to drive you?" Sofia asked. Her fingers were tracing soothing patterns on Liza's back and

Liza wanted to snap at her, to demand that she show some fucking emotion. Charlie was a friend of her family's—had been for years. Sofia had never been particularly keen on him, but she had never actively disliked him (according to Kevin anyway) after he had said some rather choice things about her during a city council meeting a few years back. "Or do you want to go by yourself?"

Sofia knew loss and injury and heart attacks. She knew what it was like to get a phone call in the middle of the night saying that someone she loved was in the hospital. She certainly had gotten worse phone calls than the one Liza had just received.

"I don't want to take your car," Liza said. She was sniffling and didn't want to get snot all over Sofia's shirt. She was clinging to Sofia like she was a lifeline, her mind racing a mile a minute, traitorous thought after traitorous thought. "And I don't want... Nathan..."

"I'll call Kevin on the way to the hospital, he knows where the key is." Sofia pulled Liza back to standing fully upright and stared at her. She brushed the tears away from her eyes with thumbs that seemed far too practiced in the motion. "He's going to be okay," she said, but Liza could see the uncertainty that was barely hidden in her eyes.

He had to be okay.

For all their sakes.

Kevin was a little drunk when Sofia called him, but Isabelle, his librarian friend, wasn't. She listened to Sofia and promised to get Kevin over as soon as possible and to stay the night if necessary. She didn't have any family in town, Isabelle explained quickly, so it really was no trouble.

Liza was half listening to the phone conversation as they drove up the narrow road that cut through the state park and over to the hospital. The roads were icy and they hadn't been plowed or salted yet. Liza wasn't even sure if they would salt this road, given that it would be Christmas Day in twenty minutes and everyone who had any family elsewhere had already left town.

"I don't want him to die," Liza mumbled. Sofia set her phone down in her lap and put both hands back on the steering wheel. Liza didn't know how to articulate her greater fear, that Charlie was the closest thing she'd ever had to a father and if he were to go...

Liza puffed out her cheeks, trying not to think about it. Sure, Kevin's dad was there, but he'd also given her back to the city when taking care of two children had started to be too much for him. Charlie had never given up on her, not once. Even now, his judgmental comments and thinly-veiled criticism of her past bled out and Liza knew, she just knew, that he hadn't given up.

Sofia's jaw clenched tight. From where Liza sat, she could see the muscles popping on Sofia's neck and in her cheek, but she couldn't tell what she was thinking. They sped up as the car hit a straightaway and Liza curled within her coat, staring out into the wilderness. Maybe this was her own twisted version of *Polar Express*; maybe there were wolves in this forest too.

"When David fell off the boat, I knew that it was over," Sofia said. Her eyes were fixed on the road, fingers white-knuckled on the steering wheel. "I..." She faltered, but sucked in a huge breath of air and continued to speak as the silent trees of the woods around Near Haven flew past the windows of the speeding car. "I had to keep Nathan safe and I just froze. He was in the water and my father was screaming for me to throw him a line to get him out of the water. My mother was below trying to radio the coast guard. There was no one else to help him. I watched him drown because I didn't dare let go of my son."

Liza swallowed nervously. "Why are you telling me this?" She didn't understand; her mind couldn't process the information and looked for a hidden meaning behind the words. She was not smart enough for that on a good day, but now, with everything that had happened, she couldn't figure it out at all.

Sofia glanced over, before she shook her head almost sadly, turning back to the road. "Because Mr. White is not in that situation. He's in a hospital surrounded by doctors and nurses and people who care for him. It isn't a split-second decision where there is no right choice. You shouldn't worry, Liza. He'll pull through."

Between them, a great divide of ever-expanding silence grew. Liza buried her want to comfort Sofia, because there was nothing that she could say. It was all in the past now. Her own memories were not why Sofia was telling her what had happened to David. She'd never asked the specifics before, only followed her own doubts of the newspaper's coverage. She didn't think that it looked right. Why hadn't Nathan been below with his grandmother? Why had they been out in weather like that in the first place? There were a million questions that she wanted to ask, but Liza didn't dare voice her fears—not right now, not when everything was falling apart around them.

"I'm sorry about Dave." Liza had said it before and she was sure that she would say it again. Pushing all the mutinous thoughts of foul play and suspicion from her mind, she tried to remember that they were all only human. She probably would have frozen up too.

"Me too," Sofia said. She maneuvered the car around the twists and turns of the dark country road with a precision that made Liza wonder how many times she had raced down this way in the dead of night.

The hospital was not the best in the state, or even the county. The harsh lights of the ER shone like beacons out of the automatic doors as Sofia swung the Mercedes into a parking space that was blissfully close to the door. Liza was out of the car in seconds, but she waited for Sofia to button her coat more closely around herself before they hurried together into the hospital.

There was only one waiting room, and Liza noticed the huddled, weary-looking form of Nancy sitting at the edge of an uncomfortable-looking plastic chair, a half-shredded paper cup in her hands. She didn't get up when they walked in. Her eyes were fixed on something that Liza couldn't see, a specter in the darkness of the night.

"Nancy?" Liza crossed to her side in three long strides, falling to her knees beside her friend.

Nancy's eyes were red from crying and she didn't seem to see anything at all, looking through Liza as though she were glass.

"Hey." Liza tried again, nudging at Nancy's hand from where it was clenched around her decimated cup. "Hey, we're here."

Nancy was still silent, but she let out a small hiccup and tears continued to run down her cheeks like streaks of black ice, just hitting the light right to spell doom.

Liza risked a panicked glance over towards Sofia, who was speaking with the receptionist. The look went unnoticed and the worried knot that had settled at the base of Liza's stomach clenched harshly. She was pretty sure she knew what had happened and all she could think to do was throw her arms around Nancy and pull her in as tight as she could.

"I am so sorry." Liza whispered the words into Nancy's dark mop of hair. She was half-hiccupping herself, tears starting to flow down her cheeks as she felt, rather than saw, Sofia come to stand beside her. There was a hesitant touch on her shoulder and Liza knew, almost without looking, that they were too late. *Oh God, we're too late.*

Liza clung to Nancy tighter and tried desperately to muster up the will to be strong. Her resolve was shaking and all she could think about was the team and wondering how she was going to tell them what had happened. Her tongue felt heavy in her throat and she didn't dare speak. She just let Sofia's fingers tangle soothingly in her hair and wished for the world to stop.

Liza didn't know how to do anything else, and not a word was said between them.

They left the hospital at five thirty in the morning, once Nancy had signed what felt like thousands of papers the hospital required in order to release Charlie's body to a funeral home and to cover their asses in case she decided to sue. They had given her only a handful of minutes alone to say good-bye to her father.

Liza had spent the better part of the night pacing the length of the hospital waiting room, telling Sofia that she had seen the signs, but that he'd brushed them off as unimportant. Sofia listened patiently to Liza's spiraling guilt and didn't say much at all, her eyes dark and full of emotion that Liza could not place.

Now Liza sat in the front seat, clinging to Sofia's hand as Nancy stared silently out of the window, her breath fogging and drawing out the smudges and smiling faces that Nathan had drawn on the window, the ones that seemed to not fit at all with the somber mood of the car.

Liza was shaking as she clung to Sofia's hand. "What do we tell Nathan?"

Sofia's eyes narrowed, and her grip on Liza's hand tightened. "We tell him the truth." She shook her head with a determined finality. "I do not lie to my son, dear."

Liza's mind was sluggish, she knew that she desperately needed to sleep, but all she wanted was to go back to this morning. It felt like a lifetime ago, but it had been so good to have a warm, pliant Sofia in her arms without a care in the world. Now she was freezing cold despite Sofia's presence and there wasn't any warmth in sight.

"I shouldn't be there," Nancy said. Her voice was hoarse from crying and lack of sleep, but she kept it steady. "I don't want to ruin your Christmas."

Liza opened her mouth to reply, but Sofia beat her to it. "I have some...experience with what you are going through, Ms. White. I don't mind your company and I don't think you should be alone."

Turning in her seat to look at Nancy, Liza took in the red-rimmed eyes and grief-exhausted form of her disheveled best friend. She tried to smile reassuringly, but it came off a little bit as a grimace. "I want to stay with you, okay?" She bit her lip. "Charlie was, *shit*; he is one of the most important people in the world to me. I can't imagine what you're feeling, but you don't have to feel it alone."

Christmas, after the morning that they'd had, was a sleepy and sad affair. Nathan was upset when they told him why his teacher was sleeping fitfully in the guestroom and why Kevin was dozing on the uncomfortable couch, but he understood loss better than most children. Liza couldn't help but feel a swell of pride when she caught him sneaking into the guestroom to sit with Nancy, holding her hand and telling her all his happy memories of Charlie.

As she puttered in the kitchen, Liza wondered how often Nathan had had to do that for his mother. She rummaged around until she found the coffee in the freezer and brewed a strong pot, handing a mug to both Sofia and Kevin, who sat up on his makeshift bed on the couch so that she could sit next to him. Cradling the coffee to her chest, she was scared to meet anyone's eyes and admit her own weakness.

Noah came over after lunch with Rachel and they took Nancy back to Noah's house to start trying to figure out how to have a funeral so close to Christmas, particularly since Charlie had been such an institution in the town. Liza helped Nathan open his presents and smiled shyly as Sofia opened the small extravagance that Liza had been able to afford to give her. It was a stone that she'd found at the bottom of one of the traps that summer, a nearly perfect garnet that a jeweler in Bangor had been able to remove and make into a necklace for what Liza hoped was a decent price. She really had no experience with such things.

"Where did you find this?" Sofia asked. The blood-red stone caught the light and glittered prettily.

Fingers wrapped around the knee she had pulled up to her chest, Liza leaned back. "It must've chipped off of a rock down at the bottom of the ocean or something. There was a big hunk of it in a pot we hauled up this summer. I just got it extracted." She shrugged. There were veins of garnet in the rocks all over Near Haven. When she and Kevin were kids, they used to go looking for it, scrambling with scraped knees and jagged rock "chisels," trying to extract the tiny red stones when they found them along the seams of the quartz and granite that formed the shores of Near Haven. "It's a part of this town," Liza added. "Like you and I are."

Sofia smiled and it almost managed to chase away the sadness in her eyes.

Liza so desperately wanted to make her happy, but their lives were plagued by sadness, it seemed. She hated it so much, hated God and whatever it was that took people from them both so violently. Maybe it was enough to have each other. Liza didn't know.

Turning, Sofia lifted up her hair and offered the back of her neck to Liza. Liza took the fine silver chain and fastened it, lingering for a moment, her lips a hair's breadth away from pressing a kiss to the back of Sofia's neck.

Nathan glanced up at her and rolled his eyes dramatically before making a loud gagging noise and flipping the Lego set he was working on over.

Liza narrowed her eyes, leaned forward, and kissed Sofia's neck. She smiled wickedly at Nathan as Sofia leaned back into her.

"Does this mean that you're going to stay here now?" Nathan demanded. He clicked the Lego into place and flipped the instruction booklet to the next page. Beside him, the small box from the basketball team lay forgotten. Liza couldn't bear the thought of opening it now, without them around her, and without Charlie. "Because I'm really, really okay with that, so long as you're not gross," Nathan added.

"Uh…" Liza said.

"Just go with it, dear." Sofia whispered in her ear.

Liza thought she could do that.

CHARLES WHITE NEAR HAVEN'S LONG-TIME COACH: A RETROSPECTIVE

Mark Sawyer

Special to *Near Haven Mirror*

December 26, 2012

NEAR HAVEN - I first met Charlie White fifteen years ago and the first thing he ever said to me has stuck with me. I was a stranger in a town where everyone knew everyone, but he greeted me like an old friend all the same. He asked me if I could have anything in the world, what would I want. I didn't know the answer at the time, and he smiled at me, telling me that it was a good answer.

He was a wise man, a student of the game he coached. White dedicated his life to improving the quality of basketball play at all ages through his school-sponsored summer camp programs and volunteering on the youth spring development leagues. He fostered coaching and playing talent in the young women of Near Haven wherever he found it.

Under his watch, Near Haven boasted a 70 percent winning record. Coaching in more than 1,000 games over his career at Near Haven High, Charlie won more games than any coach before him in varsity ball. He brought his teams to the playoffs twelve times and won it all once, a feat that brings him among the rarified air of Maine's coaches.

Three times, White turned down the opportunity to coach the boys at Near Haven; once more he turned down a chance to coach at USM. He was deeply passionate about fostering the women's basketball talent of the area and didn't care much for the politics of the game. He coached the Maine Varsity All-Stars in 2001 to a win over New Hampshire and Vermont before eventually losing to Connecticut in the New England Classic tournament to end the season that April.

White is perhaps best known for the 2002 championship squad, led by much-maligned guard Elizabeth Hawke. Under his leadership and her stellar play, the Lady Knights rose to the rarified air of state champions, a feat that had not happened since South Bristol won it all in 1992 and has not been repeated since. After that championship match, I remember him telling me that all he could possibly ever want was for his family, his team, and his town to be happy, and that in winning, he thought that he'd made everyone's hearts soar.

Survived by his coaching legacy, White stands in a rarified air among Near Haven residents. His daughter, Nancy White, has followed in his teaching footsteps, teaching fourth grade in Near Haven.

Charlie's other legacy lies in his current assistant coach. After returning to Near Haven last summer, Liza Hawke won back the trust of her former coach and took an assistant's position on this year's squad. While some questioned White's decision to accept Hawke back into the fold of Near Haven High athletics, her influence is clearly visible in the level of play of this year's team. The Lady Knights are currently 6-0, with a preseason non-conference loss to South Portland High. There is no limit to how far this squad could go, and it now falls to Hawke to lead them to wherever the season takes them.

This reporter and this town mourn the loss of one of our own, a truly great friend and coach.

**Funeral Services are arranged for December 30 at two o'clock in the afternoon. They are to be held at the high school with a private burial ceremony to follow.

CHAPTER ELEVEN

For the Team (Dec 29—30, 2012)

THE KEYS FELT AS THOUGH they weighed a thousand pounds as Liza fiddled with them, trying to figure out which one opened the equipment room and which unlocked the empty office just off the hallway that led to the high school's single locker room. She didn't want to go in there—she didn't dare, afraid that even her presence in the room would set things in motion. She was afraid that if she were to go in there, the grim reality of Charlie's death would be driven home to her in a way that sitting with Nancy sobbing in her arms never would. Liza was trying to be the strong one, after all.

Finally the right key slid home. Liza turned the lock quickly and pulled the two racks of basketballs and the basket of freshly laundered practice jerseys out of the room before closing the door hurriedly. She didn't dare breathe when she was in that room. It somehow felt dishonest to be in there, as if she was intruding on someone's tomb.

Liza had done her game prep alone. Sitting in the basement of the library in front of their shitty CRT-TV and VCR combo, she had watched and re-watched the film of their next opponent and their last game. She had written down a list of teaching points and an even bigger list of questions to ask the team about how all this was done. Although she had done this with Charlie eight times before today, it felt like a whole new sort of a ballgame now that she was on her own.

The principal of the school had called her on Christmas Day, and demanded to know if she was still up to the position of coaching. The school board, given the circumstances, had decided that it wasn't worth trying to force Liza to "better" herself through schooling if she was suddenly stuck coaching their team without an assistant.

Liza, who had been sitting with Nathan's head in her lap, reading *The Phantom Tollbooth* to him, had replied that she was more than willing to continue coaching. She wasn't stupid. She knew that if she left too, the team would be absolutely screwed.

She hadn't realized just how screwed she was at that particular point in time.

She sighed. Charlie's canvas L.L. Bean bag was slung over her shoulder and she had set up camp in a corner of the locker room, changing out of her salty, snow-covered boots into her Jordans and settling in to re-read her notes. Nancy had dropped the bag off earlier that morning and told Liza she was welcome to drive Charlie's car or the old, beat-up, bright-ass-red, VW Beatle that was just sitting, rusting, in his garage. Liza had opted to borrow the bug car until they could figure out her transportation.

What was so weird was that she had suddenly acquired a car and she was really not entirely sure what to do about it. Kevin pointed out that it needed a great deal of work.

The paint was fading and the tires were certainly not going to maneuver well in the snow. Liza could easily slide right off the road if she wasn't careful, he'd explained. Then he offered to jury-rig her some chains until she could determine whether she could afford snow tires.

The car brought a sense of freedom that Liza hadn't felt in years. She had been pleasantly surprised that her first instinct after the offer to take on the team wasn't to run screaming from this town that had filled her up with nothing but horrible memories and incredible sadness. She thought that Sofia, with her sad smile and her tentative touches, was keeping her here and firmly grounded; and Liza wasn't about to argue with the feeling of utter contentment that lingered every time Sofia came near her.

Mark Sawyer had written an article in the paper before Charlie's goddamn obituary had even been published. Liza wanted to strangle the man for doing so, but she was glad that it'd been published the day after Christmas and not rushed to be included in the Christmas Day edition. She didn't think that Charlie would have wanted to ruin everyone's Christmas with talk of him dying.

Nestled at the top of the L.L. Bean bag was the little wrapped box that the team had given her nearly a week ago. She hadn't been able to stomach opening it on Christmas Day. It'd been hard enough to look at the box and know that somewhere, Charlie had had a present just like this one, waiting for him. A present that would never be opened.

Liza bit her lip and swallowed. Nancy hadn't asked her if she would like to speak at the funeral, and Liza wasn't really sure that she should, even if Nancy did ask. She wasn't family, which Liza thought was part of the problem. She was an outcast, a little girl lost in the great wide world who'd come under Charlie's wing for the briefest of moments, only to step away from him and lose herself once more. It didn't seem right, somehow, to take her personal feelings for Charlie and to air them publicly. Liza had never really been one for expressing herself like that anyway. She chalked that up to her childhood and the constant array of faces that didn't particularly care for her, just the checks that came in the mail for her care.

Sometimes, when Liza was really down on herself, she wondered what it would have been like if that first family had actually committed to her and adopted her. She'd snooped around enough in the town records during her long hours alone in the library basement to know that the paperwork had been started to process her adoption. She knew that the family discovered they'd been pregnant not long after that, and they sent Liza away on a holiday weekend, just as spring turned into summer. It almost made sense that Liza came back to the Milton family home at the same time of year.

She remembered that cold house and the feeling of absolute helplessness. She had been so young back then. She hadn't known what was happening, but she'd kept the secret her entire life. Liza knew that she had enough to ruin Constance's hopes of a future in politics with a few well-placed words. Yet she didn't want to do it. That had never been what she'd wanted. She just wanted to understand how a woman could become so broken that she'd want to do something like that to a child—her own child, and the child of a complete stranger.

Charlie had never seen the trauma of her past, and Liza had never mentioned it. The only person who'd ever truly seen how fucked up in the head she was had been Kevin's father, recognizing a kindred soul. He'd given her things to do with her hands, taught her hand-eye coordination on the NES, and taught her how to shoot a basketball long before Charlie ever met her.

Drawing in a deep breath of air though her nose, Liza stared down at her hands. He'd taught her many things, Kevin's father had, and yet he had never been her father. Liza had never thought of him that way, even at her lowest points. She thought of Charlie as that person. She had always thought of Charlie as that person, because she liked to imagine that her father would have been like Charlie—tough, but fair. He would have raised her into a good person who made better decisions than Liza had made over the course of her life. Her time with Charlie had only been for three impossibly short years when she was a moody teenager, desperate to escape this town, but that hadn't been enough. Liza would have given anything to have had a lifetime with Charlie as her father.

Now there was just another void to try to fill, and no hope at all of ever closing it entirely.

The realization that she was falling into the abyss of this town all over again gripped her. The problem now was that she didn't think that she wanted to leave. Liza straightened up and reached for the little box at the top of the bag. She stared down at it for a moment, before she ripped the paper off with hands that were steady for the first time in what felt like *years*. It hadn't been years though, merely days of monumental change in her life.

Inside, coiled on a Near Haven purple nylon cord was a whistle. It was… *Christ*, it was brand new and gleaming in the harsh fluorescent light of the locker room. Liza picked it up and saw that there was an inscription etched into the side of the whistle. She read it with the reverence that she usually reserved for the words of Hemmingway or Melville. "To Coach Hawke on her inaugural season, 2012-13 Near Haven High Girls' Varsity." Something had lodged at the back of Liza's throat. It settled thick and uncomfortable as she struggled to read the words fully. A dry sob escaped her lips. This was her first season. It was her inauguration as a coach. And she was going to do the best goddamn job she could. Liza slung the whistle around her neck and pulled her warm-up jacket more closely around herself. She shoved her notes onto her clipboard and headed out of the locker room, ready as she would ever be for the first practice she was going to run on her own.

The team filed in a few minutes later, standing quietly on the baseline once they'd changed into practice gear. Liza was standing at the top of the key, launching shot after shot, waiting for them to arrive, and chasing down her own rebounds. When she counted ten bodies, she walked to the middle of the court, ball resting against her side, clipboard tucked carefully under her other arm.

They gathered around her, worried and sad faces looking for emotional support to the one person among them who was probably the most fucked up. Liza promised herself to have a good laugh with Kevin about *that* particular fact later that evening, and put her game face on. "How is everyone doing?" It was probably a strange question to ask with her eyes drawn and serious as she watched them all.

"Okay," Meghan said. The others echoed her sentiments. Bri was oddly quiet; she was usually the most vocal of all the players, arguing with Liza or Charlie or both of them over the play calling. She had a head for the game, that much was for sure. "It's just crazy to think that he was there and then he was gone...just like that."

Liza nodded, because she was dealing with that as well. She dropped the ball to rest under her foot, holding it steady as she'd seen Nathan do in his soccer matches and when he was practicing in Sofia's backyard. Liza folded her arms across her chest, her clipboard jammed uncomfortably against her stomach. "The doctors at the hospital said that there was no telling with something like this. So please don't think that he was hiding something from any of you. It's a risk that everyone's got to deal with, okay? We have to carry on. We've got a good season going on right now. I want to keep winning, for Charlie."

They all nodded, determination growing on their faces. Liza knew that she could do this. It was three days after Christmas and they were all here, not off on vacations with their families. They were here because they wanted to be and Liza was *so* grateful for their dedication.

She spent the first twenty minutes of the practice talking about the matchup they had on New Year's Eve. It was a stupid-ass day to schedule a game, but Liza wanted to use the fact that it was away and on a holiday to their advantage. "The crowd won't be there," she explained. "And Northlake is really, really bad. I've spent a good deal of time going over Charlie's notes on them from last year, and watching film from this year. They don't have consistent guard play and their center is barely five seven. Bri, you and Meghan are both taller than her, which works to our advantage, as she plays down to her size, not above it."

The practice that followed was hard and fast. Liza took them to the football team's weight room afterwards and didn't allow them to leave until everyone had done at least one pull-up. Bri did seven and they were all very impressed until Liza hopped up onto the bar and fell back into the easy practice of legs locked while slowly pulling her body up and down and up and down. "What?" she asked. She'd just done her eleventh rep and was hanging from the bar and staring up at them.

"It's just… *God.*" Ashleigh ran a hand through her dirty blonde bangs and smirked at Liza through her fingers. "Sometimes it's easy to forget that you got all prison fit 'n stuff."

Liza flushed violently and pulled herself up once more, straining this time as she was going from a dead lift and had no upward momentum to channel back into the lift. She let herself drop as her chin rose up above the bar and she landed with her sore hands on her hips. "We need to be stronger," she said. "I want to win for Charlie and I want to win it *all*. We have the talent to do it and I want to see it real. Starting this week we're going to spend some time here—no lifting, but I do want you guys to be ready for it. Everyone should go home and Google some core exercises that you think might help you step up your game." She surveyed her team and put her hand forward. "I'll do anything you guys do, and I have a few ideas of my own." She smirked as she said the last bit and knew that they were intrigued. They put their hands into the circle one by one.

"Team on three," Meghan said. They counted as one, echoing "Team!" into the void that existed in all of their hearts.

Liza didn't go into Charlie's office after practice. She left it just as she'd found it earlier, shoes slung over one shoulder and the canvas bag over the other. She had notes and they were going to be practicing again on Monday morning, before Charlie's funeral. Liza, like Charlie, believed in taking Sundays off.

She stood at the back door to the gym, the one that went straight out into the parking lot, and flipped off the lights one by one. The gym went dark; only the red glow of the exit sign above her head was illuminated, and Liza nodded to herself just once. She had made her promise now, she would follow through.

The old VW Beatle, according to Nancy, had been Charlie's most recent fix-it-up project. He had been into classic cars for as long as Liza had known him, longer still by Nancy's telling. It was how her parents had met. Liza still thought it a little strange that Nancy had had a mother, once upon a time. Kevin was in the same boat, but at least Liza knew the full story there. Kevin's mother was a drunk who had run away on the back of some scruffy-looking writer's motorcycle when he was four. Liza'd been just removed from the Milton's house at the time, and she had no memories of the beautiful, dark-haired woman that Kevin had always hated with such a passion.

Liza hadn't really driven in ages, and it took a few tries for the car to crank up in the cold. She was careful with the clutch, not trusting herself on a stick after driving automatics pretty much exclusively since learning to drive in high school. Charlie'd taught her how to do that too. She bit her lip, a well of sadness surging up from deep within her. She didn't know how she was going to handle the funeral.

Liza drove home gingerly, stalling out at the stop sign downtown, the bug lurching forward as she ignored the honk from the florist's van that was sitting on her ass. She resisted the urge to flip the guy off and kept driving back towards the old foundry building at her own pace.

She had been trying to give Sofia some space after the night that they had spent together. She didn't really know if Sofia was okay with what had happened between them, but Liza was not about to ask, for fear that she wasn't. What they had said to each other that night was far more than Liza ever anticipated, so early in whatever it was that was going on between them.

Maybe it was just that she was driving a borrowed car, because she felt as though she suddenly had the weight of the world sitting on her shoulders. She wasn't Atlas and the world weighed far more than Liza could have ever possibly anticipated.

Liza shivered as she stepped inside the apartment. It was as cold as it was empty. She collapsed into a chair to unlace her boots, tossing them aside before standing to pull on a sweater from the rack by the door along with her slippers. She felt the chill of the apartment seep into her bones as she moved around on slippered feet, turning on lights and tossing her keys onto the kitchen island. She was perfectly alone, and the void in her heart that she had been ignoring since Christmas threatened to overwhelm her.

Standing in the kitchen, her hands clutched at the cold porcelain edges of the sink. Her breath came in short gasps and she was desperate to keep the air inside her lungs. She was alone, so terribly alone. She couldn't do this. She couldn't lead this team. She was not ready; she was not worthy.

Bile rose in Liza's throat and she heaved what was left of her lunch into the sink. It came up easily and without much fuss, and Liza wondered if this was what true panic felt like. Usually when she got sick like that, it would be a drawn out process, her stomach's contents heaving for hours after there was nothing left. Panic, at least, seemed to agree with her regurgitation process.

The shoes she was expected to fill were so huge that she didn't think she would ever live up to the expectations. Fumbling blindly, Liza turned on the sink and put her hand under the ice-cold water that spat stubbornly out from the faucet. She slurped water into her mouth and spat it out, feeling it dribble down her chin and get into her hair.

She hated that she couldn't handle this.

Liza twisted the faucet off and turned, slumping down against the counter and the cabinets beneath it. The knobs dug into her back and she barked out a harsh noise that could have been a wail,. She pressed the heels of her hands into her eyes and tried, desperately, not to fall apart.

Charlie was *gone*. The one person that she had thought would care about her in this town was just *gone*. His presence was no longer anywhere, and Liza couldn't handle it. He was like Kevin, like Sofia, like Nancy; he could not be replaced. Liza had so few people that she could truly call her own that it felt as though she had lost far more than just one person.

From the back pocket of her jeans, her shitty pay-as-you-go phone buzzed and Liza was afraid to answer it. Still, she pushed her weight up onto one leg and reached behind her, fishing the phone from her back pocket and flipping it open. Sofia's number was displayed on the screen. Liza did want to talk to her, despite how she terrible she was feeling. "Hey," she said. Her voice sounded like she had been crying and she sniffed loudly, brushing damp tendrils of hair away from where they were sticking to her cheeks.

"Are you at Ms. White's?" Sofia asked.

Liza heard a strange echo in the phone. She looked up, glancing towards the door before she pushed herself to her unsteady feet and headed over to open it. "Yeah, I'm here," Liza was already undoing the lock.

In the darkness of the apartment, Liza could see a shadow cast against the light that was seeping in from the crack under the doorway. She pulled the door open to find Sofia standing on the stair landing in a dark grey pea coat with a bright red scarf wrapped around her neck. Liza closed her phone, hearing it click shut against her ear as she slowly lowered it and tucked it into her pocket. "Hi."

Sofia shifted uncomfortably from foot to foot. Liza was suddenly very glad that Nancy was off trying to sort out Charlie's things with Noah and Rachel and that she wasn't there. All Liza wanted to do was wrap her arms around Sofia and cling to her like a security blanket.

"Can I come in?" Sofia asked. She was in the process of tucking her phone into her purse. "I need to" Her voice trailed off.

Liza wondered if this was going to be the buildup to another revelation that her mother was coming back to town or something equally horrible. It wouldn't really surprise Liza. Charlie had been a pillar of the community for as long as anyone could remember. It would make sense for someone, even someone as influential as Constance Milton, to return home to pay her respects.

Liza stepped aside and crossed over to the sink once more. She filled up the kettle without a word and busied herself finding her toothbrush in the travel bag that she'd dumped by the door earlier. She ran it under the water and gave her mouth a good scrubbing out, trying to spit as discreetly as possible.

As she settled herself onto a stool at the kitchen island, Sofia raised a curious eyebrow. Liza shrugged, tucking the toothbrush up on a shelf, where she was sure to forget it when she looked for it later. "I just got sick," she said. "My mouth tastes like ass and I didn't want to mix it with tea."

Wrinkling her nose at Liza's language, Sofia sighed. Her whole body was wrapped up in the motion and Liza knew that something was bothering her. Sofia pursed her lips, watching as Liza retrieved mugs and tea bags and adjusted the burner on the stove. "I see," Sofia said slowly.

Silence between them had always come easily. Liza had never struggled the way she did with Kevin or Nancy, wanting to fill the silence with idle chatter. She was just content to sit and be quiet, trapped in her own head and filled with doubts. Somehow, that was always easier than talking about things.

It took until the tea kettle whistled for Sofia to shrug off her coat. She was wearing an old V-neck sweater, with just the faintest hint of something hidden and lacy underneath.

Liza swallowed hotly and concentrated on the tea. The tea she could handle, being distracted by the suggestion of something else seemed too much right now.

"Do you still like passion fruit?" Liza asked. She'd found the box at Sprat's during a shopping trip that felt like a lifetime ago, fingers trailing over the little plastic-wrapped boxes of too-expensive tea. It had drawn her back to the summer when she'd first met Sofia as a teenager, memories of making it on a rainy June day where the temperature didn't get above fifty degrees. They hadn't done much in the way of chemistry then, sitting and watching the surf from the shelter of the library's reading nook that faced the sea. They'd been so young then, faced with what still seemed like an impossible situation.

Sofia nodded, biting her lower lip and puffing out her cheeks. She looked so small in the sea of that oversized sweater. "I haven't had it in years…" She took the mug that Liza offered her and flashed a hint of a smile. "I'm sorry to barge in like this; I know you must have just gotten back from practice."

Shaking her head, Liza raised her mug to her lips. It was far too hot to drink, but the fragrant steam that rose into the air above her was wonderful and smelled like the summer that was just a flash in the pan of this seemingly never-ending Maine winter. "Why're you here?" Liza asked. Her voice was quiet, and she was trying to convey that she really didn't mind Sofia's presence at all. She was probably the one person that Liza didn't want to hide from at this particular moment. Sofia would understand what Liza was going through right now, without ever wanting to judge her for possibly encroaching on Nancy's grief.

There was the soft sound of Sofia setting her mug down on the rough wood of the kitchen island, and Liza looked up to see her pulling her purse towards herself. Sofia rummaged around for a few seconds before pulling out a single, white envelope. She held it between her hands, staring down at the smudged pencil that labeled it, before she passed it over to Liza.

The grey smudges of pencil spanned from where the words on the label, "Summer, 1986," were written in careful letters. Liza swallowed, and flipped the envelope over. There were photos inside. Two of them. They were battered at the edges and Liza wondered how long they'd been in there.

"Wow." Liza pulled them out and leaned closer so that Sofia could look too. It was only when Liza placed them under the light that she could see why Sofia had come over. There was Liza, standing on one of the rocks that jutted up out of the hill over the town. She had a tank top on and her arms stretched out on either side of her.

The air rushed out of Liza's lungs as she saw the dark patches on her neck and arms in the picture. Her body was riddled with bruises; evidence of all that was never talked about when it came to the discussion of her stay with the Milton family over that summer. "What is this?" Her fingers trailed over the dark marks and she wondered when the senator had ever gotten so careless in her abuse.

Sofia was silent, and Liza set the first photo aside and stared down at the second one. They were both so impossibly young, in bathing suits, standing up to their knees in a tide pool. Liza was holding up a tiny crab and Sofia had seaweed on her head, grinning widely at the camera. And yet here too, the bruises were evident. They were everywhere; on Sofia's back where the single braid had slipped over her shoulder, giving the camera a clear view of the evidence: thin lines of bruising all over her back and arms.

"What the hell would possess her to take these?" Liza demanded. She flipped both pictures over so she wouldn't have to look at them anymore, her stomach turning again. The tea that had once smelled so wonderful was now making her stomach churn uncomfortably and she half stumbled away from the kitchen island, away from the pictures.

"I..." Sofia took the pictures and put them back into their envelope. She moved quickly and methodically, like she didn't want to look at them any more than Liza did. "I never knew that she'd..."

Liza scowled. "Of course you knew; she did it right in front of you."

"Because you'd broken a vase!" Sofia's hands flew to her hair and she raked her fingers through it, as though she was trying to calm herself down. "That's the only time I remember," Sofia said uncertainly. "She told me that they'd found a better home for you, so you couldn't stay with us any longer."

"Do you believe everything that woman tells you?" The counter was digging into Liza's lower back, but she was still somehow not far away enough from Sofia. "Why did you show me these?"

"You never told my mother's secret." Sofia sighed and fingered the envelope. "You were removed from our house because there was worry about abuse, but you never said a thing about it. Why would you keep that secret? What did you have to lose by telling it?"

Liza shook her head. She'd hoped—oh how she'd hoped—that she'd never have to explain this to Sofia. She didn't know where to start, because her reasoning as a child had been different from her reasoning as a young adult, and it was different still as an adult. "I was nearly four; I didn't understand what had happened to me then." She spat it out like a curse and it almost felt like one. "It wasn't until I was eleven that I really understood." Liza ran tired fingers through her hair, thinking back to that lake and how easily she could have slipped beneath the surface. She could have been free of this town then, but she'd stuck around for more heartbreak. She always had been a glutton for punishment.

Liza looked down at her hands. "I read a lot as a kid, before I started to play ball. It was the one thing I was better at than everyone else. I read anything I could get my hands on, lived in the library because Mr. Rogers was way more welcoming than most of my foster families—even the okay ones. He gave me this book that was new one day; it was called *Bastard Out of Carolina*." It seemed so silly now, her grand realization of what had happened. "It's about a girl growing up in an abusive household."

Sofia looked away. "I know." Her voice was tight. "We had to read it in school."

Even though it hurt too much to say it, Liza thought that the cruel existence that they'd both known about it growing up had to be brought to light now that they were both older and could discuss it as adults. "I got to leave," she said. "I was taken out of that house, but you had to stay." Liza shifted her weight and bit her lip nervously. "I never told because I didn't want it to get worse for you. I didn't want you to end up like me."

"My father—" Sofia began, but Liza shook her head again.

"He was never there, was he? He probably knew what was going on, but he did nothing to stop it. He just shipped you off to boarding school as soon as he could, right?" Liza watched as Sofia's jaw clenched and unclenched, knowing she had nothing to say to what had been said. "He did the right thing."

"Liza, you weren't even a part of the family and she did that, how can you..." Sofia blinked furiously, as if to force down tears, "How can you possibly ever forgive me for that?" She tapped her finger on the envelope. "I found that in an old book of my father's earlier today. I think he knew that someday you...I...one of us might want proof. My mother destroyed all the others with the pictures of David from when we were younger."

It was so tempting then, to close her eyes and to not think about what Sofia was saying...to let the meaning fly over her head and not follow the thread of logic. But Liza couldn't do it; she'd tried and tried to ignore this. Dave had just been a face about town, someone she'd never quite allowed herself to hate because he made Sofia happy. She'd never really known him, never known him enough for him to be David, at any rate.

"She destroyed the pictures?" Liza asked. She still kept her distance. She didn't know why Sofia was here, or why she thought that showing these pictures to Liza now of all fucking times was a good idea. There was bile at the back of her throat and she was trying to hold onto herself long enough to force down the urge to vomit. Again. "Of you and David?"

Sofia nodded slowly, and then she reached for her tea. Liza watched her throat work as she swallowed, and she could see that it was difficult for Sofia to do it. "Thinking about Charlie's death, I found myself remembering my father. When I found those pictures, I realized that maybe it wasn't some sort of catharsis after his death, what my mother did." She looked down into the tea cup, tugging idly on the string that Liza'd wrapped around the handle. "When my father died my mother... I don't know what happened to her. I wasn't living at the house then, and I came over as soon as I found out. She was sitting in the living room, family photo albums all around her, burning picture after picture. I have some copies, but most of them were there...a lifetime of memories...gone." She swallowed again and her breath rattled around in her chest. "Nathan's baby pictures, my wedding pictures, and pictures of what might have been."

"Pictures of me," Liza said stiffly. She knew then that what had happened to David had been an accident, that even though it seemed so suspicious, there was no way anyone would wish that much death upon their family.

"I never kept them," Sofia said. "It was too painful." She picked up the envelope and stared down at what had to be her father's handwriting. "I don't think my mother knows that he saved any of these."

"Then why show them to me?" Liza had wrapped her arms around herself and felt like a total fool. This was the worst possible thing for her to hear right now, and the urge to bolt from this horrible place and all of its bad memories was almost overwhelming. Adding these terrible memories into the mix was enough to make Liza actually consider it. Sofia had terrible timing, but it seemed to Liza that her reasoning was sound. She couldn't run away, no matter how much she wanted to. "Why now of all fucking times?"

Shoulders slumping, Sofia sighed. She pushed the envelope with one finger into her purse and bridged her fingers together around her crossed legs. "I... I don't know. I found them and I thought—I stupidly thought that you'd want to see them."

Maybe it was because Liza had had enough of alienating people who made her feel emotions, but she pushed herself forward and stepped towards Sofia. If it was revelation time, Liza had one of her own, and it was one that she thought Sofia needed to hear to understand why she had never told. "When I read that book, I realized what happened to me in that house. I went up to the lake." She gestured vaguely to where the lake (which was really more of a pond) was located, up over the hill and away from town. "And I tried to sink down into the water there."

There was a pallor that came over Sofia's face then. She was gifted with her father's skin, olive-colored and gorgeous even when the winter pale set in for most people.

Now though, she looked as white as Liza, shock coloring her features. "You...you were a child."

"No one would have missed me." Liza took another step forward, her hands resting on top of where Sofia's were bridged on her knees. "I had no Charlie then, no Kevin—shit, not even Kevin's fucking dad at that point. I had Beth, the worthless social worker, and the harsh reality that no family in town wanted me. Mrs. Hubbard's group home got real old after a while." Sofia's hands were shaking under Liza's fingers and she kept her gaze steady. "They'd just told me I was being shunted away again, into a new home that could take me for a while. Not permanently, mind you, never permanently. And I just wanted it to stop."

"But you didn't..." Sofia started.

"No, I didn't." Liza's cheeks were burning when she admitted this next bit, her deepest secrets were all bubbling up to the surface today, it seemed. "I thought about you and how even though I threw off the balance in your house, you always welcomed me. I was not even four years old, but still I knew that you were there and that you would feel sad if I wasn't there anymore."

Liza bit her lip and met Sofia's brown-eyed gaze evenly, daring her to say anything about how she was only eleven at the time, and how the hell could she possibly have known then? The accusation never came, just sadness and comprehension and the steady breath in the cold air of this poorly insulated apartment.

"I wasn't sad when you left, Liza." Sofia's voice came evenly and rose with the steam of the tea into the air. A promise of all that was, is, and could be between them. "I was heartbroken."

"I was a fool," Liza said. She had lied to herself for so long about Sofia that she was finally at the point where she could be honest. "Permanence isn't a thing I really get."

"I'd figured," Sofia said. She'd curled her fingers up to wrap around Liza's, twining them together, stripes of skin that blended into one entity. They fit together so well, and Liza realized in that moment that she had always been a fool. "I didn't want to upset you, but I…I wanted you to see them and I thought that you would have wanted to see them as soon as possible."

Liza tilted forward on slippered toes and pressed her lips to Sofia's forehead. "I'm not angry with you," she said. "It's just…those are a lot of memories for me."

When Sofia nodded her agreement and relaxed somewhat into the loose hug that Liza had pulled her into, Liza knew that they were going to be okay. She bit a piece of loose skin on her lip and buried her nose in Sofia's hair. She smelled of sunlight still, even in the dreary depths of a Maine winter just underway. And it was peaceful.

Liza didn't go home with Sofia that night, retreating to her cold bedroom and settling into an uneasy sleep instead. Charlie's funeral was going to be a challenge, and all she could think about, as she counted the exposed beams of raw wood in the ceiling over and over again, was that it was going to be a good-bye she was not sure she could stomach.

Liza was scarcely awake when Kevin arrived to collect her in the morning, inspecting the red Beatle outside and humming his approval. "You're gonna need snow tires on that wicked bad," he said. He had a cup of coffee in his hand from the diner and a suit on that looked like it was the same one he had graduated high school in. The tie, at least, was new.

She was wearing dark blue, because she didn't own a funeral-appropriate black dress. The sweater dress went down to her knees and she was wearing grey knit tights under her boots. "I feel underdressed." She shrugged on her coat, liberated one of Nancy's chunky-knit scarves from the rack, and wrapped it around her neck. Then she zipped up her jacket before taking the coffee from Kevin with a raised eyebrow. "None for you?"

"I have one in the car." He fiddled with his hook for a second before letting it drop to his side. "And no second hand to carry."

Inclining her head, Liza ushered him out of the apartment and back down the stairs and out of the building. His truck was idling, exhaust from the muffler rising with steam into the frigid morning air. "I'm not ready for this," Liza said.

She had never been to a funeral of a person that was close to her before, but she had been to so many in her life now that it seemed like a regular occurrence. Not recently, but growing up. People in Near Haven lived and died here; a never-ending cycle of small-town America.

"No one ever is, Liza," Kevin replied. There was a strange note in his voice and Liza knew that it was because he had done this before, just like Liza, for a father who'd forsaken him. "No one ever is."

They picked up Billy from his house on the outskirts of town before circling back to the high school. Billy had put his car into storage until he could officially return from Newfoundland in March—and would be carless until Kevin drove him to the airport on Thursday. Liza sat between them and listened as they chatted about the projected catch this season and if Billy thought that he could make it through without too many near-death experiences. It was all so very mundane, and Liza wanted to say that she hated it already. Today should be about Charlie and his family. The family that Liza was not a part of.

They sat in the back of the church, the three of them all in a row. Liza could see that Noah was sitting with Leslie and not with Nancy, and Liza's heart ached. This was about appearances and grief. Sofia was sitting with Nathan, alone and by herself. Her mother was nowhere in sight, thank Christ.

There was no body, which was Charlie's wish. There was only a small urn, containing all that was left of him. It was made of pewter and ornate in design, gorgeous when Liza looked more closely.

A lump welled up at the base of her throat and she tried to force herself to make sure that yes, one by one, the entire team came in. Something strange was happening. They were coming up to her, touching her shoulder and trying to keep themselves together. And it was not just them. Liza saw former teammates, kids from the rec leagues, people who had been touched by this man.

In the middle of it all, Nancy sat alone. Her mother was long gone, and now her father was gone as well. The only child of only children, she was alone in the world, mourning a father beloved by so many.

And Liza's heart broke all over again.

She leaned against Kevin's shoulder and touched his hand. "I'm sorry that I didn't come home for your dad's funeral," she said.

Billy shifted on her other side, but was silent.

Kevin's jaw was tight, but he turned and managed almost a smile. "It's hard to be eighteen and trying to deal with something like this; be grateful that Nancy's got a few years on that."

"I—" Liza began, but Kevin shook his head, effectively cutting her off.

"I understand why you didn't come back, Liza." He puffed out his cheeks as he said it, and nudged her with his shoulder. "I don't blame you, I don't think I could have handled it very well either."

"Still." Liza's eyes prickled at the corners as salty tears stung the chapped skin there. "I'm sorry all the same."

Kevin squeezed her hand and they sat in silence until the end of the service.

Later, they all ended up sitting in the living room of the empty bed and breakfast, a bottle of vodka that Rachel had found somewhere passed around between them. Nancy was leaning against Noah, but her hand was clenched around Liza's. Ted was there, but Leslie wasn't. Liza supposed that that was probably too weird for her still.

A short while later, Liza was drunkenly rambling about how this one time, Charlie threatened to make her run around the whole goddamn island to prove a point.

"Would you have done it?" Ted asked. He leaned forward, pulling the bottle from her hands. He took a swig and made a face before handing it to Kevin who tilted it back with a wink in Ted's direction and far too many lewd slurping noises for the rest of them.

They pelted him with pillows and socks and empty paper cups.

"Probably," Liza admitted. She glanced towards Nancy, catching her red-rimmed eyes and smiled, "I would have done anything for your dad. He was sort of like my dad too."

"I know, Liz." Nancy pulled herself away from Noah and flopped onto Liza.

Liza held her tight, never wanting to let her go. Nancy had been so sad, so fragile, and Liza understood it. She could be a pillar of support for Nancy, just as Nancy had one for her.

Liza was not used to being the strong one, but she thought she could be okay at it. It was in that moment, slightly drunk and surrounded by good friends, that Liza decided she was going to stay in Near Haven, once the season was over.

CHAPTER TWELVE

Piecrust Promises (Jan 23, 2013)

Athletics were founded on routine, and by habit. They were all about doing the same things day after day to create habits and translate those habits into performances on the court. Liza had spent her entire life falling in and out of carefully regimented routines. She set them up without even thinking, moving in and out of her day-to-day life knowing that the future was only as certain as she could be predictable.

They had lost one game since Charlie's death against a non-divisional opponent that had far outclassed them in almost every statistical category. The team was undefeated within their division, and Liza had been fielding calls from colleges about Bri and Meghan. They were both being recruited, as Liza had been all those years ago.

Liza's heart swelled with pride when she spoke to the coach from the University of Hartford—the coach who *remembered* the championship run from eight years ago—and told the woman a bit about Bri's numbers and her measurable statistics and overall player ability. Bri was tearing it up right now, and Liza knew that she could

translate her play into a ticket out of Near Haven, out of
Maine, and maybe even out of New England entirely. Liza
wanted that for her, because Bri was so much bigger than
this tiny town in this backwards state.

Liza had spent the morning very pointedly not
watching tape or preparing for practice. It was the first
time since Charlie's death that she hadn't ventured into the
basement of the library to use their TV. Instead she spent
the morning sitting in the corner of the shared conference
room down the hall from Leslie Burke's office, helping
Kevin set up the projector and video conferencing system
that they had borrowed from the high school. Her leg was
bouncing a mile a minute and Liza could feel her heart
thudding in her chest. She was nervous, almost desperately
so, and she wanted this to be *over*.

"Are you ready for this?" Kevin asked. He jabbed
the power button of Leslie's laptop with his thumb and
positioned it so the far end of the table was clearly visible
to the webcam that they had attached to the top of it. "Billy
said you told him you weren't sure it was going to work."

Crossing her arms across her chest, Liza snorted.
"Billy's got a big mouth." She scowled pointedly. He had
been gone for close to two weeks now, back off to Canada
where there was more money than God to be made,
provided you didn't fall off the damn boat in the process.
"And all I said to him was that I was worried that this
wasn't going to work out. The judge is a wicked hard-ass,
and he's been dragging his feet something fierce on this.
This is the second time we've tried to do this."

"Oh, I am aware." Kevin waggled his eyebrows
suggestively and then turned, blinking at the computer.

He only had one hand to operate it, but it was going pretty smoothly, all things considered.

Liza resisted the urge to smile. She didn't think it would look right if she did though, and her nerves were getting to her as it was.

"I think I have this set up correctly this time, at least."

"I'll have Leslie check it when she gets in," Liza said. She tugged at the sleeves of the slightly too short blazer she was wearing and worried at her lip. The anxiety that had twisted into a painful knot at the base of her stomach had only intensified as the day went on. The blazer was Nancy's, old and vintage and probably from that thrift shop over in Bar Harbor that she liked so much. Liza had thought about asking Sofia if she could borrow something a little more modern, but it just seemed wrong, somehow, to ask for something like that. Nancy was more her size, anyway. Sofia had less in the shoulders and more in the breasts. Nancy was a better fit for Liza—her style, however, was not.

Liza sighed and leaned back against the wall, her arms crossed over her chest. She was trying to ignore the ache of her muscles and the bags under her eyes that she had smeared with far too much concealer in the bathroom just now. She wasn't sleeping, not really anyway. She was making promises to herself like it was going out of style. Promising that she would stop lying to herself about how nervous she was, and how she wished that she could stop ending up on Sofia's doorstep, desperate and alone, night after night. She promised herself she would not knock, she wouldn't wake Sofia up, but somehow Sofia was always there and pulling her inside without complaint.

They were more than fooling around now. Liza was breaking another promise to herself. She had sworn that she was going to be respectful of Sofia's need for space.

And somehow, it all felt heavier.

"Do you think that you'll be able to get through this?" Kevin's tone was even, but he knew Liza better than most, and was able to pick up on her moods. He could sense when she wasn't coping well with stress. "I mean... It's your freedom."

Liza stood stock still, picking at some imagined lint on her jacket as the chat program booted up and the camera came to life and she was face-to-face with the blank grey background. The Skype icon was just below the trashcan and she wanted, desperately wanted, to delete the program and be done with it. Maybe if it wasn't there, she wouldn't have to face this.

Kevin stepped forward, his hand resting on Liza's shoulder, and pulled her into an awkward, one-armed hug. He smelled like the sea and wood smoke from the stove that heated his house; like home and comfort and everything that Liza still wasn't quite sure she deserved. "You'll be fine," he said. Liza gave a slight hiccup and tried to back away. "You're a fighter."

Fighting was what she had been raised to do. Fight and scrape and bargain for every bone that was thrown her way. She was the boxer in that song, but her story, unlike the one described in the song, was told often and it was that constant retelling that had gotten her into a world of trouble. She rested her forehead against Kevin's shoulder. "I told Sofia not to come, today."

"They're not going to ask for character references?" He sounded more curious than anything else, and when Liza shrugged, he offered to stick around. "I haven't got anywhere to be until three, anyway."

"No, it's okay," Liza said. If it came to needing references, she already knew who she wanted her references to be. She and Leslie had discussed it with the principal of the high school and Sofia, if it truly became necessary. Liza wanted the references to come from people with whom she didn't have strong connections, people who could look past her and be objective about the whole thing. "We were going with Noah and Mrs. Hanneway anyway—they're both relative outsiders who didn't know me before I came back." Liza lowered her voice conspiratorially. "Leslie actually suggested Mr. Spencer as well."

"But he's an ass" Kevin shook his head. "I can do it if you want, Liza, but I get why you'd want objective people involved."

"Yeah, it sucks, but I'm glad you understand." Liza rubbed at the back of her neck and backed away from Kevin's hug.

Leslie came into the room, bearing an arm full of papers and wearing leggings with thick wooly socks and a smart business suit jacket and blouse. Liza wondered if she wasn't bothering with pants just because they were going to be sitting, and she wanted to be comfortable—since this was fake court anyway. "Mr. Jaspen." Leslie offered him a hand.

He swept away from Liza to take her hand and allowed Leslie to set down all of the papers in her arms before he smiled charmingly at her.

"Do your best," he said earnestly. "For Liza and for the rest of us. She fell off my boat in November! I can't have such a liability on my crew if she can be doing other work."

"Hey!" Liza protested. "I didn't mean to fall off."

"Oh, I know." He laughed. "You have the sea in your veins, that's for sure."

Leslie watched them laugh with a mild expression of amusement on her face. Since they met each other, Liza had learned that it took a lot to set Leslie into anything that could be considered a mood; she was even-keeled and hard to upset. Liza liked that about her, because it meant that she could take Kevin's good-natured ribbing for what it so transparently was. He was trying to draw both of their minds off of what was about to happen, trying to put her back into the moment without pulling her aside and promising her things that he could not deliver upon.

"Are you ready for this?" Leslie asked. She settled the stack of papers around her in a way that looked prepared and professional, watching as Liza crossed the room and pulled Kevin into a tight hug. She was in borrowed clothes, just like the last time, but at least she wasn't scared and alone. She nodded to Kevin, who saluted her with his hook, before turning on his heel and walking out of the conference room.

"I think so." But Liza was being less than honest, and another promise to herself crumbled around her. She was trying to be more confident, to channel Charlie when she could not think of anything else to do. Charlie would have never backed down from a fight, or a bad call. He got T'ed up more times than Liza (or Charlie had) cared to admit, but it had all been for a good cause. Bench warnings and technical fouls were his bread and butter. He fought for the kids on the team because he had to; he was their leader and he had to make sure that they were cared for to the best of his ability. He had to do that, even if it meant getting ejected from the game, as he had that one memorable time. They'd ended up playing man defense for the rest of the night because the assistant coach at the time was a total moron.

Liza had to be like Charlie now, because this was her future.

The judge in Oregon was incredibly understanding about the fact that they were three hours ahead of him and completely across the country. There were three thousand miles between them, and somehow, as the Skype call rang, Liza couldn't help but feel like it was not far enough. She was face-to-face with a man who worked for the same people who had ruined her life, once upon a time, and she could hardly bring herself to keep from recoiling away.

Leslie had her hand on Liza's leg, stilling it as it started to bounce nervously. Leslie made pleasantries and waited while the judge started his recording program. She was already running her program in the background.

"This is highly unusual." The judge chuckled. He was a round-faced man with dimples at the corners of his mouth. His hair was shaggy and greying, swept back with gel that made him look menacing, rather than the youthful look Liza was pretty sure he'd been going for. The years hadn't been kind to him, Liza realized. When she'd first met him, he'd been significantly less grey about the ears. "But the circumstances dictate that we should do it this way."

Leslie inclined her head, "Thank you for your consideration, sir."

Liza shifted, the whole world seemed to have come down to this one moment. Leslie was a warm presence beside her, reassuring as she spoke through her points and talked about how Liza had established herself with a strong support network here in town and how Leslie thought that it would work a lot better for Liza in the future if there were less obstacles to achieving gainful employment.

It was hard to think about how much Liza had bounced around, watching faces and names and the people of her life drift in and out. She had lied to herself about Sofia for so long that she had almost convinced herself that it wasn't real, and Sofia's hurt eyes haunted her even now.

"Well, Ms. Hawke, what have you been up to for the past few years?" The judge asked the question, and Liza could feel her jaw working and saw herself visibly swallow in the small window at the bottom of the screen showing them what the judge saw. Nervousness overtook her. She didn't know how to explain what she had been doing, just that she had never been able to shake the feeling of being an abject failure at everything

Leslie touched her thigh, steadying it from its bouncing, and nodded once. They had talked about this. They had planned this down to every angle, every second, every last moment. She had to demonstrate who she was and explain to him why the record had become a scar on her life that she could never escape.

"I've been traveling." Liza started ticking off her destinations on her fingers.. "When I was released, I had my bus ticket printed up for Vegas. I wanted to go someplace where I could be completely anonymous after being in prison, you know?"

The judge nodded and made a note; Liza bit her tongue and the implications of all that going to Las Vegas might have meant fell silent around them.

"I got a job in a diner on the edge of the city. We got truckers, mostly, a few tourists. I think I worked there for six months before they realized that I had a record and told me I couldn't work there anymore. I'd saved up some money, plus I had the settlement money, so I bought a bus ticket to St. Paul and lived in a sustainable energy community—"

"Come again?" the judge asked.

Liza glanced over to Leslie, her eyes wide and fearful.

Leslie nodded encouragingly and Liza sat up a little straighter and began to explain once more. "A sustainable energy community. We tried to have as small a carbon footprint as possible. It was pretty cool, but I couldn't find a job and eventually left. I got another job waiting tables in Chicago, which lasted nearly a year before someone googled my name and I got found out again."

"Did you ever lie on a job application?" the judge asked. He leaned forward slightly.

It was a reasonable question to ask, and one that Liza had been prepared to answer for some time now. She had never actively lied on any legal document and she had never left anything out. It was more of a situation of, they didn't ask and Liza didn't tell. She thought that that was a totally reasonable thing to do, honestly. She was just worried that it wouldn't seem that way to anyone who hadn't been in her shoes and understood just what sort of desperation bred the want to lie in the first place.

She shook her head. "No, sir, I didn't. These jobs were all word-of-mouth. There was never a formal application process. I filled out a W-4 in Vegas, but the restaurant in Chicago paid me under the table. I paid my taxes on my tips, before you ask."

"I have the records right here, Ms. Hawke." The judge chuckled.

Liza's heart ached for the other grouchy old men in her life. Charlie was gone, though, and while Chet was older and definitely grumpy, he was way more of Nancy's friend than Liza's. She had earned the dubious title of his homebrew tester, however, and Liza was pretty sure that pork spices should never go into beer, ever.

"And I have done my homework on your case. It seems like you've been trying to find yourself for a while?"

"I think that's a good way to put it," Liza agreed. "I spent some time in Knoxville and then I moved on to Raleigh, before I finally realized that I needed more help than I could provide myself." She looked down at her hands and sighed. This was over a webcam, everything she said sounded tinny and somehow insignificant, but she was doing this for her life. "I came back here because it's the only place where I still have roots, and I was getting sick of not having any."

"And now you're working for the high school there?"

"Yes." Leslie cut in smoothly and Liza shot her a grateful glance. "Ms. Hawke was offered an assistant's post on the basketball team here, she has since inherited full coaching responsibilities following the head coach's fatal heart attack."

"I'm very sorry to hear that," the judge said.

Liza was shocked to hear a hint of kindness and actual, real-sounding sympathy in his voice. She didn't know that people were capable of empathy, especially a judge who sent people to jail on a daily basis. It didn't seem real, somehow.

"And this position is steady?"

"When the season ends I'll probably go back to helping out on my friend's lobster boat," Liza said. "And then I was thinking about taking on the summer camps that Charlie used to teach about fundamentals—of basketball that is." She shrugged then, borrowed jacket riding up her shoulders and scratching at her ears uncomfortably. It was probably from the eighties, buried in some thrift store that Nancy had found, because she was good like that, and Liza was pretty sure that if she didn't scratch that itch soon she was gonna go nuts. She took a deep breath and pulled herself back to the moment. "The reason I want my record expunged is so I can be a legitimate employee of the school district. Because of Charlie's—" She choked up, the words dying in her mouth as she said them. She had never actually said them, and her eyes darted desperately to Leslie, who smoothly segued into discussing their reasoning for trying to get her record expunged.

Liza tuned it out for the most part, pressing the palms of her hands into her eyes again and trying to force herself to think straight. Charlie had been dead for a month now. The team was rolling through the conference. Liza wanted to feel like she was carrying on as well. She wanted to feel a lot of things; but, despite her want for normalcy, she didn't think she was holding herself together very well at all.

However, Liza thought of Charlie and what he would have wanted from her in this moment. He would wish that she'd concentrate on what was going on. Liza sniffed to cover up a quiet chuckle that threatened to bubble out from within her and looked up at the screen once more. The judge was looking at some papers. There was a pen in one hand and he was ticking off what looked to be a checklist as Leslie talked, slowly and steadily.

It was strange really, that Liza had found herself back in this town, and no matter her intentions upon arrival, she found herself wanting to stay. She had promised herself, initially, that she would only stay long enough to get herself back on her feet, but she knew now, there was more to it than that. Near Haven was the sort of town that drew its residents into its perpetual cycle of hell. You never wanted to leave after a while it seemed.

"I can fax you the paperwork?" Leslie asked. There was a pleasant tone in her voice and she was smiling, wide and triumphant.

The judge was shuffling the papers in front of him, setting them into a neat stack. He looked up and met Leslie's eyes with a pleasant smile all his own.

Liza *felt* that smile, even though it was all pixelated and small. The surge of approval welled up within her and she found herself smiling brightly back at the judge, even though the smile was directed not at her, but at her lawyer. She felt as though she had waited almost eight years for this sort of acceptance, for the understanding that this had never been her fault in the first place. She was, after all, the perfect patsy.

No matter how many times she thought about it, Liza hated how easily she had allowed Jared to manipulate her. She had been so desperate to forget, completely absorbed in her need to be a person that wasn't some nobody from Near Haven, Maine. Jared had swept in with a charming smile and had chased all the regret from her mind. She was able to be a new person with him, one who wasn't ruled by a terrible childhood and the misfortune of falling in love with the wrong person at the wrong time. And she'd almost been able to forget, to downplay how she felt about Sofia into nothing more than the woman who'd tutored her to get her a passing grade in chemistry and biology. She'd almost managed to fool herself with Jared, even though it had all been a lie.

"Thank you," Liza said to Leslie later. They were sitting in her office, feet up on the desk and a bottle of wine between them. Liza was not much for wine, but she had decided not to turn it down, because Leslie had offered and she did feel like celebrating. "I had no idea it would be so easy."

Leslie shrugged, straw-colored hair falling over her shoulders against the coal grey of her jacket, like sunlight creeping into the darkest of spaces. "There's a lot of precedent—mostly for drug-related cases, but it's easy to point out where judges have done similar things for the wives, girlfriends, and probably even the drug runners of much bigger fish." She tilted her head back, and her smile was easy and kind.

Liza felt the wine's buzz at the back of her head and she couldn't help but feel that even though she was sitting here celebrating the expunging of her record, she was still out of place. She was the fallen son, the failed child who had come crawling back to what was known and what was easy when everything else blew up in her face. And yet, here, in that moment, she felt joy at that failure and she didn't understand why.

She knew that Leslie helped her with her case to distract from her own personal problems. Leslie's divorce was final now, and there were signs emerging everywhere that indicated both she and Noah had moved on. Ted wasn't afraid to be seen with Leslie in public anymore, and people didn't whisper behind their hands nearly as much as they used to if Nancy and Noah happened to go hiking together.

The entire town knew that Leslie had cheated, though, and Liza wondered if helping her was Leslie's penance. Perhaps this was Leslie's attempt to find redemption from her own perceived slight against the town as a whole. Liza hated that small-minded mentality, because small towns were so irritatingly insular, that something as innocuous as falling out of love with someone was under a microscope from the first stirrings of problems. They blamed Ted more so than Leslie, but Liza had seen the judgmental old ladies down at the diner and at Sprat's sometimes, looking at Ted and Leslie together and shaking their heads. They made Liza want to scream, because they were all so closed-minded.

"I sort of hate this town," Liza said. Leslie had refilled her glass and raised it in a toast to their success.

"Oh?" Leslie's eyebrows shot up. "Why? Is it the smell? Or the fact that no one can get the hell out of here?"

Liza stuck out her lower lip and chewed on it thoughtfully, debating actually drinking the wine in her glass. She probably shouldn't, since she still had to get home to tell Nancy how things went and would see Sofia later. She could hardly sleep alone these days.

"They're so...judgy," Liza said. Leslie threw her head back and laughed, long and loud. It felt good to hear her happy, and Liza grinned widely.

"It's a small town, Liz; it's sort of how it goes." Leslie glanced at her watch and made a comical face of alarm at it before downing the rest of her wine in one prolonged gulp. "Speaking of, I have to go give them something to talk about."

Liza tilted her head to the side. "What?"

"Noah and I are having dinner tonight. We were always better as friends, even in high school." She laughed and then shook her head ruefully, reaching for the wine cork. "I have no idea why we got married. Guess it was the thing to do after college, since we'd stayed together that long."

"Guess so," Liza said. She downed the rest of her wine and reached for her coat, pulling it on over Nancy's stupid itchy jacket and scowling as the tag scratched the base of her neck. "You'll have the town all a-twitter before the night's out." She grinned.

Leslie caught her by the arm at the door and smiled widely at her. "Thank you for letting me work on this case. It...well, I guess it provided a good enough distraction that I was able to be objective about what was happening between myself and Noah."

The smile that Liza returned was small, mostly because she was fully aware of how it must look, to take charity like this. The town would probably talk of nothing else until she won another five games in a row or something equally insane and unlikely. "Thank you. I don't think I could have done this without your help."

"I think you'd be surprised," Leslie quipped. She gathered her coat and slipped her feet into the salt-splattered pair of winter boots that had been drying over the air vent since Liza's arrival earlier that morning. "You're pretty capable, Liza. Just look at the basketball team."

Liza supposed that she was right. The team was rolling and would probably win the regular season title in two weeks. After that, it was the playoffs and they were anyone's guess. She had always hated the playoff system, but she knew that doing well in it would be good for Meghan and Bri. Liza was still a little bit in awe at some of the schools that were looking at Bri—and seriously considering offering her a spot on their squads, at that. Bri's numbers were outstanding and she had a chance to play at a really high level if Liza put her in touch with the right people. She felt as though she spent the better part of the past month trying to remember her own recruitment, and how Portland State had been able to win her over. Bri hadn't taken any official trips yet; she had said she was waiting until after the season was done because of travel and academics. Liza just hoped that she actually got to see some games when she did go on official visits.

Liza's mind was wrapped up in thoughts of the team and the missed calls and voice mails that were left unheard on Charlie's desk phone at the high school. Liza didn't know his password and she didn't want to. That was still his space. She refused to trespass there. Besides, the team was totally cool with Liza running her office out of the basement of the library most days anyway. A lot of them had younger siblings in Kevin's after-school program, so even the parents were behind the idea of Liza working there, since she didn't have a TV at home to watch film on.

With a nod and a grin at Leslie's bright smile, Liza headed out. She left Leslie to lock up and picked her way back towards the old foundry building, knowing that Nancy, and probably Kevin, would be waiting for the results of the hearing. She had texted them already, relaying the short version of events, but there was a nagging feeling she couldn't shake that she really shouldn't be telling anyone such important news in a text.

She knew that they were going to want to see her, but somehow...somehow it didn't seem right to go to them first. Liza's boot planted itself into a snow bank and she turned, a glance at her watch telling her that it was five thirty and knowing that there was a really good chance that Sofia was still at her office.

The city hall was covered in snow, and the windows were mostly dark. There were a few lights on here and there, but the building just loomed large and dark as she approached it. Liza wanted to swallow nervously as she slipped through the door and into the building. City Hall smelled like an elementary school, it always had; the scent of old crayons and damp rugs permeated the place. Liza wondered if she would find a stash of crayons as old as the building itself, the wax melted into a swirl of color along the pipes if she were to lift up the floorboards.

Sofia's office door was cracked open, and she was sitting in a pool of light from her desk lamp. Her fingers were tangled in her bangs as she read a report, her lips pursed and her brow creased. Even drowning in work, she looked beautiful. Liza's breath caught, just looking at her.

Liza nudged the door open with her foot, sticking her head in. "Hey." She knocked after the fact, as the door swung open.

Sofia looked up sharply. Her expression softened as she saw Liza, and Liza scooted around the door and closed it behind her.

"How'd it go?" Sofia set her paper down and pushed the stack before her into a more neat and orderly pile with her index finger.

Liza knew that Sofia was trying to sound blasé, and that she was glad that Liza had come. Sofia wanted to know, Liza knew that she did, and she was tempted, oh so tempted, to play coy with her, just to see what would happen. Liza jammed her hands into her pants pockets, standing in the middle of Sofia's office and smiled at her. She was caught up, thinking of that summer day that felt like ages ago, when Sofia had told her to go see Leslie. She wondered if she would feel vindicated at the news. "My record is expunged; they're signing the paperwork tomorrow, probably. After that it's a two-week wait for all the federal and state databases to update and remove my arrest record from their systems."

A smile blossomed on Sofia's lips and Liza found herself grinning brightly back at her, the large desk separating them. Liza shifted from foot to foot and her grin widened.

"So you were never arrested," Sofia clarified.

"Not according to the cops and any background check service that knows how to use Google," Liza replied. She chuckled at the idea, but she knew that it was still a really big concern. Everyone googled people these days; it was bound to be a problem at some point in the future. "Leslie thinks that I should talk to Mr. Sawyer at the paper and do a sidebar sort of piece if the season continues as it is going. She thinks that getting the word out publicly will help to establish that I... I guess that I turned my life around." Liza rubbed the back of her neck, feeling stupid even saying it that way.

Sofia stood up, gathering her stack of papers and tucking them neatly into her briefcase, logging off of her computer with one hand. "It's a good idea," she said. She zipped the leather case shut and stood there for a moment, her hands resting on top of it, just looking at Liza. There was a tension about her neck and shoulders that set Liza on edge, and she wondered if it was because of the implications of what a clean record meant for her. "I'm happy for you." Sofia's smile was almost sad.

"Thanks," Liza said.

Liza felt a surge of sadness when she saw the look in Sofia's eyes. It was as if Sofia knew that Liza had also been thinking about what this all meant, as if she too had thought about it. Liza hated that Sofia even had to question her, but truth was that she had a history of running from things when they got too hard and too complicated. Liza knew that this was what she deserved.

Sofia looked down and fiddled with the zipper on her briefcase. "Are you going to leave then, since you're free of the burden of your own poor choices?"

Even though she had been expecting it, Liza winced. If there was anyone in town who would treat such happy news with trepidation, it would be Sofia. "I…" Liza started to speak but swallowed as the words welled up and got stuck in her throat. She knew that Sofia was just barely managing to ask her question without losing her cool, and Liza knew she shouldn't stumble in her response. The words tumbled from her lips, unbidden and angry. The emotion of the day was all wrapped up in one outburst. "I did that once; I would never do it again. I swear it."

"That's a piecrust promise," Sofia said quietly. "Easily made and broken."

"You have *got* to stop watching that movie." Liza folded her arms over her chest and scowled.

Sofia glowered at her from behind the shadow of her bangs, which had fallen into her eyes and made her look far more upset than she sounded.

"I don't want to leave, seriously. For the first time in my life, I like my life. I like what I'm doing right now; what I did over the summer with Kevin was great too. The school board probably wants me to take over for Charlie. You're here. Nancy's here. I have…God, I have you and I never dreamt that I could have you." She deserved the doubt, because she was always running away from her problems—Sofia most of all.

"I think I'm falling in love with you." Liza was babbling now, not really following what she was saying. She just knew that it was the truth and it *had* to be said. "Again, I mean. I really think that this has a shot at working, and I want to…I want to see it through."

Sofia looked up at her, eyes dark and unreadable. "Are you certain?" She looked back down, her cheeks coloring a bit. "I told myself that I'd never let myself fall for you again. And yet here we are…"

Liza nodded. She took a step forward, and then another, circling around Sofia's desk and coming to stand in front of her. Sofia's breath was warm against her cheek and her fingers reached forward to grab the lapels of Liza's jacket. Her hand was shaking, and Liza placed her hand on top of Sofia's. "I am."

And when Sofia kissed her, Liza wrapped her free arm around Sofia's shoulders and drew her in tight. She was afraid that she would let go, and that this would all be another of her horrible dreams, a forgotten moment as soon as she woke up. She couldn't have that. This wasn't a piecrust sort of a promise. This was a future that stretched out forever.

POST

HAWKE CONFIDENT IN LADY KNIGHTS' PLAYOFF CHANCES

Near Haven Mirror
Feb 2, 2013

NEAR HAVEN - As the regular basketball season comes to a close, the playoff picture is becoming clearer by the day, and the interim coach of the Near Haven Lady Knights likes her team's chances, based on conference standings as they are now.

"We're going to have to play West Point in the opening round if things continue as they are now," Hawke explained during a telephone interview following her victory over a talented Bangor team that is currently in hot pursuit of the Lady Knights' number one overall record. "We played them back at the beginning of January, and matched up well against them.".

Barring a catastrophe, Hawke has helped to coach this team into a strong position, within striking distance, again, of a state title. If the team continues on their current path, it will be a tribute truly fit for late coach Charlie White.

SIDEBAR: A NEW START

Near Haven Mirror

Feb 7, 2013

Everyone knows the story of Liza Hawke's fall from grace in a city across the country. Once considered an embarrassment to the very name of the town she once called home, Hawke has worked her way steadily back into Near Haven's good graces.

It hasn't been an easy road for Hawke. Growing up an orphan who was shunted from home to home within the community, Hawke was part of a Maine Child Protective Services pilot program that kept her central to a community, rather than a string of group homes and fosters all over the state.

"In a sense, it was that program that has given me roots," Hawke explains. "I met a lot of other foster kids after I left Near Haven, but none of them had roots like I did. None of them had a place that they could definitively say, 'Yeah, I'm from there.'"

Hawke was offered a position by her former Coach Charlie White as an assistant in September, taking over for Finn Mulligan, who accepted a position at UMass Lowell as an assistant. With Mr. White's unfortunate death in December, the responsibility of taking on the stewardship of this talented Lady Knights team has fallen firmly onto Hawke's shoulders.

Despite her less-than-warm welcome upon returning to town, Hawke is thankful for the challenge of coaching. "I'm grateful for the opportunity to provide a service to the school and the community. Charlie left behind a great legacy, and I only hope that I can come close to his success."

So far, since Hawke has taken over, the team hasn't lost a single conference game. They are firmly in first place in the AA Varsity division, with their closest completion three games back. With only five regular season games remaining before the playoffs, Hawke is liking her chances.

NEAR HAVEN'S STAR GARNERING TOP OFFERS

Kennebec Journal
Feb 12, 2013

NEAR HAVEN - Briannan Montclair, starting guard for the Near Haven Lady Knights (15 points, 6 assists, 1.7 steals) is starting to attract attention as her team continues on its historic run through the season. After former head Coach Charlie White suffered a fatal heart attack, the team has rattled off seven wins and only one loss to an out-of-conference opponent, Portland High School. These wins are drawing attention to the 5'8" senior, who is looking to play ball in college next year.

Sources close to Montclair say that she has been approached with offers from the University of New Hampshire and the University of Hartford, the latter of which has posted at-large NCAA Tournament bids out of the America East conference twice in the past five years.

Coaches say that they like Montclair's measurables and hustle on the court, and say that they think that a run through the playoffs could garner some offers from higher-profile schools.

NEW ENGLAND BASKETBALL RECRUITING ROUNDUP

Rivals
Feb 17, 2013

NEAR HAVEN, ME - 5'8" Senior Guard Briannan Montclair (15 points, 6 assists, 1.7 steals) has received offers from Hartford, New Hampshire, and, most recently, Boston College. This ACC offer constitutes the only major conference basketball scholarship out of the state of Maine since Montclair's coach, Liza Hawke, was offered one by Fresno State.

HAWKE'S TEAM TAKES OPENING ROUND

Portland Press Herald

Feb 19, 2013

BANGOR – It isn't Charlie White's team anymore. The late, great coach of the Near Haven Lady Knights left his team in the capable hands of a former protégé, Liza Hawke, a member of his lone state championship team. Hawke coached a nearly perfect game, led by the impressive double-double performance by starting point guard Briannan Montclair.

Montclair hit her first four 3-pointers and was nearly lights out in the paint as well. She recorded 2 steals and had 12 assists in the Lady Knight's 75-52 rout of West Point High School's eighth-seeded team. Meghan Matthews recorded 11 rebounds, a career high, as well as 8 points that helped to put the game away for Near Haven.

The team will play again tomorrow night against the winner of the Bangor/Bar Harbor two-seven matchup *(more after the jump).*

CHAMPIONS ONCE MORE

Near Haven Mirror
March 1, 2013

NEAR HAVEN – After nearly a decade, Near Haven stands supreme once more, first among women's basketball in the state of Maine. The overtime victory over a talented Bangor team that scored a last-second 3-pointer to force the game into extra minutes will go down in the annals of Near Haven's history as one of the most exciting that has ever been played.

Bri Montclair shot 8 to 12 from the field with 8 assists as well as 5 rebounds and a single steal. This performance, as well as the performance of Meghan Matthews and Jess Pinkerton were enough to secure a 68-65 victory over Bangor at the Lady Knights's home court last night.

Interim Coach Liza Hawke was beside herself following the game. "I told the kids in December, I told them that if we did this, we'd do it for Charlie. I'm just so proud of them, really. They played a great game against a really good team, and even if it took five extra minutes, it was well worth it."

COACHING RETROSPECTIVE, HAWKE'S PERFECT SEASON

Near Haven Mirror
March 15, 2013

If one were to look up Near Haven's notable daughters, Liza Hawke would probably be at the top of the list, as she is the one who fell from grace and dared to come back. Over the course of history there have been heroes and villains in this town, and for the longest time, Liza Hawke was cast firmly in the role of the anti-hero.

Now though, she is a hero to the town once more, but not for the reasons that one might think. Sure, winning a state championship in the face of such adversity is an accomplishment in and of itself, but what Hawke has done with her time in Near Haven is even more remarkable than that.

"I was offered a second chance by everyone in this town, and I took it," Hawke said following her overtime victory over Bangor.

Working with a local attorney, Hawke was able to establish a case to have her name exonerated for the crime for which she was convicted, but did not commit. The paperwork was signed in late January, just as the Lady Knights were poised to start their championship run. Hawke has never commented publicly on it, but friends close to her say that she is going to use the change in her societal status to return to school and pursue an education degree over the summer and then hopefully return to coaching next fall. This reporter, at least, hopes the best for her return to Near Haven.

ABOUT ANA MATICS

Ana Matics is twenty-six, a long-time writer, and sometimes bank employee. When not writing, Ana enjoys running with her dog and exploring the vast countryside that her current state of North Carolina offers.

CONNECT WITH THIS AUTHOR:
Tumblr: anamatics.tumblr.com/

OTHER BOOKS FROM
YLVA PUBLISHING

www.ylva-publishing.com

BARRING
COMPLICATIONS

BLYTHE RIPPON

ISBN: 978-3-95533-191-7
Length: 374 pages

It's an open secret that the newest justice on the Supreme Court is a lesbian. So when the Court decides to hear a case about gay marriage, Justice Victoria Willoughby must navigate the press, sway at least one of her conservative colleagues, and confront her own fraught feelings about coming out.

Just when she decides she's up to the challenge, she learns that the very brilliant, very out Genevieve Fornier will be lead counsel on the case.

Genevieve isn't sure which is causing her more sleepless nights: the prospect of losing the case, or the thought of who will be sitting on the bench when she argues it.

BITTER FRUIT

LOIS CLOAREC HART

ISBN: 978-3-95533-216-7
Length: 244 pages

Fuelled by booze and boredom, Jac Lanier accepts an unusual wager from her best friend. Victoria, for reasons of her own, impulsively challenges Jac to seduce Lauren, her co-worker and a young woman Jac's never met. Under the terms of their bet, Jac has exactly one month to get Lauren into bed or she has to pay up. Though Lauren is straight and engaged, Jac begins her campaign confident that she'll win the bet. But Jac's forgotten that if you sow an onion seed, you won't harvest a peach. When her plan goes awry, will she reap the bitter fruit of her deception? Or will Lauren turn the tables on the thoughtless gamblers?

MAC VS. PC

FLETCHER DELANCEY

ISBN: 978-3-95533-187-0
Length: 148 pages

As a computer technician at the university, Anna Petrowski knows she has one thing in common with doctors and lawyers, and it's not the salary. It's that everyone thinks her advice comes free, even on weekends. That's why she keeps a strict observance of her Saturday routine: a scone, a caramel mocha, and nobody bothering her. So when she meets a new campus hire at the Bean Grinder who needs computer help yet doesn't ask for it, she's intrigued enough to offer. It's the beginning of a beautiful friendship and possibly something more.

But Elizabeth Markel is a little higher up the university food chain than she's let on, and the truth brings out buried prejudices that Anna didn't know she had.

People and computers have one thing in common: they're both capable of self-sabotage. The difference is that computers are easier to fix.

STILL LIFE

L.T. SMITH

ISBN: 978-3-95533-257-0
Length: 352 pages

After breaking off her relationship with a female lothario, Jess Taylor decides she doesn't want to expose herself to another cheating partner. Staying at home, alone, suits her just fine. Her idea of a good night is an early one—preferably with a good book. Well, until her best friend, Sophie Harrison, decides it's time Jess rejoined the human race.

Trying to pull Jess from her self-imposed prison, Sophie signs them both up for a Still Life art class at the local college. Sophie knows the beautiful art teacher, Diana Sullivan, could be the woman her best friend needs to move on with her life.

But, in reality, could art bring these two women together? Could it be strong enough to make a masterpiece in just twelve sessions? And, more importantly, can Jess overcome her fear of being used once again?

Only time will tell.

UNDER A FALLING STAR

JAE

ISBN: 978-3-95533-238-9
Length: 394 pages

FALLING STARS ARE SUPPOSED TO be a lucky sign, but not for Austen. Her new job as a secretary in an international games company isn't off to a good start. Her first assignment—decorating the Christmas tree in the lobby—results in a trip to the ER after Dee, the company's second-in-command, gets hit by the star-shaped tree topper.

Dee blames her instant attraction to Austen on her head wound, not the magic of the falling star. She's determined not to act on it, especially since Austen has no idea that Dee is practically her boss.

COMING FROM YLVA
PUBLISHING

www.ylva-publishing.com

TURNING FOR HOME

CAREN WERLINGER

Like her mother before her, Jules Calhoon couldn't wait to escape her small Ohio town. Unlike her mother, though, Jules couldn't disappear forever. When she's called back for her grandfather's funeral, the visit unleashes a flood of memories and starts her on a lonely—and familiar—path.

Her partner, Kelli, feels Jules slipping away but can't figure out how to pull her back. In desperation, she turns to Jules's oldest friend—and her ex—Donna. The problem is, Donna never could figure out why her relationship with Jules ended so long ago, and she never stopped loving Jules.

When a lonely, confused teenager reaches out to Jules for help, the past and present are set on a collision course, igniting a chain of events that will leave none of them unscathed.

BEGINNINGS

L.T. SMITH

1974. The Osmonds, space hoppers and climbing trees, all grounded in the ultimate belief that life was perfect. Childhood filled with tomorrows and a friendship built to endure anything. Or was it? Lou Turner loves Ashley Richards. Always has and always will. This is Lou's story...a story spanning thirty years...from the innocence of youth to the bitterness of adulthood. But can Lou use her beginnings to shape her future? Only one woman can answer that question. Childhood and friendship...love and belief...hope that yesterdays can be what futures are made of. And Lou's future began the day her world fell from a tree.

THE CAPHENON

FLETCHER DELANCEY

On a summer night like any other, an emergency call sounds in the quarters of Andira Tal, Lancer of Alsea. The news is shocking: not only is there other intelligent life in the universe, but it's landing on the planet right now.

Tal leads the first responding team and ends up rescuing aliens who have a frightening story to tell. They protected Alsea from a terrible fate—but the reprieve is only temporary.

Captain Ekayta Serrano of the Fleet ship *Caphenon* serves the Protectorate, a confederation of worlds with a common political philosophy. She has just sacrificed her ship to save Alsea, yet political maneuvering may mean she did it all for nothing.

Alsea is now a prize to be bought and sold by galactic forces far more powerful than a tiny backwater planet. But Lancer Tal is not one to accept a fate imposed by aliens, and she'll do whatever it takes to save her world.

The Return
© Ana Matics 2014

ISBN: 978-3-95533-234-1

Also available as e-book.

Published by Ylva Publishing, legal entity of Ylva Verlag, e.Kfr.

Ylva Verlag, e.Kfr.
Owner: Astrid Ohletz
Am Kirschgarten 2
65830 Kriftel
Germany

www.ylva-publishing.com

First edition: November 2014

Credits
Edits by Nikki Busch and Astrid Ohletz
Cover Design and Formatting by Streetlight Graphics